# TRIGGER POINT

## A TOM ROLLINS THRILLER

### PAUL HEATLEY

INKUBATOR
BOOKS

Published by Inkubator Books
www.inkubatorbooks.com

Copyright © 2025 by Paul Heatley

Paul Heatley has asserted his right to be identified as the author of this work.

ISBN (eBook): 978-1-83756-518-4
ISBN (Paperback): 978-1-83756-519-1

TRIGGER POINT is a work of fiction. People, places, events, and situations are the product of the author's imagination. Any resemblance to actual persons, living or dead is entirely coincidental.

No part of this book may be reproduced, stored in any retrieval system, or transmitted by any means without the prior written permission of the publisher.

*For Aidan*

# 1

Tom Rollins has been off-grid for three months. He wanted some time to himself. To get back to nature. He'd found work with a logging company in Oklahoma after a busy few weeks in San Francisco and Texas. His body had been put through a lot with fights and explosions, and the logging work didn't give him much time to heal. He was always so busy.

After he'd made a little money and he left Oklahoma, he drove north-east until he reached Green Mountain National Forest in Vermont. He needed to get somewhere quiet, somewhere he could be alone. Somewhere for his body to rest and for his mind to clear. It was late February when he arrived, and there was snow on the ground. He'd bought equipment on the way – a thermal jacket and trousers with ratings high enough to withstand up to minus twenty Fahrenheit, along with a couple of sweaters. He bought a bigger backpack to carry his new equipment, including an insulated sleeping bag, and a portable propane stove, along with a pot and a pan to cook upon it. He got a small tent, too, and a camo tarp to drape around the perimeter of his camping site, making him harder to spot. He bought copious amounts of dried mushrooms and berries. Ordinarily, if it were spring or summer, he'd live off the land, but with snow covering everything that wasn't going to be an option.

He put his car into storage and hitched a ride to the forest. He walked out into the trees, most of them barren, their branches empty, but still thick and overgrown enough to conceal him. He spent the following three months alone. Just himself and his thoughts. He caught fish from the rivers, and set traps for the rabbits and wild turkeys. He cooked them over low, controlled fires, always careful and vigilant not to set the whole forest ablaze. When he wasn't concentrating on food, he took in the nature that surrounded him. He swam and floated in the cold, cold waters, emerging feeling refreshed, his aches and inflammations numbed and reduced. He watched moose through the trees, and fed a deer berries from his hand. When spring came, he avoided the black bears emerging from hibernation. He stayed away from their trails and they never gave him any trouble. He sat upon a fallen bough and breathed deep the clean, crisp, sweet air, meditating for hours on end.

Through it all, he stayed hidden from the rangers. He regularly moved his campsite. He cleaned up after himself and never left any sign that he'd been present. They never searched for him. They never even knew he was there.

It's May now. The days are still cold, but they're milder now than when he first arrived. The trees are slowly turning green again. Tom doesn't know where he's going next, but he's decided it's time to move on. He's walked down through the forest and back to the main road, thumbing while he walks alongside it. Down here, the snow is mostly gone.

Tom has lost a little weight, he knows, and his hair and beard are both longer, but he feels better. He feels lighter, and he feels stronger. Nothing hurts. His head is clear. His thoughts are ordered. His lungs are full of clean air.

He manages to get a ride and they drop him off in the next town, where his car is. It's late evening by the time he reaches the storage, and it'll be dark soon. There's no one working the front gate, but he has a key. He lets himself in and goes to see the security guard. He fills out a brief form and pays for his three months of storage. He retrieves his car from where it's parked in a gated enclosure at the rear. It's a black Toyota Corolla. He picked it up in Lubbock after his Ford was totalled. As with most cars he buys, he picked it up pre-owned and cheap. Tom has never been a car guy. All he needs a vehicle for is to get him from A to B. He does a lot of driving, and taking care and pride in his vehicle would be next to impossible. Too much rough ground. Too many miles. Plus, quite often he sleeps on the backseat. Finds a quiet spot and curls up when he doesn't feel like spending money on a motel.

He takes advantage of the electrical outlets in the storage area and charges up the cell phones that were in his backpack. As they come to life, he checks them over, each of them marked up with who has the number for it. He had them in the forest with him, but there wasn't any signal and they all soon ran out of battery. Looking now, he sees that no one has tried to get in touch. This is good. No news is good news.

The car starts when he turns the ignition. The battery is still alive. He's pleased. There's still a full tank of gas. While the engine warms up, he looks at his reflection in the mirror. His hair is longer than he usually keeps it. He's bearded, and that's longer than he'd usually wear it, too. This is the first time he's seen his reflection in anything other than a pool of water in three months. He grins at himself then leaves the storage area and stops at a nearby Goodwill to drop off his camping equipment, including the bigger backpack. He doesn't need it now. He has his smaller backpack, with which he has criss-crossed the country. Next, he goes to a drive-thru to get food. He sits in the parking lot and eats it as the light fades and it gets dark. It's a clear night. He looks up at the stars. They're not as bright here, in civilization, as they were in the forest where there were no other lights.

A car pulls into a space a couple over from Tom. A couple of teens, a boy and a girl. They don't have any food. They leave the engine running, and as soon as the car has stopped they set upon each other, kissing with wide, wet mouths. Tom starts the Toyota and pulls out of the lot, dropping his waste in the trash on his way out.

It's dark when he hits the road. He heads west. He's spent enough days in Vermont. It's time to go somewhere else. He'll need to find work. Something to bring in money and, more importantly, to fill his days until he's ready to move on to the next place.

He drives along a road lined with trees, and deep, dark woodland beyond on either side of him. He can't see the stars here. The only light comes from his headlights stretching out before him. It's quiet. There's no one else on this road, and no sign of any other headlights either ahead or behind.

Tom is about to reach for the radio, to put on some music, when he notices something up ahead at the periphery of his headlights' reach. At the right side of the road, the bushes are trembling. Tom slows, foot tapping the brake pedal, expecting an animal to emerge and run across the road. He doesn't want to hit it.

Except, what emerges isn't an animal. It's a woman.

She falls through the bushes and lands on the road on her hands and knees. She stops, her head turning, looking toward Tom's car. She pushes herself up, unsteady on her feet. Her blonde hair is wild. Her make-up is streaked and running down her face. The headlights light her up, and Tom can see scratches on her cheeks. Thin trails of blood run from them. She's frantic, waving her arms trying to get him to stop. Tom opens the door and steps out.

The woman is crying out to him. She looks young, late twenties maybe, and she's clearly in trouble. Tom has heard about women emerging on dark roads, pretending to need help as a setup for men lying in wait nearby to jump the concerned passerby and jack their car, but he doesn't think that's what's happening here. The woman's bruises and cuts are too convincing. She's not trying to set him up for anything. She needs help.

"Please!" She's calling to Tom. She draws closer, falling onto the hood of the car, bracing herself with both hands. "Please, help us!" She looks back the way she came, down the road and toward the bushes and trees. "My son," she says, turning back to Tom, coming to him now. "I've lost my son! He was with me. I had his hand, but then he fell, and then I fell, and I got all turned around, and I don't know where he's gone –"

"Try to calm down," Tom says, placing firm hands upon her shoulders. "You've lost your son? He's in the woods?"

The woman doesn't calm. She's almost hyperventilating with panic. "They're coming," she says. "They were right behind us."

Tom's eyes narrow at this. He looks to where she emerged, but he doesn't see anyone there. "Who's coming?" he says. "I need you to make sense. I can't help you if you don't make sense."

There's a rustle from the bushes behind him. They both hear it. The woman peers past him. Her eyes go wide. She's scared. Whoever is there, it's probably the person she was running from. This is enough for Tom. He lets go of her and he spins, ready for action. A squat man with a shaved head in overalls. In his right hand, Tom notices he's carrying a flashlight, but it's not turned on. The man sees Tom. He sees the woman. His face is grim.

"My sister's off her meds," the man says, holding out his hands. He continues to step forward, taking his time like he's not wanting to pose a threat. Tom notices how tightly he holds the flashlight. "I need to get her home before she can hurt herself."

"I'm not his sister," the woman says to Tom, sticking close to him. "I've never seen this man before today. He and his brothers took me, and they took my son. They killed –"

"Come on now, Ella, that's enough," the man says, still coming. "You're talking crazy. You're saying upsetting things. This nice man doesn't need to hear none of that crazy."

Tom remains between them. He eyes the approaching man, keeping one eye on the flashlight.

"Mister, if you just step aside, I'll get my sister and we can go on home."

"She said she's lost her son," Tom says.

"I'm sure she did," the man says. "She says a lot of wild things. Truth be told, she don't have a son. She don't have any kids."

"Please don't believe him," the woman – Ella – whispers to Tom.

The man is close enough for Tom to reach out and touch now. Tom doesn't. Not yet. He waits. Watches. Tom believes the woman more than the man, though he knows he has to entertain that either one of them could be lying.

But then the man decides to take a swing. He brings the flashlight around, aiming it for Tom's face. Tom blocks the attempted blow with his left forearm. He sees the man's eyes widen, shocked at the speed of Tom's reflexes. Tom slips his left arm around the man's right, pinning it to his ribs, controlling him. Tom jabs him in the centre of his face, and again, harder, in the chest. He lets go and the man stumbles back, the flashlight dropped, one hand to his chest while he coughs and gasps for breath. He drops to a knee, looking like he might throw up.

Then, from behind, the woman lets out a muffled cry. Tom spins. Two more men have emerged. One of them has Ella from behind, a thick arm wrapped around her waist and a meaty hand clamped down over her mouth. The two new men look similar to the one Tom has just dealt with. The one who isn't holding Ella, however, is much bigger than the other two.

And he's already in motion. He's bringing down a flashlight of his own. This one is turned on. It connects with the side of Tom's skull. He hears the batteries rattle inside it. The light momentarily blinds him. As he goes down, he sees that the blow has broken the flashlight.

Tom hits the ground, landing on his back. He manages to keep the rear of his skull from bouncing off the road. He tries to roll onto his side and get back up, but his limbs are suddenly leaden. The bigger man is looking down at him.

"Tyrus," he calls to the man Tom put down. "Get your ass up and help Billy-Ray haul this bitch back to the house."

Tyrus stumbles back into view. The two men are circling in Tom's vision. "What about the kid?" Tyrus says, his voice rough from Tom's blows.

"Cyril's got him," the bigger man says.

Tyrus looks down at Tom. "You all right on your own with this one?"

The bigger man smirks. "He ain't no trouble at all." He raises a boot and brings it down into Tom's face. This time, his head bounces off the road. Darkness soon follows.

# 2

Tom awakes to the sound of laughter.

It pierces through his skull like a knife. The front and back of his head throb mercilessly. He opens his eyes only a little, not wanting anyone to notice he's regained consciousness, but even this is enough for the light to blaze and burn across his retinas. He closes his eyes again and breathes long and slow, settling himself and the sickly feeling in the pit of his stomach. He wonders what time it is – if it's still night, or if it's early morning. The lights are on, which means it must still be dark. When he feels better – as good as he's going to get in the current circumstances – he half-opens his eyes again.

He's in a cabin. The smell of wood is strong in the air. It's a good smell, and it reminds him of his time in the forest, but he knows this is not a good place. It's a big cabin. The main area is all open-plan. There are a few rooms running off it, but the kitchen and living room are all in one large connected space. Turning his head just slightly, Tom takes in the area where he is. It's an annexe at the rear of the cabin, probably used for sitting in a rocking chair and looking out the window. Tom wonders if they're still near the woodland, surrounded by trees, or if he's been taken further afield. From where he is on the ground, he can't see much out of the window. Only darkness – either it's still night, or it's the very early hours of the morning.

The annexe does not have a door. It connects to the rest of the living area. Tom, however, is tightly bound – his wrists and ankles are tied tight with rope, and a length of it is wrapped around his chest, pinning his arms to his side. Tom realises he's not alone here. He sees a familiar mane of wild, dirty blonde hair laced through with twigs and leaves. A woman dressed in jeans and flannel. The woman who emerged from the woods. The woman he stopped to help. A name comes back to him – Ella? The first man who appeared after her called her that. He wonders if it's really her name.

She's tied up, too, but she's not on her back. She's propped upright, looking in the direction of the raucous laughter. Under it, Tom can hear the rattle and spin of something metallic being dropped. Before he can raise his head to see what is happening, Ella turns toward him. She sees that he's looking back at her, even through his half-closed eyes. Tom opens them all the way to see her properly. The make-up that was running down her face when he first saw her has been roughly wiped away. She opens her mouth to speak but Tom shakes his head. He makes sure no one is looking their way, then mouths, *Don't make a sound.* He doesn't want the men to know he's awake.

She nods that she understands, then she turns away from him, back toward the noise.

Tom looks that way, too. He sees the back of a young boy with dark hair in need of a cut. He sits at a desk and his back is to Tom and Ella. From behind, unable to see his face, it's hard to guess his age. Tom thinks he looks less than ten. He wonders, too, if this is Ella's missing son. In front of him, on the other side of the desk, four men stand close. They're the ones doing the laughing. Tom recognises three of them. He saw them on the road last night. He sees the man in the overalls whom he beat up, and there's bruising across his nose and under his eyes, and crusted blood on his nostrils. He sees the big guy who knocked him unconscious with the flashlight and his boot. He's laughing the loudest. He sees the man who grabbed Ella. Tom notices that they all look alike. The fourth man, the man he hasn't seen before, looks just like the others. They're all too close in age for one of them to be the father, or potentially an uncle. They must be brothers.

The bigger man looks like the oldest. He scoops up whatever he's dropped in front of the boy. He reaches into his back pocket, adds something to it, and then shakes it all in his fist. Tom strains his ears, trying to hear better.

"Every time!" one of the younger brothers says. "Every goddamn time! How's he doing it?"

The bigger, older brother doesn't answer. He drops whatever he's shaking onto the desk in front of the boy again. Tom catches just a glimpse as they land. They're coins. The boy glances down, just briefly, and almost instantly says, "Two dollars, seven cents."

The brothers laugh again. One of them leans forward and counts up the coins to make sure the boy is correct. "Right on the money," he says.

"I'm running outta coins," the oldest brother says.

"Anyone got more? Pitch it in – let's make it a big one. Let's make it difficult."

The brother who spoke earlier eagerly pulls coins from his pockets and hands them over. "He'll get it," he says. "I'll bet anything. He's never got it wrong yet."

Tom realises there are two other men in the cabin. They're not partaking in the guessing games going on at the desk. One of them stands close, his face set, grim, staring like he's waiting for them to get bored and wrap up. His arms are folded. He wears dark jeans and a khaki shirt. There's a handgun on his hip. It's the only gun Tom has seen on show in the cabin. There could be more, but they're not in the living area. Everything about this man's demeanour screams of impatience. It's hard for Tom to tell at this distance, but he sees a likeness in the profile of this man's face as with the brothers, though he's younger and slimmer and better dressed than they are.

This man clears his throat. "You all aren't bored yet?"

The bigger brother turns to him. Glares at him. The man stands his ground, but he withers a little. Tom notices it, and he thinks the bigger brother does, too.

The man has to swallow before he speaks again. "Deke, I'm just saying, we've been trusted with this. There's more to do. We can't get hung up on some savant kid guessing at the outcome of some dropped coins."

Tom has a name now. The oldest brother – *Deke*. He remembers he heard names at the roadside, too. They're coming back to him, his memory jogged now. Tyrus was the one he beat down. Billy-Ray grabbed Ella. The one he didn't see must be Cyril.

He remembers something else, too. Something that Ella

said. She wasn't able to finish her sentence before Tyrus cut her off. She said that they'd killed someone.

"We got time," Deke says. "What's that stuck-up prick you work for gonna do? Bitch and moan that we took our time?" Deke sucks his teeth. "Fuck him. By the time he gets back out here, there's gonna be nothing for him to complain about. And you ain't gonna talk any shit about your cousins, are you, Jake?"

Another name – Jake. A cousin. Explains the similarities, and slight difference, in their faces.

"You all are trying to get work with that stuck-up prick," Jake says. "And I vouched for you. Don't let me down on this."

Billy-Ray speaks up, but it has nothing to do with Deke and Jake's conversation. "Hey, I think we've got a load of dice in the game closet," he says. "Should I grab it? Maybe the kid can do the same with dice?"

Deke slaps him on the back, staring at Jake while he does so. "That's a great idea, Billy-Ray," he says. "You go on and get that dice. Many as you can find. We wanna challenge the boy, don't we?"

Jake bites his lip. He takes a step back. He doesn't argue. It's clear he's already lost.

The other man in the cabin, the sixth, doesn't look anything like the others. He stays away from them, too, sticking to the other end of the cabin. He watches them, worrying at his bottom lip. His face doesn't betray frustration – instead, he looks concerned. He looks down at his watch, worried about the passage of time.

Billy-Ray hurries off to find the dice. He passes by the annexe. He glances in. He looks straight at Tom. Tom doesn't move. Keeps his eyes half-closed. Billy-Ray doesn't see that he's awake. Billy-Ray turns his attention to Ella, grinning at her. "Don't you worry," he says. "We haven't forgotten about you."

"Please don't hurt Kit," she says. Kit must be her son. The boy at the table, guessing the sums of the dropped coins.

Billy-Ray doesn't respond to this. He laughs in the back of his throat and continues on.

He passes by the sixth man. The man avoiding the others. There's a whiteboard close to him. It's covered in writing – they look like squiggles. Tom risks opening his eyes a little, to see if they start to make sense. They don't. He sees letters, numbers, dashes. It's a formula of some kind. Mathematical, maybe. Tom doesn't know what it means. Math was never his strong point, especially not once letters got involved.

However, on the ground behind the whiteboard, he spots canisters. He sees them marked up with warning symbols – toxic, corrosive, and others like this. Billy-Ray runs back by the annexe, hurrying to the desk, his hands laden with dice now. Tom stays very still. He continues to look behind the whiteboard. In front of the canisters, propped against them, are some bags. About a dozen of them. They look like flour bags. Their contents are written across the front. Sodium fluoride.

Tom thinks about this. Sodium fluoride goes into toothpaste. He stares at the canisters behind it.

Before he can fully register what they are, what they contain, he hears another burst of laughter at the desk with Kit.

"He just don't miss!" Cyril says.

"We should've started with dice," Billy-Ray says. "Roll them again."

Jake reaches into his pocket suddenly and starts waving for them to be quiet. "I'm getting a call," he says. "It's Lincoln."

Deke shrugs. "So?"

"So I need you all to shut the fuck up for a few minutes," Jake says. "You think you can do that?"

"A few minutes, sure," Deke says. He grins at his cousin. "You'd best just hope it's a quick phone call, because in a few minutes, I'm gonna start rolling dice again."

## 3

Jake Underhill breathes deeply before he answers the call. He steps away from the brothers, and the kid, and crosses the cabin until he's closer to Ian. He exchanges a quick glance with Ian. Neither of them is happy with how things are right now, but neither of them is in a position to say or do anything about it. They're outnumbered.

He stares at the screen. At Lincoln's name. He glances at Ella, who is staring at her son. He looks at Kit, too, and the new arrival, whoever he is. There wasn't any ID on him. He's a complication that Jake doesn't need. This whole day and night has turned into a complication that Jake doesn't need. It wasn't supposed to be like this. It was supposed to be an easy trip. An easy task. An easy way for him to prove himself.

It was supposed to be an easy way for his cousins to prove themselves, too. To step up and show themselves capable of being a part of Lincoln's organisation. And then, suddenly, there's a tiny complication in the form of an attractive blonde, and Deke and his clan lose their fucking minds. They stop listening to reason. They *won't* listen.

And now they're entertaining themselves with some kid doing quick mental math, like it's the best and funniest thing they've ever seen in their lives. Jake supposes his cousins live in the backwoods of Vermont – maybe it *is* the best and funniest thing they've ever seen. They don't get out much.

One thing that this night has made very clear to Jake, however, is that his cousins are not professional. They're not reliable. They can't be counted on, not even for him, and he's their blood. They're a backwoods clan, and they're always going to be just that. Nothing more. Without admitting to how much of a mess things have become, Jake is going to have to make it clear to Lincoln that Deke and the others are not a right fit.

He answers the call. "Sir," he says.

He hears Lincoln's familiar London accent. "Took you a while to answer there, Jacob."

"Sorry, sir. I was – I was dealing with something else."

"Mm. How are things going out there, sweetheart? Everything sorted? Nice and neat with a bow on top?"

Jake hesitates.

Lincoln seizes on it immediately. "Oh dear," he says. "That pause is alarming, Jacob. What's going on?"

"Everything is...in hand. Things are being dealt with."

"In progress?" Lincoln tuts. "It's been hours, Jacob. This isn't what I was expecting to hear."

"The boy doesn't really speak," he says, not mentioning how he's only spoken to answer the dropped coins and dice. "He's pretty much nonverbal, most of the time. I don't think we have anything to worry about from him."

"Pretty much isn't *completely*," Lincoln says. "And you're

missing an important point, Jacob – I don't *care*. I don't care if he's mute. They saw too much. I want him dealt with. And I want his mother dealt with, too. They already should be. Explain to me why they're not."

Jake looks around the cabin. He sees his cousins looking back at him. The boy sits very still at the desk. He stares at the mix of coins and dice before him. Jake turns away from them.

"My cousins," he says. "Uh, they don't get much female company out here, if you catch my meaning. They, uh, they wanted to have a little fun with the mother. She's, y'know, she's an attractive woman, and they want to take their time."

Lincoln is silent for a moment. Jake doesn't like it. Lincoln isn't happy, and nothing good can come from this silence.

"Did I hear you correctly?" Lincoln says.

This time, Jake is silent. There's no right answer.

"I'm not a bloody pimp, Jake," Lincoln says. "This wasn't *arranged* for them. I don't care what they want, and I don't care how they spend the rest of their time – right now, they're on my payroll. They have one job left to do – I want the woman and her kid taken care of."

"Yes, sir," Jake says.

"What about at the woods? Were the bodies properly disposed of?"

Deke told Jake that they were. At the time, Jake was preoccupied with Ella and Kit, and was still inclined to believe what his eldest cousin told him. "Yes, sir," he says. He has to believe that his cousins would at least do this *one* thing correctly, but now he has some doubts. Doubts he can't share with Lincoln. He'll have to go back out there and check for himself, just to be absolutely sure, once everything in the cabin has been dealt with.

"And how's Ian?"

Jake glances at Ian. Ian is looking back at him. "Ian's fine," Jake says. "He's ready to begin."

"He hasn't started yet?"

Jake realises he's said the wrong thing. "Uh, we've just all been a little preoccupied with things out here –"

"That shouldn't be the case," Lincoln says, and Jake can hear that he's speaking through his teeth.

"I know, sir. I'm sorry. I'll make sure things are wrapped up here and that Ian gets to work."

Lincoln lets out a long exhale, calming himself. "Are there any *other* issues I need to be made aware of?"

Jake looks toward the man in the annexe close to Ella. "No, sir," he says. "And I promise – everything will be resolved soon."

"I certainly hope so, sweetheart," Lincoln says. "For your sake. Otherwise, I may have to put you in a small room with dear Arthur and you can explain to *him* what went wrong and how things took so long out there."

The call ends. Jake closes his eyes and breathes deeply. He swallows. The last thing he wants is to be alone in a room with Arthur Langstrom, Lincoln's right-hand man. He's bigger than Deke, and far more dangerous.

Jake can feel eyes upon him. His cousins, watching his back. Ella too, probably. When he opens his eyes, he sees Ian looking expectantly back at him. The two men exchange a glance. Jake nods.

He turns to his cousins. He needs to be strong. His whole life, he's backed down to Deke. Not only is Deke bigger, he always had the numbers on his side, too. His brothers back him up. Always have.

But things have changed. Jake isn't a kid. Hasn't been for a long time. He's a man. He was in the Air Force. He's proven himself. Now, he needs to handle this situation. He needs to be careful, but at the same time he has to assert himself.

He faces each of the four brothers, eyes settling finally on Deke. "That was Lincoln," he says.

"We guessed," Deke says, smirking.

Jake ignores him. "It's time to get serious. We need to wrap things up here."

"Is that so?"

"Yeah, that's so." Jake stands his ground. He stares back at his oldest cousin. He doesn't back down. Doesn't blink. He's more scared of Lincoln – and Arthur – than he is of Deke. "So if you wanna play dice with the kid, go ahead and waste your time, but you haven't got much longer to fuck around. I'm in charge here, and you all need to remember it."

Deke chuckles. "What'd he say to you on your little call there?"

"It's nothing to do with what he said," Jake says. "It's what he reminded me. We ain't backwoods dwellers with nothing better to do than piss off the local town. We're *professionals*. I've let you have your fun, and it's gone on long enough. Now, I need to work. Ian needs to work. The four of you can't handle that..." Jake shrugs, holding out his hands.

Deke eyes him. He almost looks impressed, or at least as close as he'll ever get. "All right," he says. "But our fun ain't over." He flicks his head toward Ella. His tongue wets his lips.

"Fine," Jake says. "There's time for that, if you're quick. But right now, that's not your priority." Jake points to the mystery man. "He is. I need to know where he's come from, and where he was going. I need to know who's going to miss him, and if they're gonna come looking. Pick him up."

Deke cocks his head.

Before he can speak, Jake cuts him off. "Unless you think Cyril might be better suited?" Cyril is the second-oldest of the brothers. Only slightly smaller in stature than Deke.

Deke narrows his eyes at this, as Jake knew he would. "I've got him," he says, moving away from the desk and heading to the annexe.

Jake smiles, pleased with himself. "Take him into your bedroom. Cyril, you should probably join us on this, too." He wants the two biggest brothers with him. The intimidation factor will help loosen the stranger's tongue. "Billy-Ray, Tyrus, the two of you stay here, keep an eye on things."

"What should we do with the boy?" Billy-Ray says.

"Keep throwing him the dice, or tie him up." Jake shrugs. "The boy's not a concern. It's his mom I want you to watch."

"Should I get started?" Ian says.

Jake turns to him. "Not yet. Let's deal with things here first. You're gonna make enough of a mess. We don't need this chaos going on behind you."

"I could start prepping the area?"

"Sure," Jake says.

Deke has hauled the mystery man from the ground. He's carrying him over his shoulder. He carries him toward his bedroom. Jake follows. It's the biggest of the bedrooms. More space for the four of them to fit in.

# 4

Tom is sat in a chair. The rope around his chest has been loosened and retied, this time around the back of the chair so that he's pinned to the seat. He lets his head loll, his chin hanging down to his chest. He's heard everything. He knows why he's here. Knows what they want from him.

Jake pulls his head up with a handful of hair and starts slapping his cheek. "Hey," he says. "Hey, wake up."

Tom blinks like he's only just regaining consciousness, wincing against the blows. He swallows, looking around, taking in the three men standing before him. His back is to the wall in the corner. Behind the men and to the right is a chest of drawers with a television on top. A couple of the drawers aren't closed all the way and socks and underwear poke out. On the left is a king-size bed, unmade, the blanket dishevelled and the sheet has come away from the top corner, exposing the stained mattress beneath. Above the bed, taped to the exposed wooden beams, is a poster of two naked women pressing up against each other, staring into the camera with their best fuck-me eyes. The top right corner of the poster has come loose and hangs down. The room smells of sweat and the underlying stink of a few open beer bottles down the side of the bed.

The three men don't speak, not straight away. They stare down at Tom, giving him a moment to fully wake up and take in his surroundings.

Tom thinks how best to handle this. He can be belligerent, try to piss them off, make them sloppy. He's already beaten up Tyrus, so they know he's capable of handling himself. Or, he can play it scared, try to put them at ease, make them careless that way. Up close, he can see that it's a Heckler & Koch VP9 on Jake's hip. If Tom pisses them off too much, there's nothing stopping Jake from just pulling his handgun and putting a bullet through Tom's head. The ropes are tight, and he can't get free. He's at their mercy, for now. Subtly, trying his best not to move his body too much and give himself away, he works at the knots at his wrists.

He plays it scared, and confused from the strike to the head. "Where am I?" he says. "Who are you?"

Jake starts to smile. He stands closest to Tom. "I think, given our current positions, that I should be the one asking the questions."

Tom notices that the brothers don't speak. They're too busy trying to intimidate him. They stare at him, eyes narrowed and mean. Cyril pops his knuckles.

"Okay," Tom says.

"Do you remember how you got here?" Jake says.

Tom nods.

Jake smirks. "You mustn't have hit him hard enough," he says, turning to Deke.

"I hit him plenty hard," Deke says, almost growling the words.

Tom notices a new swagger, a new attitude displayed by Jake since he took the phone call. His cousins have noticed it, too, and they don't look pleased by it.

"What's your name?" Jake says, turning back to Tom.

"David," Tom says.

"Just David?"

"David Thoreau."

"Is there any reason why you're not carrying any ID, David Thoreau?"

"I didn't know I'd need any."

"Uh-huh. Where were you coming from?"

"Green Mountain National Forest."

"What were you doing out there?"

Tom shrugs. "Just, you know, forest stuff. Listen, whatever's going on here, I promise I won't say anything, okay? You don't need to worry about me. If you let me go, you'll never see or hear from me ever again."

The brothers laugh. Jake grins. Tom isn't surprised. He didn't expect this to accomplish anything. It was all part of his character. He doesn't want them to think of him as competent. Wants them to figure what happened with Tyrus was just a lucky strike.

"Sure," Jake says. "We'll see. But you need to finish answering my questions first."

Tom swallows and nods.

"You're not from around here, are you?"

Tom shakes his head.

"Where you from?"

"New Mexico." There's no point in lying.

"You're far from home."

"I've been up here a while." Tom continues working at the knots. They're a little loose. He can get his right middle finger between them. Soon, they'll be loose enough. He'll no longer be so helpless. The binding on his wrists is separate to the rope holding him to the chair. He just needs to keep them talking. Keep them distracted.

"Where were you going tonight?" Jake says.

"I was just going home."

"And where's home?"

"Rutland."

"Not too far to go. You lived there long?"

Tom slips his index finger into the gap he's worked free in the knot. Slowly, he starts to unthread it, but makes sure to not let the rope fall from his wrists. He knows that they're going to kill him, but they're not going to do it in here. Not inside the cabin and especially not in Deke's bedroom. They're more likely to take him outside, where the mess will be manageable. They might even make him dig his own grave first. He needs to be ready for when that happens. "Six months."

"Who do you live with?"

"It's just me."

"No wife, no girlfriend?"

Tom shakes his head.

"Any kids?" Jake wants to cover all bases.

"No."

"What about friends? You gotta have friends, right?"

"It – it can be hard to meet new people in a new place."

Jake glances at Deke. Tom can guess what they're thinking. So far, so good. They like what they're hearing. This is what they needed to know. If he disappears, no one will notice straight away. No one will come looking for him.

"Your family still back in New Mexico?" Jake says.

Tom nods.

"And what about work? What do you do in Rutland?"

"I stack shelves."

Cyril snorts.

"That's not very exciting," Jake says.

"I guess it's not," Tom says.

"I think that's all we need to know, David. I'll have a couple of my cousins escort you back to your vehicle."

Tom doesn't believe this for a second. He has the knots loose. He holds the rope in his hands, makes it look like he's still bound.

"It'll be Billy-Ray and Tyrus," Deke says. "I'm staying here with the girl." He looks at Jake. "You got a problem with that?"

"No," Jake says. "Take it in order. Oldest to youngest. I don't care. Just have your fun and get it over with. Get him out of the chair. I'll get your brothers."

Tom swallows as Deke and Cyril approach. He sits rigid in the chair. They smirk at him, at his fear. If he keeps them distracted thinking that he's scared, if they're pleased with themselves, they're not going to notice that he's gotten free of the ropes.

Sure enough, they take it from around his chest. They undo his ankles. They stand him up. "What about my wrists?" Tom says.

Deke slaps a heavy hand down on his shoulder. "When you're at your car," he says. "We don't want you doing anything stupid, now, do we? We saw what those fists did to our little brother. We don't want to see him get hurt again."

As if on cue, Tyrus and Billy-Ray appear in the bedroom. They look displeased at having been dragged away, at having to do the dirty work. Deke pushes Tom toward them. Tom stumbles, but he manages to remain upright, and to maintain his grip on the rope in his hands. Tyrus shoves him from the room. He hears Deke and Cyril chuckling behind him while their younger brothers glare at them.

Tom snatches a quick look around the room. Kit remains at the desk. There are dice and coins scattered in front of him. He stares at them. Ella is in the annexe, still. She stares back at him, worried. Ian remains at the far side of the cabin, close to the whiteboard and the chemicals. He's disinterested in Tom. He's looking at his watch. He wants to get on with his work, whatever that may be.

Jake stands by the door. "All right, let's go," he says, and Tom notices how his hand is resting upon the handgun.

Tyrus grabs Tom by the arm and marches him forward. He leads him to the door. Billy-Ray follows close behind. Jake opens the door. Tom looks back, toward Ella. Deke and Cyril have left the bedroom. They're advancing upon her.

"You hold her down," Deke says. "Once I'm on top, she ain't going anywhere. You keep an eye on the boy. I don't reckon he'll try anything, but just in case."

"You don't have to worry about her," Jake says to Tom. Tom is at the door now. Tyrus pushes him through it. Jake follows them out. "It's time for you to go home."

## 5

It's still dark outside. Still night. There's a chill, but not cold enough for the men to see their breaths.

While he's dragged along, Tom quickly surveys the area. There's a wide clearing in front of the cabin. Off to his right is a dirt track for vehicles to travel down. He spots a couple of trucks, as well as his Toyota.

They take him to the left.

He doesn't mention that he's spotted his car, and that he knows they're not taking him to it. He never thought they were. As suspected, they're going to kill him. They drag him to the rear of the cabin, to the trees. Nearby, he spots a shelter stocked with firewood. Close to it, there's a heavily scarred tree stump, an axe resting against it. They're going to pass by it on their route.

Tom knows he needs to act fast. He can't wait to reach wherever they're going. He needs to catch them by surprise. While the brothers aren't armed, Jake has his Heckler & Koch VP9. Tom can't give him a chance to pull it from its holster.

But he has more than just himself to think about. There's Ella and Kit inside the cabin, too. He needs to get back in there before they can be harmed.

They're getting close to the stump. Tyrus holds his arm still. He has it tight.

Tom tears his arm free from Tyrus's unsuspecting grasp, pretending he's rolled his ankle and he's falling. He cries out, just to make it seem good. Jake, leading the way, spins and freezes, hand upon the gun. The two brothers look down at where Tom has fallen. Tom keeps his hands behind his back, resisting the urge to catch himself. He lands hard on his front. It only hurts a little. The axe is right in front of him.

"Ah, *shit*," he says, trying to push himself up, rolling onto his side and stretching out his left leg. He flexes his left ankle. "I think there was a hole in the ground."

Billy-Ray grunts. "Goddamn moles, probably," he says.

Tyrus looks back, squinting at the ground, searching for a hole.

"It doesn't matter," Jake says, stepping forward. "Just get him up."

Tom makes like he's still trying to push himself up. He gets onto his back. Pulls his legs up, like he's trying to get them under him. Tom angles his body so he's aiming toward Jake. Tyrus reaches down, his body blocking Jake from view. This is what Tom wanted. He raises both legs and kicks at Tyrus, pushing him back and away, toward Jake. The two men collide and fall to the ground, Jake trapped under his bigger cousin and unable to reach for the gun.

While they topple, Tom pulls his hands from behind his back. Billy-Ray is close. Tom throws a punch between his legs. Billy-Ray's knees invert. His legs buckle. His mouth makes an O. He's low enough now that when Tom stands, he's able to bring his knee up under Billy-Ray's chin.

With Billy-Ray subdued, Tom turns to Tyrus and Jake. Jake has pushed Tyrus off him. He's pulling his gun free. Tom kicks it from his hand. It flies away into the darkness, away from the light cast from the cabin's windows.

Tyrus is coming. He charges. Tom still has the rope, dangling from his wrists. He pulls it taut and catches Tyrus across the throat. Tyrus's eyes pop. Tom uses his momentum against him, wrapping the rope around his neck, then pressing against him so they're back to back. He pulls on the rope.

In front of him, Jake is on his feet. Tom spots something gleam in his hand. Short, but lethal. A concealed knife that Tom hadn't seen. Hidden in his boot, perhaps. He lunges for Tom. Tom spins. He hears the knife go into Tyrus, and he feels Tyrus's body go rigid against him. Tom spins again, yanking the knife from Jake's hand, keeping it inside Tyrus. He drops Tyrus as he turns, coming face to face with Jake again.

There is blood on Jake's right hand, but he's not stunned at what he's done. He knows he can't linger over it. He strikes at Tom. Both men exchange blows, each ably blocking the other. Jake is trained. He's a fighter, not a brawler.

But his eyes betray him. They flicker to the left, over Tom's right shoulder. Tom hasn't forgotten about Billy-Ray. He twists to the left as Billy-Ray swings down the axe Tom was soon planning on grabbing for himself. Its head embeds itself high in Jake's chest, through his collarbone. Blood sprays. It soaks his face. Jake makes a gargled cry in the back of his throat, falling to his knees, his back arching as if he still has time to avoid the blow.

Billy-Ray looks at what he has done, hands out to his side, eyes wide. He doesn't have to think about it for long. Tom grabs him from behind and snaps his neck. Billy-Ray collapses into a heap.

Tom turns back to Tyrus. The rope is still around his neck, but it's loose now. He's on his front, but he's lifted himself from the ground, trying to reach for the knife in his belly. His arms are trembling. Tom places a boot on his back and presses him down, driving the blade in deeper. Tyrus shakes harder, but the blood is seeping out of him, soaking into the dirt. His shakes slow as his blood leaves.

Tom turns to Jake. He's on his back now, staring up at the night sky with frozen eyes. In the end, Tom never needed to use the axe. Not personally, anyway, and not out here. His work isn't done yet.

As if to remind him of this, from inside the cabin Tom hears a scream. Ella. Tom goes to Jake and presses a boot into his chest, taking the axe handle in his right hand and pulling it free.

He goes back into the cabin.

## 6

Ian spots him first. Sees the flecks of blood upon his face, and the bloody, dripping head of the axe.

Ian doesn't try to warn the others. He flees, heading out the back door of the cabin. Tom has to let him go for now. Deke and Cyril are his priorities.

They've taken most of the ropes off Ella, but her wrists are still bound behind her. Cyril holds her from behind, sitting with her between his legs, an arm clamped across her chest. She struggles, trying to get free, but the men are too big and too strong for her. Deke is in front of her, on his knees. He's working at the belt and button of her jeans.

"You ain't gotta relax," Deke says, and Tom can hear the grin in his voice. "I like the way you thrash, girl. I like it when they struggle. It's more fun for me."

Kit is at the desk still. He stares down at the objects in front of him and doesn't turn to what is happening behind, in the annexe.

Deke and Cyril have not noticed Tom's entrance. He doesn't make them aware of his presence. He crosses the cabin to them, and as he gets close he raises the axe in both hands. He swings it into the back of Deke's skull.

The scene freezes, Ella and Cyril looking up at Deke. He's frozen. Tom tears the axe out of his skull. Blood spills out of the wound as he slumps to the side. Cyril looks up at Tom. He tries to push Ella away. His mouth is open, about to speak, or to scream. Tom aims for it. He swings the axe into his mouth, shattering his teeth and driving it all the way through to sever his skull from the top of his spinal column, and pinning him upright to the wall of the cabin.

He leaves the axe in Cyril's mouth. He goes to Ella, looking her over for any damage. There's nothing new that he can see. Her clothes remain intact. "Are you all right? Did they hurt you?"

Ella shakes her head, blonde locks waving in front of her face. "Not yet," she says.

Tom kneels beside her and undoes the knots on her wrists. When she's free, she hurries to Kit and wraps him in her arms, holding him tight while she kisses the top of his head.

Tom goes to the back door. He looks out, but there is only darkness and woodland. No sign of Ian. He's gotten away.

When he turns, Ella is close behind him, holding Kit's hand. "Thank you," she says. "Thank you so much – they were going to kill us."

They were going to do worse than that, Tom thinks, but he doesn't say anything.

Kit is staring unblinking at the whiteboard, and the writing there.

"We need to get out of here," Tom says. "One of them got away. He might come back with more. We need to be clear of here when he does. My car's outside. The black Toyota. You should take the boy outside. Wait by the car while I search the cabin for my keys."

Ella nods. She starts to turn.

"And keep his eyes covered," Tom says. "There's more outside."

Ella does.

It doesn't take Tom long to find his keys. They're in the kitchen, sat atop the counter. There's no sign of his bags. They must have left them in the car. If they'd searched them, they would have found his Beretta and KA-BAR. They would have had more questions for him. He's not surprised they didn't. They were lazy. Unprofessional. They weren't planning on keeping him alive and so they didn't care what they might find. He grabs the keys and leaves the cabin.

# 7

Ella and Kit live ninety minutes away, in a small town called Benton. Tom drives them. He's told Ella his name – his real name. She sits up front with him, running her hands up and down her arms like she's cold, despite Tom having turned up the heat. She looks back every so often, checking on Kit. The kid is silent, and Tom doesn't know if he's sleeping or awake.

"Is he okay?" Tom says. They haven't spoken for a while. He's given them a chance to calm, to gather themselves after what they've been through and what they've witnessed.

Ella doesn't answer straight away. She watches her son, her lips pursed. "It's always hard to tell," she says.

"How old is he?"

"He's seven."

She turns back around. Tom doesn't say anything. He can sense that she's about to speak more.

"You might've noticed that Kit is...quiet," she says.

"The brothers seemed impressed at how fast he does math," Tom says.

"Mm," Ella says, her face twisting at the thought of the brothers. "Kit is…he's on the spectrum. We're just not sure where he falls. Doctors say more tests are needed before we can be sure."

"He's autistic?"

"Like I said, he's *somewhere* on the spectrum. He's neurodivergent, but I don't have any specifics beyond that. Sometimes, he disassociates. Like now. It's understandable. But earlier today –" She glances at the clock. "Yesterday, I guess. Yesterday, he was…warmer. He was more engaging. He never speaks much, but he can be engaging. That's how it was yesterday, before…"

Tom waits a moment. He hears Ella swallow.

"How did you get caught up with the Underhills?" Tom says.

Ella blows air. "We were on a picnic," she says. She shakes her head. "That's all. I took my son for a picnic, far from home in a place in the woods where my parents used to take me, and we had a lovely time together, just the two of us. And then there were gunshots."

"What happened?"

Ella breathes deeply. "While I was clearing up, Kit wandered off. That's not like him. I figure he must've seen something, and he followed it for a closer look. An animal, maybe. Or maybe it was the men, I don't know. Almost as soon as I realised he was gone, before I could even panic, I heard the gunshots. Three of them. Ordinarily, they'd be the last thing I'd want to hear. They'd be the last thing I'd heard toward, but I ran straight for them. I needed to know that Kit was okay.

"Kit was there. He saw what happened. It was Jake and his cousins, the four brothers. Ian was there, but I didn't notice him straight away. I think he stayed away from the killing. He wasn't like the others. I got the impression he was a chemist or something, just from what I heard and things he would say. But the others, Jake and his cousins, they'd killed three men. Those were the gunshots I heard. They still had the guns out. They were pointing them at Kit, and then they were pointing them at me."

"Do you know who they killed?"

"No idea. They just looked like regular guys. I think there'd been some kind of buy happening – I don't know if something went wrong, or if Jake and the others just didn't feel like paying."

"A buy? Did you see what was being sold?"

"I couldn't tell what they were. They weren't my main focus when there were guns pointing at me and my son. Whatever they were, Ian had them. They looked like flour bags."

Tom remembers the bags from the cabin. The sodium fluoride. He frowns. Why would Jake and the others kill some men just for sodium fluoride? Why would they set up such a clandestine meet in the first place?

"It sounds like you're lucky they didn't shoot you there and then," Tom says.

"I was lucky *you* showed up when you did," Ella says. "There was nothing lucky about what they were planning on doing to me."

"And that's the only reason they didn't kill you?"

Ella nods. "And they kept Kit alive to keep me complacent. They would threaten him if they ever felt like I was getting worked up or about to step out of line."

"How did you manage to escape?" Tom says. "When I found you at the roadside, what had happened?"

"They were arguing," Ella says. "Jake and his cousins. Ian kept out of the way, but he was watching them. He was always very quiet. They'd threatened him earlier – the brothers weren't happy about him. But while they were all arguing, and while Ian was distracted, I managed to get loose, I grabbed Kit and we fled. You know the rest. But that's why we were so tightly bound after they caught us again, and you. I'm amazed you were able to get loose."

"I'm lucky they wanted to ask me some questions. If they hadn't moved me, taken the ropes off my chest and from around my arms, I might not have been able to." Tom returns to something she said. "Why weren't the brothers happy with Ian?"

"Because he spoke to their boss," Ella says. "About me, and Kit. After they'd killed the men in the woods, and they'd captured us, Ian made a phone call and told their boss *about* us. The brothers weren't happy. They were wanting to keep us a secret."

"When I heard Jake on the phone, talking to whom I assume was their boss, he seemed to be aware of yours and Kit's presence. Jake never mentioned I was there, though."

"I heard the name Lincoln," Ella says. "I think that's who they worked for. I think that's who wasn't happy Kit and I had seen things and were still alive."

"Did you hear anything else about Lincoln?"

"No," Ella says.

"Is there anything else I need to know about what happened in the woods, and in the cabin?"

She looks at him. "I think I need to know more about *you*," she says. "Right now, you're like two separate people. The scared guy who was begging for his life back at the cabin, and the cool, collected guy who killed –" She looks back at Kit. "Who *killed* five men and got us out of there. I feel like this one, the latter, is more the real you."

Tom doesn't respond.

"Who are you? I don't feel like you're just some random passerby."

"Well, I was," Tom says. "I wasn't driving along that road thinking I was going to come across a kidnapped woman and her son."

"But there's still more to you," Ella says.

"Let's just say that if there had to be someone stumble across what was happening, it's good that it was me. I've had training. I can handle myself. I'm more than capable of handling men like them. And I'm capable of helping you and Kit, too."

"We're thankful for the help you've given us so far," Ella says. "Kit won't express it, so I will on his behalf."

"So, was there anything else that happened before I was there?"

Ella thinks for a moment. They're not far from Benton. "They took my ID," she says. She remembers something. "*Shit*. They gave it to Ian. He was carrying it."

"He knows where you live," Tom says. "This changes things."

"What should I do?"

"You need to stay somewhere else for a few nights. I'll take you to your apartment, you can pack a couple of bags for you and for Kit, and then I'll take you to a motel. From there, you can call the cops, tell them what happened."

Ella is silent while she takes this all in. Tom leaves her with her thoughts, lets her think.

"After you drop us off," Ella says, "where are you going?"

"I don't have anywhere I need to be," Tom says.

"No? Will you…"

"I'll stick with you," he says. "If that's what you want. I don't want any involvement with the police, but I'll stay close."

"What'll I tell them about you?"

"That you don't know my name, and that I left."

"Why won't you talk to them?"

"Because it takes too long," Tom says. "I don't want to get caught up with them and their official way of doing things. They'd have questions for me, especially after what happened back there. I'd spend a night or two in their interrogation room. I'd probably have to pay for a lawyer. I don't need that hassle. I'll stay close, for you and Kit, but there's nothing I can say to the cops that'll actually help them. When they get out to the cabin, see everything out there, they can deal with the rest themselves."

## 8

Lincoln wasn't happy to hear from Ian. He wasn't happy to hear about what had happened in the cabin, or the mystery man whom Jake deigned not to tell him about.

He takes Arthur Langstrom with him to Vermont. He trusts Arthur. Arthur is his right-hand man. He's a Yank, from Idaho, but Lincoln doesn't hold that against him. Lincoln has known him longer than anyone else in his organisation, especially since…since Stan's death.

Arthur drives. He's a big guy, just shy of six-five. He's broad across and barrel-chested. His biceps bulge at the sleeves of his T-shirt. Lincoln gives directions along the backroads, following the co-ordinates Ian Farrow has sent for his location. "We're not far now," Lincoln says. "Not far at all."

"It's gonna be light soon," Arthur says, his voice deep. "If we have clean-up we need to get on with at the cabin, we're gonna have to get there soon. Our runaways could have called the cops by now."

Lincoln stares at the GPS in his hand, on his phone, and tries not to think about this. "We can beat them out there," he says. "We have to. All right, stop the car. He's close."

Arthur pulls to the side of the road. There's no one else around. Lincoln looks into the trees, peering through them. He can't see anyone. Ian will be lying low. Lincoln calls him.

"Is that you?" Ian says. "Black BMW?"

"It's us," Lincoln says. "Come on out. We've still got a lot to do."

Lincoln hangs up, and a moment later Ian emerges from the trees, dishevelled and worse for wear after a night out in the open. He climbs into the back, groaning as he does so. Arthur turns the car around.

"Well, well, sweetheart," Lincoln says, turning to see Ian. "What's all this then?"

Ian swallows. "I tried to stop them," he says. "Jake did, too. We tried to get them to behave, but they were like animals. They wanted the woman, and no matter what we said, they were going to have her."

"Forget about the woman for now," Lincoln says. "Who was the man? Why wasn't I told about him?"

"I don't think Jake wanted to upset you. I think after the stuff with Ella and Kit, he already knew you weren't happy."

"How'd he end up part of this at all?"

"Ella and Kit managed to escape." Ian bites his lip. "I don't know what happened out there. When they came back, they had this guy with them."

"Another thing kept from me," Lincoln says, clucking his tongue and shaking his head.

"Like I said, Jake knew you already weren't happy."

"Uh-huh. And why didn't you tell me?"

"Because after I called you the first time, they took my

cell off me. *They* really weren't happy about that – the cousins, I mean. I managed to grab it before I ran, when the man came back in with the axe and started killing them." Ian hesitates, running the back of his right hand across his mouth. "Lincoln, I didn't sign up for this. I'm a chemist, I'm not here to watch a bunch of inbred fucking brothers rape a mom in front of her autistic kid. You promised me you run a professional operation."

"And I do," Lincoln says. "Jake vouched for his cousins. I trusted Jake. I'm disappointed. But you don't need to worry anymore, sweetheart." He reaches back and pats Ian on the cheek. "Those big bad brothers are all gone now. Who was our mysterious stranger? What do you know about him?"

"Nothing," Ian says. "He wasn't carrying any ID. They took him into a bedroom and questioned him, but I didn't hear anything they asked, or what he answered. Besides, anything he said, it was probably all lies. He was pretending he was someone he wasn't, making out like he wasn't a threat."

"Mm," Lincoln says. "This is a problem we're gonna have to deal with."

Ian shifts his weight, lifting one leg, and reaches into his pocket. He pulls out a purse. "The woman's ID," he says, holding it out to Lincoln.

Lincoln smiles when he takes it. He holds it up. "This is very useful, Ian. I'm glad, despite everything else, you were able to keep your head about you." He turns back around. "I'll place a call. Get a team out there, keep an eye on things. While you've been waiting, Ian, have you heard anything? Any cops?"

"Nothing," Ian says. "It's been quiet."

"Good. How did the 'buy' go? Did they get rid of the bodies?"

"They said they did."

Lincoln frowns. The Underhill brothers did not prove themselves to be reliable. "Did you see it?"

"Jake sent me back to the cabin with the sodium fluoride. He came back not long after me. The brothers promised him that they dealt with the bodies."

They're not far from the Underhill cabin. It doesn't take them long to arrive. Arthur parks down the road. They continue on foot. Lincoln carries a Sig Sauer. Arthur has a Glock. They approach with care, stepping lightly, sweeping the area. It's clear. Ian follows close behind, though it's clear he doesn't want to be back here.

They find the bodies of Jake, Tyrus, and Billy-Ray, first. They're close to the woodshed. Lincoln pokes at Billy-Ray's body with the toe of his boot. "Bloody idiots," he mutters. He turns to Jake, and kicks him a little harder. "And *you*," he says. "I'm very disappointed in *you*, Jacob. You and your moronic cousins."

Arthur has continued on into the cabin. "Jesus Christ," he calls back from inside. "It's a slaughterhouse in here."

Lincoln heads in to take a look for himself. Ian stays close, pinching his nose to avoid breathing in the heavy smell of death. Lincoln places his hands on his hips and looks the room over. He sees Deke and Cyril's bloodied bodies. Sees the axe still lodged in Cyril's mouth, pinning him to the wall behind him. He sees all the ropes scattered across the cabin floor.

"Well," he says. "This is no good, is it?" He picks up a piece of rope. "Doesn't even look like they can tie a decent knot. Can tell they were never at sea..." His eyes narrow as they zoom in on the whiteboard in the corner. He goes to it, and sees the formula written upon it. He recognises its symbols by sight, though they mean little to him. He points to it, turning back to Ian. "What's this doing on here? Bit careless having it out in the open, isn't it? This isn't something we want everyone knowing."

"Jake asked me to write it out," Ian says. "He said if he was going to be helping me make it, he wanted something to refer to."

Lincoln waves his hand in front of the whiteboard. "This wouldn't make any sense to him."

"He wanted me to teach him."

"Jake was no chemist. Why didn't you just say no?"

"Because he had a gun," Ian says, his temper clearly rising. "And because his cousins were assholes, and because you left me alone out here with these fucking idiots."

Lincoln doesn't appreciate the tone, but he supposes Ian has a point. He jerks a thumb back at the whiteboard. "But you know this, don't you?"

Ian nods. "There's only two of us who do."

Lincoln turns to the whiteboard and wipes the formula off it with his sleeve. "I don't want it out in the open like this," he says. "The vast majority of people aren't going to know what it means, but we don't need it to be found by the one or two who can work it out. In a week or so we'll have time to find some more chemists we can trust. You can teach *them*. Until then, it stays in your head." He turns to Arthur. "We don't have long. Do you think you can get this place cleaned up?"

Arthur has been surveying the scene. "It's not gonna be perfect, but I can get rid of the bodies and the blood. Make it so the only way they'll find anything is if they bring in a hardworking team of forensics, but by then it won't matter." He tilts his head toward the open front door, toward the outside. "The brothers' trucks are still there. I'll load their bodies into the back and then wipe this place down. I can get rid of the bodies elsewhere."

"It'll be light soon," Lincoln says. "Can't be driving around with a pile of dead bodies in the back."

"I'll throw a tarp over them," Arthur says. "There's one already in the bed – I spotted it on the way in. What're you gonna do?"

"Well, first of all, I'm going to call up some more of our boys, get them to come here and keep an eye on things, see what happens when the police show up. See if they bring Ella or our mystery killer back with them." Lincoln claps a hand on Ian's shoulder. "And then I and the prof here will get these bags and canisters back to the Beamer," he says.

"I was an assistant," Ian says, shrugging his hand off. "I never made professor."

Lincoln slaps him on the back, harder than necessary. "Congratulations. I've just promoted you."

Ian swallows. He looks around, holding out his hands. "Where am I going to work now?"

"It won't be here. But don't you worry about that – I'll find you somewhere nice and new. Now let's grab these bags and canisters and get out of here, otherwise, sweetheart, our work's going to be over before it can even begin."

## 9

It's dawn when Tom gets Ella and Kit to their apartment building. Tom heads inside with them. He gets his Beretta and his KA-BAR from his backpack, but he's subtle about it. Keeps both weapons concealed. Doesn't want to spook mother and child.

He goes in ahead of them, making sure it's clear. It is. He tells Ella to pack quickly. They don't want to be here for long. While she does, he stands by the window, looking out. Ella's apartment is at the back of the building. There's woodland behind the parking lot. The trees there are thick and lush, and hard to see through. If someone were observing the building, waiting for their return, that would be the best place to hide. Tom watches it. He watches the road, too. He doesn't see anyone appear.

"Okay, I'm done," Ella says, two bags slung over her shoulders, one for her and one for Kit. Tom takes them from her and they leave the apartment, heading back outside to the Toyota.

While he drives, Tom watches his mirrors. No one

emerges from the woods behind the apartment building. No vehicles slip into line behind them, following. It's still early, and it's quiet.

"Is there a motel nearby?" Tom says.

"Just outside of town," Ella says.

It takes them fifteen minutes to get there. They book into a room. Tom tells them to stay by the door while he sweeps the area. When he's satisfied it's clear, and that no one has followed them, he returns.

"I called the sheriff's department on the landline while you were outside," Ella says. "I figured we didn't want to waste any time."

Tom nods. "I'll wait in the car until after they leave. Are they far?"

"Kind of," she says. "They're just outside of Benton, but on the other side of town. I don't think it'll take them long to get here. Plus, I know one of them – I spoke to him on the phone. Teddy Fuller. We went to high school together."

"You get along? That's good. They're liable to be more helpful for someone they know. Do you have a cell phone?"

"They took it last night."

Tom takes a burner from his backpack. He punches his number into it and hands it over. He notices that Kit is watching him. When Tom looks at him, Kit looks away.

Tom leaves the motel. He returns to the car. He's parked at the rear of the parking lot. He sits low in his seat and watches the road. It doesn't take long for the cops to arrive. Even if one of them didn't know Ella, if the department is on the other side of town it would still be a short journey. Benton, Tom has noticed, is a small place.

The two cops head to the motel room. They knock. Ella answers and they head inside. Tom waits. He watches the motel room, and he keeps an eye on the road, too. It's quiet out here. It's close to morning rush hour now, but there's still not many vehicles on the road. He's seen a couple of logging trucks pass by, going in opposite directions.

The deputies are in the room a half-hour. Tom can't see them through the windows. They leave, still talking to Ella in the doorway. When they walk away, she closes the door. One of the deputies is younger than the other. Tom assumes this could be Teddy. He looks a similar age to Ella.

When they're gone, Tom gets out of the car and returns to the motel. He knocks, and Ella calls through to make sure it's him. She lets him in.

"It was Teddy," she says, wrapping her arms around herself. "And another deputy I didn't know. I told them what happened. I told them they spoke to a man called Lincoln on the phone, but that I didn't know if that was his first or last name. I also told them where the cabin is. They said they'll head straight out, take a look."

"Anything else?" Tom looks toward Kit. He's sitting on the chair in the corner. There's a colouring book open in his lap. He colours in a picture of a bear surrounded by trees. Even from a distance, Tom can see that he's neat. The colours stay inside the lines.

"They asked about you," Ella says. She stifles a yawn. "I told them what you said to. That I didn't know who you were, and that you'd brought us here after you freed us, and then you disappeared. After they left, I saw them go and talk to the receptionist, probably to ask about you, but they never came back to me after that, so I've got to assume the receptionist either didn't remember you, or didn't care to. Anyway, other than that, they just said that they'll be in touch. They said it might be a few hours."

"You should sleep," Tom says. "Both of you. It's been a long night."

"We need to *shower*," Ella says. "And then sleep sounds good." She looks toward the door, and then at Kit. Her teeth worry at her bottom lip. Her eyes are narrowed, probably thinking about last night. She looks back at Tom. "You'll wait here?"

"If you want me to."

She nods.

She takes Kit into the bathroom with her, along with a change of clothes for them both. Tom locks the room's door and stands by the window, watching outside. The road remains quiet. He thinks about what happened last night, and what he saw. He wonders what the men were planning. Wonders where Ian could be now, and if he's called others. They know there's at least one more man they were in contact with, a man they seemed to answer to called Lincoln.

The police are involved now. If they're lucky, they'll find the bodies, trace their known associates, and that'll be that. Ella and Kit can put this nightmare behind them. Tom can hang around until they feel safe. There's nowhere else he needs to be.

Ella and Kit emerge from the bathroom, their hair wet and slicked back from their faces. Ella wears an oversized T-shirt and a pair of grey jogging pants. Kit is in pyjamas. There are two single beds in the room. Ella takes Kit to one of them and tucks him under the blanket. "I know it's daytime," she says to him, "but we've been up all night, so we need to sleep, okay?"

Kit looks back at her. He doesn't speak.

"We're both very tired. We need to get some sleep." Her face is close to his. Kit reaches up with both arms and hugs her around the neck. She hugs him back, then kisses his forehead. "I love you, Kit." He takes his arms back, turns onto his side and closes his eyes.

Ella looks back at Tom. "Are you okay?" she says, standing. "You've been awake a long time, too."

"I'm all right for now," Tom says. "I can watch from out in the car, if that's better for you."

"Stay in the room," Ella says. She says it fast. She takes a deep breath, smiles at him. "Please," she says. "If…if it's okay with you."

Tom saved them from something awful. She feels safer with him around. "I'll be right here," he says. He nods toward the other bed. "Get some sleep. If the cops come back, I'll slip out the back, but I'll let you know first."

Rounding the bed, she hesitates before she climbs into it. She steps closer to him. She wraps her arms around him and embraces him quickly. "Thank you," she says when they part. "If you hadn't come along…"

"Don't think about it," Tom says. "It's over now. And you don't need to thank me. Just get some sleep."

For their sake, he hopes it's over. But truthfully, after what he saw and heard, he's not so sure.

## 10

Lincoln is thinking of his brother.

Stan Collyer hasn't been dead long. Just a couple of weeks. The grief is still raw. Lincoln keeps himself busy. Distracts himself with his work. Part of what makes it difficult is that Lincoln hasn't been able to bury his brother. Hasn't seen his body since he was shot dead. Hasn't been able to take him back home to England, to London. To Walworth, where they grew up. Burying his brother – that's when he'd expect to grieve. Except, he'll never get to bury him. His body is still in the possession of the US government. For all Lincoln knows, they might have cremated him already. They might have discarded him.

But every so often, he thinks he's going to turn around and his younger brother will be next to or behind him in the car, or a door will open and he'll come walking through it, wearing that cheeky grin he always had, and he'll ask Lincoln why he looks like he's seen a ghost.

Or sometimes his phone will ring, like now, and he'll check the screen and expect it to say Stan, but it doesn't.

Because Stan will never ring him again. Instead, the screen reads Neil Dunham. Neil is at the Underhill cabin with a few others. Lincoln is in Benton, with a few others of his own. They've come to Ella's apartment. They're sitting outside right now, watching the building. They've already been inside. Picked the lock to get in, only to find that it's empty.

There were signs someone had recently been inside. A closet door was open. Clothes were missing. He assumes it must have been Ella and Kit. They came back, packed, and left in a hurry. Now Lincoln and his men wait outside, hoping that someone might return. Lincoln knows it's a slim hope, but this is a thread that needs to be tied up. He doesn't know how much Ella and the boy have seen and heard, how much they know. This mystery man, too. How long was he around? What did he learn? Lincoln can't afford to leave these people running free. There's too much at stake. Lincoln personally can't hang around here forever. He has too much to do. Sitting in a parking lot and staring at a building isn't a productive use of his time, but he'll partake while he's still in town. Arthur cleaned up at the cabin and he's already left Vermont, getting things ready for what's next. Finding a new workspace for Ian chief among them. The men with Lincoln will have to stay behind after he goes, which will be soon. The apartment is a lead – their only lead right now – and they can't just give up on it at the first hurdle.

Lincoln answers the call. "Neil, precious, talk to me."

"Cops are here," Neil says, keeping his voice low. "We've got eyes on them."

"How many?"

"Half a dozen," Neil says. "Few cruisers. They've taken a look inside, and they're looking the grounds over."

"Are you safely out the way?"

"I'm at a safe distance. Watching through binoculars. If they come this far out I'll be surprised."

"Okay, that's good. How's it looking? Have they given up yet?"

"It's hard to tell. They've made a few calls. It looks like they're taking her seriously if six of them have come out here in the first place."

"Mm," Lincoln says. "That had crossed my mind."

"What do you want us to do?"

"Don't engage with them," Lincoln says. "There's nothing there for them to find. Arthur has got rid of the bodies. He cleaned up. I trust his work. Keep an eye on the cops. If they leave, follow them. They might lead you to the woman. Keep in touch with me."

"Got it."

Lincoln hangs up. He looks at the other men with him. "That's promising," he says. "We'll sit tight and see how this plays out."

## 11

It takes the deputies longer than a few hours to return. Ella and Kit are awake now, and Tom still sees no sign of them.

Ella and Kit are both dressed. Kit sits on the chair in the corner again. He's drawing, or doodling. He doesn't have a colouring book this time. He has a notepad of blank paper. He's engrossed in it, his pencil rarely leaving the page.

Ella sits at the foot of the bed closest to Tom. She sees where he's looking. "He loves to draw," she says. "Give him a pen and paper, and he can entertain himself for hours."

"Is he a good artist?"

"*Really* good," Ella says. "Especially for seven, but they say that's one of the signs of neurodivergence. But he's my little artist. He'll draw anything. Everywhere we go, when we get back he'll draw me some pictures of things he's seen. Almost like a photograph, sometimes."

"That's impressive." Tom watches him. "I'm not much of an artist myself, but it looks to me like he might be writing."

Ella nods. "He writes, too. Not, like, stories or anything. He'll write down conversations he's heard."

Tom nods. "If you don't mind my asking, it's just you raising him?"

"Yeah." She doesn't look at him when she answers. Tom senses an air of sadness when she says this. He looks toward her left hand. There's no ring there, nor a tan line or an indent in her finger where she used to wear one. Of course, that doesn't mean anything. Not everyone who has kids gets married first.

"Do you mind if I ask about his father?" Tom says. "If you don't want to answer –"

"He died," Ella says. "Kit was one. He won't remember his father, but he knows who he is. He sees pictures of him, and he knows who he is. I'm not sure if he fully understands that he's never coming home."

"I didn't see any pictures in your apartment."

"They're in our bedrooms. You never came into our bedrooms."

Tom nods. "I'm sorry for your loss. Both of you. What happened? Again, you don't have to talk about it."

Ella takes a deep breath. "I can talk about it," she says. "It's been six years. It still hurts, and it always will, but it's not how it used to be. Me and Eric, we were together for five years before I got pregnant. When he died, I wasn't sure how I would go on, especially with a one-year-old. But I had to, because what would happen to Kit if I didn't pull myself together? Sure, my parents helped, and Eric's parents helped, but they struggled with him. Because of how he is, they didn't know how to cope. So I had to pull myself together and take care of my son, all by myself, just because some asshole got drunk, ran a red and T-boned my boyfriend." Her eyes are dry, but she runs her index fingers under both of them to make sure they stay that way. "I was told he died instantly. I think that was supposed to make me feel better, but I'm not sure how much I believe it. Instantly, in a car crash? He would have felt the metal wrap around him, felt it crushing him. He would have known what was coming, and that he only had seconds left. That he'd never see Kit again..."

"You've had to be strong for a long time," Tom says. He tilts his head toward Kit. "But you're doing a good job. He's healthy. He looks happy enough with what he's doing. And from what I hear, he's a hell of an artist."

She smiles at this, but it remains a sad smile. "It never feels like I'm doing a good job. I'm sure it's probably the same way for all moms – for all parents, for that matter."

"You do the best you can," Tom says. "That's all anyone can ask for, or expect. The best you can do looks different for everyone."

"Do you have any kids?"

Tom shakes his head.

"You married?"

Tom shakes his head.

"Single?"

"There's been women, but it's been a long time since I last had a girlfriend."

"Do you really live around here?"

"I don't have a set address," Tom says. "For the last three months I've been living in Green Mountain National Forest."

Ella frowns. "*In*? Like, as a ranger?"

"No," Tom says. "Just living in it."

She laughs. "You get caught?"

"No."

"What were you doing out there?"

"I just needed some peace and quiet."

"Ah – so you were coming *out* of a relationship."

"Not quite," Tom says. "I travel. That's what I do. I don't have anywhere to be. That's how I'm able to be here with you and Kit right now. And if I come across people who need help – like you and Kit – I try and help them."

"That's a very altruistic way to live. Does it keep you busy?"

Tom grins. "Busier than you could imagine."

"How do you make a living?"

"I have savings. I pick up jobs here and there."

"I think what I meant was, how do you make time for your own life?"

"It *is* my life," Tom says.

Ella smiles at him. "You're an interesting guy, Tom," she says, standing. "I don't mean to sound rude, but do you know if *you're* on the spectrum somewhere?"

Tom shrugs. "We all are somewhere, right? Are you hungry?"

She blinks. "I hadn't really thought about it. There's been so much going on, we slept so late and my mind has been in so many places, I haven't stopped to think about food. I guess so."

"I have jerky in my backpack," Tom says, reaching for it. "Not a lot, but enough for right now." He pulls out a handful of strips, hands enough to Ella for her and Kit both.

"You're not hungry?" she says.

"I already ate while you slept."

Ella goes to Kit. She perches on the arm of his chair, looking down at his drawings. Her eyes narrow. She points at something on the page. "What does this mean, Kit?"

Kit doesn't answer.

Ella looks at Tom. "What is it?" Tom says.

"You should look at this," she says. She doesn't sound alarmed, just confused. "He's written the same thing over and over. Does it mean anything to you?"

Tom looks down at the paper, peering over Ella's shoulder, making sure not to get too close to Kit, not wanting to invade his personal space. On the paper, Kit has drawn a scene from the cabin. The Underhill cabin. This isn't what Ella is pointing at. In all the spaces around the cabin, Tom sees the same phrase – a word, and four numbers: *Fordham 1605*. Kit has written it over and over, in every gap in his picture.

The picture itself is of the inside of the cabin. Like Ella said, he's a good artist, even for a quick sketch. He's drawn Deke and Cyril, presumably standing in front of him from his POV sitting at the desk. They're laughing, and rolling dice.

Ella ignores the picture. Understandably, she never wants to see Deke and Cyril, and their likeness, ever again. "It must be from the cabin," she says. "Did you see or hear anything like that while you were there?"

"Fordham 1605?" Tom says. "No. I assume you didn't, either."

She shakes her head. "Should we be concerned? Kit found the men before I did. It might've been something they said there, before I arrived." She wraps an arm around Kit, squeezes his shoulder. "That's a great picture," she says. She points at a *Fordham 1605*. "What does this mean?"

Kit stares at her finger. He's stopped drawing. He stares at the word and numbers.

"Do you remember?" she asks him. "*Fordham 1605* – what does it mean?"

"He's saying it wrong," Kit says, surprising them both. He puts a finger next to Ella's, pointing at the phrase, just like she is. He turns and looks up at his mother. "He's not from here," he says. "He's saying it wrong."

Ella and Tom exchange glances. Ella is frowning. "Who is, Kit? Who's saying it wrong?"

He doesn't answer. He turns his attention back to his drawing.

"Could that be something he heard in the woods, too?" Tom says.

"I don't know," Ella says. "Maybe? I guess it could be."

Before they can ponder it any further, Tom hears a vehicle pulling up at the front of the building. He goes to the window and peers out. A sheriff department cruiser. "Your friend is back," Tom says, heading to the rear window. "I'll be in my car. You know how to reach me."

Ella stands from the chair, leaving Kit alone with his pencils and paper. She nods at Tom as he slips out of the window. He hears her close it after him while he walks away, heading down the back of the motel to circle to his car.

## 12

Tom leaves, and a couple of moments pass of Ella waiting impatiently, watching the door. Finally, there's a knock. She goes to it. Before she can answer, she hears Teddy Fuller calling through. "It's just us back, Ella," he says. "Me and Craig."

She opens the door. Teddy's boyish face is smiling back at her reassuringly. Craig is older, and he stands with his hands in his pockets, his grizzled face looking back over his shoulder across the parking lot. Looking past both of them, Ella can't see Tom. She imagines he'll be careful about getting back to his car. He'll wait until the deputies are inside the room. She holds the door wider. "Come in, come in," she says.

They step inside and she closes the door.

"You were gone longer than I expected," she says.

Teddy and Craig stand in front of the dresser and television stand at the foot of the bed. Neither of them tries to interact with Kit. Teddy is already aware of him, knows he doesn't like interaction and doesn't always respond. He's probably told Craig about this, but Craig looks like he doesn't like talking to kids, anyway.

"Do you want to take a seat, Ella?" Teddy says.

She cocks her head and remains standing. "Why?" she says. "I don't like the sound of that."

"It's nothing like that," Teddy says. "We've just got a lot to talk about and I thought maybe you'd wanna get comfortable. There's a lot to run by you."

"I think I'll stay standing, if it's all the same to you."

Teddy holds out his hands. "Sure," he says. He clears his throat. "So. We went out to the cabin."

"And?"

Teddy sucks air through his teeth. It makes a squeaking sound. "There was nothing out there."

Ella blinks. "That can't be right."

"No bodies," Craig says, speaking for the first time. "No blood. No chemicals, either."

"Are you saying you don't believe me?" Ella says, suddenly adamant, feeling her body tighten, feeling herself drawing up, standing straighter.

Teddy holds out his hands again, shooting a look at Craig. "No, no, we're not saying that at all," he says. "Just telling you how it was. I'll tell you what we *did* find, though – I found a big wedge cut out of the wall in the annexe where you said the guy swung the axe through one of their mouths. We also saw that a truck was missing, and its tracks were fresh. Looked like it'd been driven out of there not long before we arrived."

"You think someone came and cleaned it up?"

"Well, you said there were five bodies and a whole lot of chemicals, and now they're missing," Teddy says. "So, like my partner here so indelicately put it –" He shoots Craig another look, but Craig is unfazed. "Yes, the bodies, the blood, and the chemicals were gone – the axe, too, come to think of it – but that doesn't mean we don't believe you. We *do* believe you, of course we do. I know you, Ella. I've known you a hell of a long time." He winces and looks at Kit. "Excuse my language."

"He heard worse last night," Ella says. She wonders too, not for the first time, how much of the slaughter he actually saw. So far as she could see, he kept his back to it, but she was distracted by what was happening. He hasn't drawn anything, though, and that's a good sign.

Teddy nods, face solemn, sympathetic. "I'm sure, and I'm sorry about that." He clears his throat before he continues, getting them back on track. "What we're thinking is, if someone took the trouble to come and tidy up, they probably didn't want us getting any IDs off those bodies. We've called in forensics, but they haven't arrived yet. Said it could be a few more hours yet. Truth be told, by the time they arrive and find anything worthwhile, it might be too late to matter."

Ella takes a seat now, mulling this over. "What about Ian?" she says. "The man who got away. Have you found him?"

Teddy shakes his head apologetically. "I'm afraid not, but we're still looking."

"He has my ID," she says. "The people that turned up to clean, they probably picked him up too, right? So now *they* have my ID. They know where I live. I can't go home." She bites her bottom lip, working at it distractedly until she tastes blood.

"We've thought of that, too. We've arranged a safe house for you and Kit until we can get this whole thing resolved."

Ella looks at Kit. "How long will that take?"

"We won't know," Teddy says. "We're doing all we can, but we can't give any kind of timeframe. For all we know, they could have gone and moved on. They've maybe discarded your ID and you'll never see them again."

She looks at Teddy, narrowing her eyes to show how doubtful she finds this. He nods. He understands. He's just trying to make her feel better. "Kit's going to struggle being away from home so long," she says. "He can do a few days here and there, but if it's too long he starts to get fidgety and difficult."

"I understand, and I'm sorry, but this is the best we can offer until we can find your attackers."

"We're doing all we can for you here," Craig says. His tone isn't as gentle as Teddy's. "You know how much it's going to cost the state putting you and the kid up in a safe house indefinitely?"

Ella looks at him. She holds his gaze. "Oh, I'm sorry," she says, though she's anything but and she wants him to be clear about that. "Next time my son and I are kidnapped in the woods we'll be sure and let them kill us then and there to save the state on the expense."

She sees the sinews dancing in Craig's cheek while he clenches his jaw. "And that's another thing," he says. "This guy that killed them – *why'd* he up and leave so abruptly? What is it you ain't telling us?"

"What do you think I have to gain from not telling you any more about him than I already have?"

Again, Teddy has to raise his empty hands and get between them, calming the situation. Ella is grateful for

Teddy's presence. If the rest of the deputies have even half as bad an attitude as Craig, she's not sure how she could talk to them.

"That's enough, Craig," Teddy says. "Ella has been through a lot. Show some compassion, huh?"

Craig grumbles and folds his arms. He leans back against the dresser and says nothing further, but he doesn't look happy about it. He hasn't looked happy since he got here.

"We did find something else," Teddy says, turning back to Ella. "In the woods, where you first came across the kidnappers. We found the bodies of the men they killed. More precisely, our sniffer dogs found them. The bodies had been disposed of carelessly. They'd been buried, but not very deep. It didn't take us long to dig them out and get a positive ID on each of the three men."

"Who were they?" Ella says.

"You know about the toothpaste factory over near Brandon?"

Ella frowns. "Sure, I've heard of it."

"They were janitors there. We contacted the factory, and they told us large quantities of their sodium fluoride stock was missing. The janitors must have taken it to sell to these men. How did it look to you? Like a buy gone bad?"

"I – I turned up late. I thought maybe that's what it was, a buy gone bad, but I didn't see any money, though. The way I saw it, they shot those men dead. Money didn't even come into it."

"Could've shot them rather than pay them," Craig says. "Lure them out with a promise of a big payday, then just pepper them with lead instead."

"And you never heard them say what they were planning on using it for?" Teddy says to Ella.

She shakes her head. "They never said, but I got the impression that's what Ian was there for. I doubt they were making toothpaste. They were going to mix it up with whatever else they had out there. I don't know what was in the canisters, but it couldn't have been anything good."

"I know we asked earlier, but did you get his surname? Ian's?"

"No," she says. She wonders briefly if Tom heard it. If he did, she can always pass it on to the deputies later and make out like it just came back to her. "Not that I remember."

"All right," Teddy says. "That brings you about up to date. If you want to get yourself and Kit packed, we can transport you to the safe house."

They're already packed, but Ella doesn't say this. She needs to alert Tom. To tell him what's happening, where they're going. She doubts they'll let her send a quick message before they go. They won't want her to let anyone know where they're taking her. She needs to get them out of the room.

"I'll need to talk to Kit first," she says. "Explain to him what's happening so he doesn't get upset. Do you mind waiting outside a few minutes?"

Craig looks like he might protest, but Teddy is already nodding. "Sure," he says, ushering his partner toward the door. "Take as long as you need. We'll be right outside when you're ready."

When they're gone, Ella goes straight to the phone. She messages Tom, tells him what's happening.

He responds almost instantly.

> I'll follow. Don't worry – they won't see me. I'll stay close by until we're sure this is over.

Ella feels relieved at this. Her breath clears and she fills her lungs, realising that since Teddy and Craig arrived and told her of what they found – or *didn't* – out at the cabin she hasn't taken a full breath.

"Kit," she says, gently. "We need to go."

## 13

Neil called when the deputies left the Underhill cabin. He and the others with him followed the cruiser. Neil isn't driving. He says Dean is. Neil keeps in touch with Lincoln.

"The cops have just come out of the room," Neil says.

Lincoln is still outside Ella's apartment building. She hasn't come back. There hasn't been any sign of her, and now Lincoln suspects he may know why. "Have you seen who they're talking to?"

"Not yet, but they haven't left."

"Does it look like they're about to?"

"One of them's got back in the cruiser – the older guy. The younger one is still outside. He's looking at the motel room. Whoever's in there, I think they're waiting for them."

Lincoln grips the phone tight, hoping it could be Ella and Kit. The mystery man too, if they're lucky. He's circulated Ella's image from her ID. Every member of his group – all two dozen of them – has responded that they've received it. Her face is known.

A couple of minutes pass. Lincoln waits. He glances at the other men in the car with him. They watch him expectantly.

Neil comes back on the line. "The motel door is opening," he says.

Lincoln waits.

"All right, I've got eyes on her," Neil says. "It's Ella Wiley, and the kid."

Lincoln closes his eyes, pleased. One less thing to worry about.

"They're going to the cruiser," Neil says. "They're getting in the back. The younger cop is holding the door open for Ella. He's talking to her."

"Any ideas?"

"Nothing. I can only see the back of his head. She isn't speaking. She's nodding. The kid's already in the car."

"Any sign of a man with them?"

"Just the woman and the kid," Neil says. There's a pause. "All right, they're both in, now. Cop's in, too. The cruiser is leaving the parking lot."

"Don't lose them," Lincoln says.

"Wouldn't dream of it. Dean's just allowing them some space." A pause. "All right, we're in pursuit. I'll send you a pin. You can follow us."

"Brilliant, Neil. We'll be with you shortly." Lincoln hangs up the phone. The pin comes through promptly. He watches it moving on the GPS. "Okey dokey, gentlemen," he says. "Progress is being made." He slips his cell phone into its holder on the dashboard, angling it toward the driver. "Follow that pin."

## 14

Tom saw the vehicle that pulled into the motel parking lot soon after the deputy cruiser. He was in his car at that point, sitting low behind the steering wheel. A black Hyundai, it appeared after the deputies had entered the motel room. It parked at the opposite end of the parking lot to Tom. He slid down behind the steering wheel, stayed out of view, and kept an eye on them. Saw how they never got out of the Hyundai. Saw how they were watching the cruiser, and the motel room. The man in the front passenger seat was on the phone, too.

When the cruiser leaves the parking lot, the Hyundai doesn't move. It watches, though. Tom waits them out. He doesn't want to give himself away. Finally, the Hyundai starts rolling. It's left a big enough gap on the road, but the cruiser remains in view. As the Hyundai passes, Tom counts four men inside.

Now it's his turn to wait. The Hyundai pulls onto the quiet road. There's nothing between it and the cruiser, but there's distance, and it does nothing to close it. Tom gets lucky. A Chevy pickup goes by, and he slips out behind it. The Chevy sticks to a steady speed. Tom can see past it. He keeps both the Hyundai and the cruiser in view.

Somehow, it looks like the friends of Ella's kidnappers have managed to track her down. He thinks about how that could have happened. A mole in the sheriff's department? He hopes not. Ella said one of the deputies – Teddy – was a friend. But then Tom knows plenty of people who have been betrayed by supposed friends.

The Hyundai followed the cruiser here. Could be that they were out at the cabin, tailed them from there. They're keeping their distance now. They probably did that coming here. It looks like they know what they're doing. They're being careful not to give themselves away, to alert the people inside the cruiser.

The cruiser joins a busier road and the others follow. The Chevy turns off, but more vehicles arrive, pulling out of junctions, filling the gap between Tom and the others. He doesn't lose them. Keeps them in sight.

They drive for an hour. They reach a small town called Carlise. The main street is not busy. Tom spots a coffee shop and a bar and an apothecary. There's a few people walking between them. There's a supermarket further down. There's a little more activity around here. He sees a hotel on the corner, too. The vehicles bypass all of these buildings. The cruiser turns down a road leading to a quiet suburb. The houses here are modest and uniform, stretching for as far as Tom can see.

It's harder to follow here without being noticed. The Hyundai pulls all the way back, and Tom does the same. He stops outside a house, as if about to get out and visit. The Hyundai continues to crawl. When it's far enough away, Tom follows. He's lost sight of the cruiser at this point, but he's certain the Hyundai can still see it. He follows their lead.

Sure enough, when he gets around the corner, he sees the cruiser on a house's driveway. The house is in darkness. The curtains are drawn. There are no other vehicles in front of it, or signs of life. The front lawn is longer than other lawns in the neighbourhood. Tom can see the occupants of the cruiser getting out. The older deputy goes to the front door. He's pulling out a key. Teddy opens the rear door of the cruiser and takes Ella's bags.

The Hyundai drives on. It doesn't stop in front of the house. It keeps going, passing it by. It continues down the road and takes another turn, disappearing from view behind a row of houses. The Hyundai is gone, but Tom doesn't believe that it's left the area entirely. They're doing the same as he's about to – staying out of sight, making sure they're not seen.

Tom takes a right turn, away from the street where the cruiser has parked. He keeps going to the dead end at the bottom of the road. There's no houses here. He parks and gets out of the car. He has the Beretta and KA-BAR on him, concealed beneath his jacket. He puts his hands in his pockets and keeps his head down as he walks back the way he came. He spotted bushes and hedgerows on the street with the safehouse – plenty of places for him to conceal himself.

He thinks about messaging Ella, about telling her about the Hyundai that followed them here. As unlikely as it seems, it could be a false alarm. Just one big coincidence. He doesn't believe this. At the same time, he doesn't want to spook Ella. And what about how the Hyundai was able to follow the cruiser in the first place? He doesn't like it, but he has to entertain the notion that whoever these people are, they could have an insider in the sheriff's department. His mind races. If the men are here, he can't just wait for them to do something. Ella and Kit are already in danger, but it puts the cops at risk, too. There's no guarantee that they're dirty at all.

Casually, he strolls to the end of the road and looks right, toward the safehouse. They're inside now. The cruiser is empty. There's no sign of the Hyundai, either, but it would be foolish for them to show themselves again. They're doing the same as him. Parking up, hiding out, then they'll come back on foot. Tom doesn't see anyone, but they could be out there already.

Or maybe they're waiting for reinforcements. They have the address – they don't *need* to come back here. Looking around, he can't see anyone else on foot. A car drives by and Tom looks down at his phone, busying himself so as not to seem suspicious.

He messages Ella. As much as he doesn't want to scare her, he has to. Has to make sure she's aware. He tells her to keep it to herself, but they were potentially followed here. Tells her he's outside and not to panic. Tells her to act natural. That if anything happens, he's right here.

He hesitates, then adds:

> Give this number to Teddy. Only Teddy. We need to talk.

## 15

Ella doesn't see Tom's message straight away. Doesn't feel the phone vibrate in her pocket while she moves around the safe house and tries to get Kit settled.

It doesn't take her long. She sits him on a chair in the living room with his blank notepad and his pencils and he busies himself drawing. He doesn't seem too perturbed by their new location. Not yet, anyway. He's too focussed on the blank paper. Ella sees, with concern, that the first thing he writes down is *Fordham 1605*, but she tries not to dwell on it right now. She thinks about presenting it to Teddy, but she doubts he'd be able to decipher it any better than she can.

The safe house is sparse. Wall-to-wall carpets. A few mirrors on the walls, but no portraits or artwork. A television in the corner of the living room with a thick sheet of dust on the screen. Furniture that looks like it was picked up in a thrift store. None of it matches, and it's all worn out.

There are three bedrooms. The master bedroom has a king-size bed, the second biggest bedroom has a double, and the smallest bedroom has two single beds. She and Kit will probably sleep in the smallest. She wants to keep him close. Wants to be able to see him if she wakes up in the middle of the night, and wants to be nearby should *he* wake up in the middle of the night and realise he's in a strange, unfamiliar place.

Ella is exhausted. Despite getting some sleep and waking up not so long ago, she doesn't feel at all rested. Her stress levels are high. Since Teddy and Craig returned, she's been constantly on edge. It's wearing her out. The only time she felt relaxed, safe, was when Tom was with them.

The thought makes her check the phone. That's when she sees the message. She holds her breath as she reads it, over and over, the words taking a moment to sink in. They've been followed? Even out here, in the safehouse, they're not secure.

Tom also says he's close by. That he'll be watching. This gives her some relief, at least, but not enough. She's on edge again. Her shoulders rise and tense. Her body feels rigid. She reads the part, once again, where Tom tells her to keep this information to herself. Then she re-reads where he says to give his number to Teddy.

She slips the phone away before either of the deputies can spot it. They're looking through the house and checking the backyard. While they're busy, Ella goes back to Kit and tears out a blank piece of paper from his notepad. She uses one of his pencils to write Tom's number down, then folds the paper and secrets it in her palm.

The deputies finish their sweep and Teddy comes through to find her. There's no sign of Craig. "I know it's not ideal," Teddy says. "But this is the best place for you to be right now."

She bites her lip but says nothing.

"I'm going to head back out, but Craig will be staying here. He'll be in the kitchen if you need him. There'll be a new deputy out to replace him in the morning."

Ella steps closer to Teddy, lowering her voice so Craig, wherever he may be, can't hear. "Why does he have to be the one who stays?"

"I know, I know," Teddy says, placing his hands on her shoulders. "I volunteered, but the sheriff thinks it's a conflict of interest, seeing as how we're friendly and all. But I'll be out there, working on this thing. We'll find these people and we'll bring them in, and when it's all over I'll drive you home myself, okay?"

Ella clenches her jaw.

Teddy sees how tense she is. He feels how tight she is under his hands. "I get this is a stressful situation," he says, "and that you're gonna be tightly wound, but just try and relax, okay? We're on this. We're doing everything we can."

Ella feels the folded slip of paper concealed in her hand. She makes sure Craig is still not anywhere close, then holds it out to Teddy. "You need to speak to this man."

Teddy frowns. He takes the paper and looks down at it. Just numbers, no name. "What do you mean?"

"He said only you," Ella says. "I've made it clear I know you – I *trust* you. He wants to talk to you, only you, about something he's seen."

Teddy blinks. "I don't understand."

"Just call the number," Ella says. "When you leave. Don't let Craig know, or the sheriff – just do this yourself."

Realisation dawns on Teddy's face. "Is this the guy...?"

Ella nods.

Teddy still looks unsure, but he slips the paper into his

pocket. His face is concerned. It's clear that he's thinking. Deliberating. "I'll talk to him," he says, keeping his voice lowered. "But I don't understand why all this secrecy."

"Neither do I," Ella says. "But he said only *you*. I guess he'll explain."

"All right, but it better be good. I can't withhold information from the sheriff. I could get in a lot of trouble for that." He pauses, looking at Ella, and past her, to Kit. He sighs. "Just...just try to relax here, okay? Everything will be all right. I'll...I've got to talk to Craig, and then I'll be on my way."

"Don't tell him," Ella says.

"I promise," Teddy says.

He heads through to the kitchen. Ella hears the two men talking. She takes a seat on the sofa, hearing the cracked leather creaking beneath her. She runs her hands down her face. A couple of minutes later, she hears Teddy leaving.

## 16

Tom waits in the Toyota for Teddy to call. He's in the front passenger seat. The phone is out in his hand. When it rings, he answers straight away.

"Who is this?" Teddy says.

"Are you alone?" Tom says.

"Yeah, I'm alone."

"You haven't spoken to anyone else about this number?"

"I promised Ella I wouldn't."

"Are you still at the safehouse?"

There's a pause at this. "How do you know...?"

"Pull around the corner. Black Toyota Corolla. Pull up on the passenger side. We'll talk." Tom hangs up. He watches the mirror. It's angled toward the corner. It doesn't take long for the cruiser to appear, crawling along the road. Tom puts the window down. Teddy pulls up alongside him.

"All right," Teddy says, getting a good look at him. "First things first – who are you?"

"I'm a friend of Ella's, just like you," Tom says. "That should be enough for now."

"I want a name."

"I'm not giving my name," Tom says. "You don't need it. It's not important. What *is* important is what I have to tell you."

"You alone out here?"

Tom nods.

Teddy watches him with narrowed, suspicious eyes. "How am I supposed to trust you?" he says. "You're being awful sneaky for someone who's claiming to help. Why do you keep hiding out?"

"Do you want this information, or not?"

Teddy stares, weighing up his options. Finally, he sighs. "Fine," he says. "What is it?"

"You were followed here," Tom says.

"No shit," Teddy says. "I'm looking right at you."

"Not by me," Tom says. "A black Hyundai. Four men inside. Followed you from the motel parking lot. They were careful. I wouldn't be surprised if you never spotted them."

Tom can see from the look on Teddy's face that he didn't.

"They followed you *to* the motel, too. Where'd you come from? The cabin?"

Teddy nods.

"That's what I thought. Seems like you didn't see them out there, either, but they saw you."

"Where are they now? I never saw anyone on the street when we arrived, or when I left."

"Hiding, so far as I can tell. They continued on down the road, disappeared around the corner."

"What do you want me to do? Go talk to them?"

"I want you to be ready for them," Tom says. "They could be waiting for back-up. You need more deputies out here. You need to be ready for them. Tell the sheriff that you spotted the Hyundai. That it looked suspicious to you."

Teddy grits his teeth, thinking.

"You can end this," Tom says. "Get some other deputies. We can't be sure where they are or who they are, or how many of them there might be. You need to come in force, lie low, same way they are right now. When they make a move, *you* make a move. End this all. Make your arrests. Make sure Ella and Kit are safe."

Teddy looks at him. "I'll have to run it by Craig," he says. "He was right there in the car with me. He's not going to back me up if I suddenly come out with this story like I knew we were being followed the whole time."

"The other deputy? Forget about him. He doesn't back you up, so what? That's not important. Ella and Kit are important."

"I know that," Teddy says, setting his jaw.

"Then act like it," Tom says, holding his eye. "If you think Craig's gonna have a problem, deal with that later. You seem like a smart guy – I'm sure you'll think of something."

"And you want your name kept out of this?"

"You don't know my name."

"You know what I mean."

"I'll *be* out of it," Tom says. "But I'll be close by."

"I can't recommend that."

"I'll take that into consideration," Tom says. He grins.

Teddy can see Tom isn't taking him seriously. "All right," he says. "I'll do it your way. I'll go talk to the sheriff. I'll keep you out of it."

"You need to be fast. I'm assuming they won't try anything until it's dark, but that's no guarantee."

"I'll be as fast as I can," Teddy says. "But when it starts going down, you really do need to stay out of our way."

Tom holds up his hands. "Fine. Do your job, and I won't need to do mine."

Teddy's eyes narrow. "And what's your job?"

"Making sure nothing happens to Ella and Kit."

"Then it sounds like we have the same job," Teddy says. He puts the cruiser in reverse and pulls away from the Toyota. In the mirror, Tom watches him go.

## 17

As much as he'd like to, Lincoln can't hang around. He has too much to do. He needs to get Ian set up. They've left the street with the safehouse. They've parked down the road, where it's quiet, under some trees. Two men have stayed behind, to observe the house. Out here, by the side of the road, there are two cars. Two teams of four, including the two men on recon but not including Lincoln himself.

Neil and Dean are present. Lincoln is confident leaving this operation in their hands. He talks to them outside of the car. "Arthur's on his way to pick me up," he says. "I need to go and get Ian set up and get him to work. With everything going on, we're running behind schedule now. We're going to have to work double-time to get caught up. It's not long until we need to put a show on, and I need to ensure everything's on track. Now, I'm relying on you two boys to get things nice and tidy for me here, all right?"

"You can count on us, sir," Neil says.

"Good chaps," Lincoln says. "Now listen, try and keep it

quiet, sweeties. This is a residential area, after all. Too much noise, and they're going to start calling the police. And here's the other thing – we know that the man who killed the Underhills and Jake isn't here, and maybe he's left, never to be seen again. But have a word with the bird, all right?"

Dean cocks his head. "The…bird?"

Lincoln rolls his eyes. "The woman," he says. "Ella. Talk to her. Find out what you can about him. If she has any answers, and if he's nearby, we can track him down and deal with him. But if he's no longer going to be an immediate problem, I don't want to worry about him any further. For personal reasons, we can always deal with him down the line. Right now, we need to think about our upcoming paydays, and making sure he can't interfere with that. Sound good to you chaps?"

Neil and Dean nod along. He knows they struggle with the things he says sometimes, like referring to women as 'birds.' They share a language, but his English is different to their English. He does it on purpose, throwing in slang and colloquialisms. It's for his own amusement. If he used real Cockney rhyming slang, they'd never understand a word he said. Sometimes, he and Stan would talk like that when they were around the Yanks. It was like their own private code, and they could say whatever they wanted.

"So, to review," Lincoln says, counting off his points on his fingers. "Wait until it's late. Dark. Keep it quiet. Talk to the woman. When you have answers, get rid of her and the kid. Relay any pertinent information to me. Then, finally, tidy up after yourselves. We're nice clean boys, aren't we?" He grins. "After that, you come join the rest of us. Simple, eh?"

Neil and Dean are still nodding.

"I'm trusting you, sweeties. I know you won't let me down." He checks his phone. Arthur is five minutes away. "I'm off to meet Artie. I'll talk to you soon."

## 18

It's late. The early hours after midnight. Tom is tired, but he's alert. Forces himself to stay awake. Focussing on the safehouse helps. Lying on his stomach under a bush, branches poking uncomfortably into his back, helps too.

He's smeared dirt across his face as further disguise. A few cars have passed by, but no one has seen him. The bush is thick, and he's deep within it. It's a quiet neighbourhood. At rush hour it was a little more active, people coming home from work. Tom didn't hide under a bush with dirt coating his face then. He would have been too obvious. He strolled the block instead, hands in his pockets. He didn't see anyone. The Hyundai was gone. He hasn't seen it since they all first arrived here. The missing Hyundai didn't bring him any relief. It increased his concern. Made him feel that it's more likely they've gone for reinforcements.

He's done a few sweeps since it got dark, too. Again, he found nothing. He wonders how far the Hyundai, and the men within, have gone to bulk up their numbers. They know where the safehouse is now. They don't need to hang around for it. Tom remains on edge, keeping watch, knowing that when they return there could be a new vehicle – multiple new vehicles – and he won't know what they are.

A couple of hours ago, he got a call from Teddy. "I spoke to the sheriff," he said.

Tom was under the bush at that point. He turned down the glow of the phone's screen and pressed it tight to his ear. "And?"

"He believed what I told him," Teddy said. "We're out here now – we've been back out for the last hour. I've had to wait for a chance to call you."

"Where are you now?"

"I said I had to take a piss. I'm in the woods."

"The Hyundai has disappeared," Tom said. "I've done a few sweeps. The vehicle is gone. There could still be people around, well-hidden. I haven't seen anyone that's made me suspicious. I haven't seen anyone at all. This is a quiet place. How many men are you?"

"There's six of us," Teddy said. "Including me and the sheriff."

"That might not be enough."

"You just said you can't see anyone."

"They're going to come back. They know where it is."

Teddy said nothing for a moment. "It's the whole department," he said finally.

"Does Craig know?"

"He's been made aware. Told to be extra vigilant, and not to alarm Ella."

"Did he have any objections to your story?"

"No, but I think he'll have some questions when this is over."

"How far out are you? I haven't seen any cruisers."

"We're out of uniform," Teddy said. "And we've come in unmarked vehicles. We're parked right outside of the neighbourhood. If Craig sees anything, he calls us and we swoop in."

"I'll do the same," Tom said. He had his Beretta and knife with him, but no idea what kind of weaponry the other men might be carrying.

"Message me if you need me or if you see anything," Teddy said. "I don't need any more questions than I'm already gonna get."

It's been silent since the phone call. At one point, the owner of the house whose bush he's hiding in came outside to drop a couple of bags into the trash. He stopped by the front door and had a cigarette, looking up at the night sky. Tom lay very still, watching him out the corner of his eye. The man took his time with the cigarette. He blew smoke in long, wide plumes. Finally, he stubbed out what remained on the wall of the house and flicked the butt onto the lawn. He went back inside. He never saw Tom. By now, he should be sleeping. The house is in darkness. All of the houses here are in darkness, save for a few porch lights.

An hour passes. A few more and it'll be dawn. The birds will awaken. The sun will begin to rise. If they reach morning and nothing happens, what then? Tom doesn't imagine that the men who followed Ella and Kit here will want to wait much longer. They know where they are *now*. If they leave it too long, they could be moved again. If it gets to morning and nothing happens, Tom will have to accept that perhaps it *was* just a coincidence. He'll struggle to believe that. The Hyundai followed with purpose. They kept their distance. They made sure they weren't seen. They came *here*, where the safe house is, and they're not at any of the houses. They're not on any of the driveways – Tom has checked.

Before he can ponder this further, he sees movement in the dark. He's instantly alert. He zeroes in on it. Four figures, all dressed in black. They emerge from the shadows and slink across the road. They have handguns, out and carried low, pointing two-handed at the ground. They come from the north. They don't cross directly in front of the safe house. They come from ahead of it, not wanting to be seen from the windows. Tom can see them. Can see everything they do. He has a clear view as they run across the front of the neighbouring lawns, sticking to the shadows. They don't make a sound. If Tom hadn't seen them he wouldn't have heard their approach.

They split. Two head toward the front of the house, and two peel off down the side, heading to the rear. Tom doesn't know if Craig will have seen them. He pulls out his phone and types fast, sending it to Teddy.

> Four on way, stealthy. Two to front, two to back.

Tom is already preparing to move. He can't wait for the sheriff and his deputies to get here. It could take too long. They could arrive too late. He can't hear their engines coming. He has a hand on his Beretta, pulling it loose as he shuffles forward, out from under the bush.

His phone buzzes. Teddy:

> On way.

He can hear the engines now, but they're still distant.

The seconds it takes them to get here can be the difference between life and death.

Tom clears the bush. Before he can stand, he spots more movement. He freezes on the ground, looking ahead into the darkness from which the first four emerged. He spots more shapes. Another four, all in black. They watch the house. He doesn't think they've seen him. He can't make out what they're carrying, but it's clear that these four have heavier weaponry. He sees the barrels of their automatic rifles.

Tom rolls to the right, away from the front lawn and where they have a better chance of seeing him. He pushes up to his feet and messages Teddy again while he runs, scaling the neighbour's fence and crossing their back yard.

> Beware – more men – ambush.

## 19

Kit is sleeping soundly. Ella is not. She's struggling to settle. She checks the time and sees that it's after three. She's lain here since ten. She's not sure if she's slept for longer than a half-hour.

The minutes tick by. She lies on her back and stares at the ceiling. She listens to every sound the house makes. Occasionally, she hears Craig moving around. He was in the kitchen earlier, making coffee. He yawned loudly. She thinks he's in the living room now. She hasn't heard him make any sounds for a couple of hours. Part of her wonders if he's still awake. He's supposed to be.

She thinks about what Tom said. About how they were potentially followed here. She doesn't think this is what's keeping her awake. Even without this information, she doubts she'd be able to sleep tonight, here, in a strange new place so far from her home. She's amazed she was able to get Kit down as easily as she did. Too tired to protest, probably. They've both been through a lot.

She wonders if Teddy called Tom. If they spoke, and

what they spoke about. She hasn't heard anything from either of them since. If Teddy passed anything on to Craig, he never relayed it to her. No news is good news, right? She certainly hopes so.

Kit was still drawing, right up until bedtime. She was happy to leave him to it, if it meant he was distracting himself from their current situation. When she finally took the paper from him and sent him to brush his teeth, she noticed he'd changed from writing *Fordham 1605*. Instead, he'd been drawing. The inside of the cabin again. This time, the area near to the annexe where Ian stood, waiting to get to work. Kit had drawn him, arms folded, looking across the room. He'd drawn the bags of sodium fluoride and the canisters propped behind them. He'd drawn the whiteboard, too, and it was this that caught Ella's eye. He'd written something on the whiteboard, in neat, small letters and symbols. It was incomplete, but it looked familiar and brought memories back to Ella. The formula that was written on the whiteboard. He was writing it out, inside his drawing. He'd memorised it, just like the rest of the scene. Ella's interruption for bedtime had left it unfinished. She stared at it, at the whiteboard and the writing upon it, wondering what it could have been for, and what it could mean to the Underhills and the person they worked for. What it meant to Ian. She put the pages back down on the chair and went and got Kit ready to sleep.

For the few hours before she came to bed, she sat in the living room, trying to distract herself, wishing she was as able to do so as Kit was. She watched Craig. He spent a lot of time at the windows, looking out, watching the street. There's sheer netting in front of the living room windows, making it difficult for anyone to see inside. This was no doubt by design. Craig had to pry them open a little so he could see out. When he realised Ella was watching him, he turned to her. "What?"

"Do you see anything?"

He frowned at her. "No," he said. "Now leave me alone. I'm trying to do my job. You're distracting me."

She sits up on the bed now, giving up on sleep. She stays where she is for a moment and watches Kit. He lies on his back, his cherubic face turned to the side, toward her. His lips are slightly parted. He breathes lightly. She watches his chest slowly rise and fall. His face is smooth and unblemished. She reaches out and strokes his soft cheek. In this strange place, she feels like she's failing him. Like she hasn't been able to keep him safe. They should be at home. They should be in their own beds.

She was just trying to take him for a picnic. She was just trying to do something nice with her son.

Closing her eyes tight, breathing deep, she tries not to dwell on it. She can't. It won't accomplish anything, and neither will lying here fighting a losing battle with the bed. She's in her underwear and the plain black T-shirt she sleeps in. She pulls on her jeans but leaves her feet bare. Looking back at Kit, making sure he's still sleeping soundly, she leaves the bedroom, careful not to disturb him.

She walks down the hall, arms wrapped around herself. She's not sure where she's going. First and foremost, she wants to make sure that Craig is still awake. She wants to look outside for herself, and make sure that no one is coming. She wants to try and see Tom. Knowing he's close by might calm her a little. Then she'll probably drink some of the coffee she knows Craig has brewed. If she's going to have to stay awake, she might as well caffeinate herself.

Halfway down the hall, a sound stops her. A chill runs down her spine, and spreads through the rest of her body. She stays where she is, one foot in front of the other, not yet fully on the ground. She slowly lowers it, and listens.

It came from the back of the house. From the kitchen. She wonders if it's Craig, except the light there is off. From the front of the house, under the living room door, she can see the glow from a lamp. As if to reassure her of his presence, Craig clears his throat. He's not in the kitchen.

Ella should go and get him. Tell him about the noise. She's closer to it, though. She's closer to it right now. She should look. Prove to herself that it was nothing – just an animal, or the house settling.

Gritting her teeth, she steps lightly toward the kitchen. Leaning against the frame, she peers inside, looking toward the back door.

And then she hears the roar of engines outside, at the front of the house. Then she hears gunfire.

All hell breaks loose.

Suddenly, the front door bursts open. At the back door, on the other side of the glass, two dark shapes stiffen, alerted to all of the new noise. Ella sees them, and she almost screams. She bites down on her tongue. Despite this, one of the men sees her. She hears gunshots. Ella throws herself to the ground. She looks up, to see that it wasn't the men at the back. The gunshots persist. They get louder, more frequent. They're inside the house, and out the front. There's a battle raging.

No longer any need to be quiet, the men at the back door cease trying to pick the lock. One of them raises his handgun, and he uses it to smash the glass. Ella flinches at the sound. Some of the shards skid across the linoleum and land close to her. An arm reaches in to unlock the back door.

Ella knows she should get up. Knows she should run to Kit, to grab him and run, get clear, but there is gunfire everywhere. Dimly, she hears Craig's voice, shouting. She wonders if he's shooting, too. Nowhere is safe. Still, she needs to get to Kit – but she can't move. She's frozen on the ground, looking up at the two men. They wear masks – balaclavas. She can't see their faces, but she knows they're looking at her.

The door is open. They're inside. Ella can't move. They're coming for her. The man at the rear points his gun at her. The man in front hurries toward her. He's reaching down for her.

Out the corner of her eye, over the shoulder of the man closest, she sees the other one disappear from the doorway, as if yanked from view. She didn't see what happened, where he went. All of a sudden, he's gone, and the man in front is blocking out all she could see, dropping to a crouch in front of her. She sees how he glances out of the kitchen, into the hallway. He seems confused by all of the noise.

Ella hears him grunt. Whatever's happening, it's not something he can dwell on. He turns back to her. His gloved hands reach for her face.

Then, before he can reach her, his head snaps to the left. Ella hears his bones crack. The man doesn't make another sound. He collapses in on himself, falling to the ground. Behind him now, there is another pair of legs.

Ella looks up. It's Tom.

## 20

Tom crouches next to Ella, motioning for her to stay low, too. He has his Beretta out and raised. He vaulted fences and crossed back yards to get here, running as fast as he could as he heard gunfire erupt at the front. Teddy mustn't have seen his follow-up message, or at least not in time. Tom reached the safe house in time to see the two men at the rear entering the kitchen.

There's gunfire inside the house, at the front. None of the bullets are coming this way with purpose; only the occasional errant shot hits the wall or doorframe. Tom risks a look out and down the hall. The two men at the front are crouching low, back to back. One of them is firing out into the street. The other aims toward what must be the living room. Craig must still be alive. He must be returning fire.

"Where's Kit?" Tom says, having to shout to make himself heard.

"He's in the bedroom," Ella says, pointing down the hallway that splits away from the front of the house. She's pale. He must be awake. The bullets are flying. Has he been hit? Is he coming to investigate?

"Go into the backyard. Wait for me there," Tom says.

"I can't leave him –" Ella begins, but Tom cuts her off.

"You're not going to. I'm going to get him. I'm faster on my own."

Ella swallows. She wants to protest, but she wants what's best for her son more. She nods. "All the way down, third door on the right," she says.

"Stay low," Tom says. "Stay away from the house. Get into the shadows. If anyone else comes around the back, you don't want them to see you."

Ella does as he says, heading to the back on all-fours. Tom notices she doesn't have shoes. He makes a mental note of this – barefoot is no good for their escape.

He peers down the hall again. Past the two men, he can see a little more activity in the street. The other four men out there look like they have the upper hand. At least one of them is getting closer to the house. He unloads a magazine toward the deputies' position, then reloads while he moves. He's coming to help the two men inside the house. He probably still thinks there's four – two at front, two at back. Regardless, they'll be aware of the noise they're causing, and how much attention this will draw. They're going to need to wrap this up fast.

Tom dives across the hall, behind the wall there. He pauses. No bullets come his way. They might not have seen him. They're preoccupied with Craig. Tom keeps moving. He needs to get to Kit. He reaches the room, third door on the right at the end of the corridor. He looks back, makes sure no one's coming. The noise at the front of the house hasn't changed, but Craig must be running low on bullets. He can't hold them off indefinitely.

Tom opens the door into the bedroom. Kit is sitting up in the bed, wide awake. His brow is furrowed. It's the most emotion Tom has seen him express.

"Hello, Kit," Tom says, not expecting a response. He keeps his tone calm and level. The gunfire is still loud, but it's more muted here. "Your mom sent me to get you. She's waiting outside. Do you want to come with me, to go to her?"

Kit stares at him, unblinking, then he pulls back the blanket and turns, swinging his legs over the side. He slides down to the floor and stands, looking at Tom expectantly.

Tom spots their bags at the feet of the beds. He sees Ella's sneakers, and Kit's. He grabs them both and shoves them into their respective bags. He picks up Kit's bag and holds it out to him. "Can you carry this for me?"

Kit takes the bag, slipping his arms through the straps and tightening it on his back. Tom slings Ella's bag onto his own back, then crouches down and holds out his left arm. "It's going to be easier if I carry you," he says.

Kit steps forward, into Tom's open arm. He wraps his arms around Tom's neck. Tom stands with him. Kit wraps his legs around him.

"Hold on tight," Tom says.

He leaves the bedroom and makes his way down the hall. Ordinarily, during a firefight, he only has to worry about his own wellbeing. Right now, there's a child on him. He's going to have to be extra careful.

He hears the assault rifle open fire inside the house. He looks around the corner. The man with the assault rifle enters the living room, either to make sure Craig is dead or to finish the job. The two men remain as they were before, back to back. Tom raises the Beretta. He fires twice, one bullet for each of them. Headshots on both. They go down. Tom crosses the hall into the kitchen. He pauses and looks back from cover. The man with the assault rifle heard the gunfire. He steps out of the living room, looking down at his two dead comrades in the doorway. Before he can look down the hall, Tom fires into him twice. Both bullets find their mark. He doesn't hang around to watch the man go down, or to see what happens next. The firefight out front doesn't sound so pitched anymore. This isn't a good sign. He gets outside, into the back yard.

Ella sees them. She emerges from the shadows next to the fence. Tom waves her back. They go to her. He lowers Kit to the ground and passes Ella her bag. "I brought your sneakers," he says.

Ella doesn't hear him. She kneels in front of Kit, looking him over, making sure he's okay. "Are you all right?" she says. "I'm so sorry, Kit, I'm so sorry. I love you so much." She hugs him briefly, tightly.

"We need to be fast," Tom says, watching the house and the alleyway down the side. "We need to get out of here. I don't think it's going well at the front."

Ella takes the bag from him and pulls out her sneakers. She pulls them on.

Tom covers the rear of the house, Beretta ready. He sees movement down the side, in the alleyway. Spots the barrel of an assault rifle. The figure is all in black. From the firefight he heard at the front, in the street, he doesn't believe the deputies have any assault rifles. He heard handguns and shotguns, nothing automatic on their end. He drops to a crouch and waits, wanting to be sure. The figure takes two more cautious steps forward. Enough light hits them for

Tom to see that they're wearing a balaclava. He fires three times, a tight grouping in their centre of mass.

Tom counted eight men. He's killed six. There should only be two left, unless there were further reinforcements that he didn't see. It's a possibility.

The shooting at the front has ended. If this man was creeping down the alley, the others are likely making their way through the house, too.

"We need to go," he says.

"We're ready," Ella says.

"Climb the fence. I'll pass Kit over. Keep going that way, through the yards."

Ella scales the fence. She's fast. Tom lifts Kit and passes him over the top. He waves for them to go to the next fence. Tom looks the safehouse over, makes sure no one is close. He looks down the alleyway, too. Clear. He hurries over the fence and drops down the other side. He sees that Ella has lifted Kit over ahead of herself. She's dropping down the other side when Tom catches them up.

They get clear of the safehouse and the chaos there. They run out of yards to cross and fences to climb, and they keep going. Tom leads them to his car, looking back all the way, checking for pursuit. He can hear sirens approaching, but they won't be deputies. State police, perhaps. Ambulances, too, more than likely. He wonders if any of the deputies have survived. He hopes they did. He hopes Teddy did.

They get into the Toyota, and Tom drives them away.

## 21

Lincoln is awoken by a phone call from Neil. He doesn't enjoy what he's told.

He has to wake himself up, patting his cheeks. He breathes deeply. "Neil, sweetheart," he says. "Run that by me one more time."

"The guy. He was there," Neil says. He's breathing hard, like he's been running. Lincoln can hear the sound of the car he's in. He's not running anymore. He's driving. "And the deputies turned up. Looked like the whole department. I don't know where they came from. They were in uniform but their vehicles were unmarked. They just turned up out of the dark as soon as we made our move. But we were careful. The motherfucker inside couldn't have seen us coming. I don't know what happened."

Lincoln clucks his tongue. "Now, now, precious," he says. "*Language.* You don't want to offend my delicate sensibilities at such an early hour." He takes another deep breath. "And my sensibilities are *already* offended. Did I, or did I not, explain what you were doing right in front of you? And did

I, or did I not, *stress* the importance of keeping things quiet?"

"We didn't have a choice, Lincoln," Neil says, harried. "The deputies showed up and they were armed. We couldn't just wait for them to shoot us first."

"Are they all dead?"

"Most of them. Last I saw, a couple of them were injured, but they didn't pose us any threat. They still don't. They'll be laid up in hospital for a while."

"And I've lost six men?"

Neil doesn't respond to this straight away. He's thinking. Finding the right words to respond. "I'm...I'm afraid so, sir."

"But you said you dealt with the deputies quite handily?"

"It was the guy!" Neil says. "Whoever the fuck – whoever the *hell* he is. Killed six of our men, and got the woman and the kid out of there."

"Well," Lincoln says. He allows a long pause to follow. He wants Neil to squirm, knowing he's displeased. "You've woken me up to some terrible, terrible news. It sounds like nothing went how it was supposed to. I sincerely hope you plan on following up with something that could soften this blow?"

"Dean's following them."

Lincoln straightens up at this. He was sleeping on a cot bed, and it squeaks beneath him when he moves. "Yes?"

"He saw what was happening. Rather than engage, he followed. He's following them right now, keeping his distance. He has them in his sights."

"Oh, Neil. It's been a terrible night, but this, at least, is promising. I'm not going to say it makes up for the failure you've executed here, but it at least numbs the sting."

"I'm sorry, sir," Neil says. "And I speak for Dean, too."

"What were you doing while he was making himself useful?"

"I performed a sweep of the property, checked it over to see if there was anything we should know about."

"And?"

"Not a great deal, but I found some drawings, and writings. I've only looked at them quickly. I figured I should bring them with me."

"Why?"

"The drawings didn't make any sense to me. They might have been the inside of the Underhill cabin – I wouldn't know, I never saw it. You'd probably have a better idea."

"Then what makes you think that's what they are?"

"Because there's a drawing of Jake Underhill, and it's almost as accurate as a photograph."

"So someone's a talented artist. So what? Are you planning on flogging these drawings off at a later date, once the artist is dead, see if you can make a pretty penny off them?"

"No, sir, that's not why I took them. It was for what's written on them."

"Do tell."

"Well, *Fordham 1605* has been written out a *lot*."

Lincoln shoots up to his feet. The cot squeals in protest as he rises. "*What*?"

"Yeah..."

"Who – whose drawings are they? Ella? Kit?"

"I don't know. The drawings are incredible, but the writing – it's kind of childlike. You said the kid was autistic or something, right? Maybe it was him."

"And he's written Fordham? You're sure?"

"I can see it right now," Neil says. "Like I said, he's written it a lot. There's no mistake."

"But how – how can he know?" He paces, wondering what Jake or his cousins might have said in front of Ella and the kid. What might they know? This has been his concern. This is why he's sending his men after them. He can't afford for them to ruin what is planned. There's too much riding on it, and too much has already been sacrificed.

*Stan...*

Lincoln runs a hand down his face. "Okay, you did the right thing. Jake said the kid was nearly nonverbal. Maybe he hasn't said anything? Maybe his mother doesn't know what it means?" He's trying to convince himself. He has to hope that this is the case.

"There's something else," Neil says.

"*More?*"

"On another piece of paper, he's drawn Ian, and I assume what was supposed to be his work area in the cabin. The drawing's unfinished, but he's drawn a whiteboard, too, and on it it looks like he's started to write out the formula."

Lincoln frowns. "GB2?"

"I think so. I'm not going to pretend I know the formula off the top of my head, but I've seen Ian writing it out, and this looks familiar. The first few symbols I recognise."

"How much of it has he written?"

"I don't know – maybe half? Just under?"

"Send a picture. I'll run it by Ian and make sure it's what you think."

"I will."

"Where are you going now?"

"Wherever you want. My first thought was to get clear, to regroup."

"All right. Stay in Vermont. I'll send a team to meet with you and you can catch up with Dean. Keep in touch with me, and make sure Dean does the same. It sounds like this little problem is becoming a big issue, and we need it dealt with ASAP."

"Got it."

Lincoln hangs up. He chews the corner of his thumb, and thinks what his dear old mum would say if she could see him now, chewing again. She'd probably give him a clip around the ear and tell him to act his age.

He takes his thumb from his mouth as his phone pings. Neil has sent him the picture. Lincoln doesn't remember all of the formula either – too many symbols – but this looks right to him, too. He takes the picture and goes in search of Ian down the hall. He'll have to wake him up to look at it. Ian won't be happy, but Lincoln doesn't care. This is important. The boy might know the formula. They can't have that. They can't have that at all.

## 22

Tom, Ella, and Kit are in a motel. Tom drove them here from the safehouse. He needed to get them far away. Once they were in the room, he swept the area, making sure it's clear. He kept the reloaded Beretta close. It was still dark. He didn't see anyone around. No masked men all in black. No suspicious vehicles.

It's morning now. The sun is rising. Kit is sleeping. Tom stays near the window, watching the parking lot at the front. He has a chair nearby for when his legs tire. He watches the road, too. Keeps an eye on the vehicles that park, and pass by, makes sure no one hangs around or keeps passing by over and over. Thus far, he hasn't seen anything that alarms him.

Ella hasn't slept. She sits on the bed next to Kit, stroking his face, her mouth working with worry. She turns to Tom, looks at him by the window. She clears her throat. "I was amazed when I saw you carrying him," she says. "That he was *letting* you carry him."

Tom glances at her.

"It usually takes a long time before he'll let anyone pick him up like that," she says. "Or even hold his hand. A lot of time and a lot of trust."

"He was probably scared of the gunfire," Tom says. "And I told him I'd take him to you."

Ella looks doubtful that this would be enough, but she says, "Maybe." She runs her hands down her thighs. She sighs. She's tired, but she's not defeated. There's a resilience about her. An inner strength that doesn't surprise Tom about a single mother. "What now? Do we just keep running and hiding until someone swoops in and makes this all better?"

"State police would have arrived at the safehouse after the shootout," Tom says. "There's a chance they might call in the FBI. I'd be tempted to reach out to them, but they'd likely just transfer you to another safehouse, and one has already failed."

"I can't do that again," Ella says. "We got lucky last night – *very* lucky. That kind of luck won't last forever. It's amazing none of us caught a stray bullet." She looks at Kit, lips pursed.

"In my experience, you can't wait for someone else to fix things," Tom says. "You have to do it yourself. If these people are going to keep coming after you, then I'm going to have to take the fight to them."

"But *why* do they want us?" she says. "All the faces we saw, all of the men at the cabin, they're all dead, apart from Ian. Is he really that important?"

"It might not be that," Tom says. "It could be something Kit saw. Something he knows. Like Fordham 1605. Whatever that is, he potentially heard or saw it out in the woods, or at the cabin, and it could be important to them. Important enough for them to want to kill you both, and to go to war with a sheriff's department."

Ella looks around the motel room, as if this is her life now – always moving, always hiding.

Tom doesn't intend for that to be the case. He's going to get them home. Back to Benton, safe and sound, without a scratch on either of them. To do that, he needs to figure out whom he's going up against. He needs to work out what they want. "Did Teddy say anything to you while you spoke?" he says.

"Oh, God, *Teddy*," she says. She's holding back tears. "Do you think he's dead?"

"We're not going to find out today," Tom says. "As hard as it is, we're going to have to focus on ourselves, and what we can do for us. Did he tell you anything that might be useful?"

Ella sniffs. She thinks. She tells Tom everything she remembers. Tells him about how Jake and his cousins killed some janitors from a toothpaste factory in the woods.

"The sodium fluoride," Tom says. "I saw the bags."

Ella nods.

"That doesn't give us much to go on," Tom says. "Just raises more questions."

"So what do we do?"

"For now, we rest. We wait. And we think about Fordham 1605, and what that could be."

"What do you think Kit meant, when he said 'he's saying it wrong?'"

"I don't know," Tom says. "But we'll have to keep *that* in mind, too. Get some sleep for now. A couple of hours, and then you can take watch. I'm close to empty. We're no good if we're out on our feet."

"All right," Ella says. "It might take me a while to fall asleep, though. I'm feeling wired right now."

"Just do your best. I'll wake you in a few."

Tom watches out the window. He hears Ella tossing and turning on the bed for a while, and then she settles and her breathing deepens. The adrenaline wears off and she's out.

Tom keeps himself alert. Focusing on everything outside of the motel helps. Watching vehicles, and people coming and going. He gets up and paces every so often, keeping his blood pumping, not allowing himself to become too settled and risk drifting off. He feels a deep tiredness in his bones.

He hears movement behind him and looks back to see Kit standing nearby, watching him and rubbing at his eyes. Tom glances toward Ella. She's still sleeping. He turns back to Kit. "You're awake, huh?"

Kit doesn't answer. Doesn't move. Just watches Tom.

"That was a close call we had last night, wasn't it?" Tom says. "If I were you, I'd still be sleeping it off."

Kit turns away from him, but he doesn't walk away. He looks around the room. He sees his mother sleeping. He watches her for a moment, and then turns back to Tom.

"I don't have anything for you," Tom says. He tries to think, wondering what Kit might want. "You hungry, that it? I might have a granola bar in my backpack. I'm all out of jerky."

Kit comes closer, but he doesn't give any reaction to the mention of food. He stands in front of Tom and looks out of the window.

"You want to help me keep watch?" Tom says.

Kit turns back to him.

Tom smiles. "All right," he says. "Come here and take a seat." Tom stands and pats the chair. Kit looks at it, and then climbs onto it and sits. Tom crouches next to him. He points out of the window. "So what we're doing is, we're looking out for anyone that shouldn't be there. Anyone that looks like they might be a danger to us. Like the men from last night."

Kit stares straight ahead, through the window.

"But sometimes they won't be on foot," Tom says. "Sometimes they'll be in vehicles – nondescript cars or vans, usually. And if you see the same vehicle pass by over and over again, or spend too long in the parking lot with a person sitting inside, that's something you want to pay attention to. You got that?"

Kit says nothing.

"So if you see anything," Tom says, "you just let me know. Give me a pat and then point it out. And then later, when your mom's on watch, you can do the same with her."

Kit nods, just once. At first, Tom isn't sure if he moved at all. He doesn't question it. He goes with it. "Well, all right," he says. "Now that you've had the lesson, it's time to put it into practice. Eyes forward."

## 23

Lincoln spreads his arms, showing Ian his new workspace. "Ta-da," he says, wriggling his eyebrows. "Not too shabby, eh? If anything, I think it might even be an improvement on the cabin. We're not meth cooks, after all. We're more sophisticated than that. I say we act like it."

Ian looks the area over, chewing on the inside of his cheek.

Lincoln's arms drop. He feels his face drop, too. "*What?*"

They're not in Vermont anymore. They're far from it. Here, they don't have to worry so much about what's going on there. Arthur found an abandoned building for them to set up in and hide out. It used to be a warehouse. It's full of open spaces, and smaller, secure rooms, like the one where Ian can work. They've already changed one of the bigger offices into a lab for him. They've moved in tubes and beakers, and a couple of stainless-steel tables for him to work at. There's a storage area. There's a whiteboard. There's everything he needs. And, next to the door, there's a long glass window for Lincoln to observe Ian's progress.

Ian, however, looks concerned. "It's fine," he says. "It's a perfect space. I'm worried about our window of time."

"What about it?" Lincoln says.

"It's not enough. We've lost a couple of days because of what happened in Vermont. That means I'm going to have to go faster, work longer. This isn't a process I can afford to be careless with."

"It is what it is," Lincoln says.

"Can't you push it back, even just a few days?"

Lincoln arches an eyebrow. "Push it back? Do you understand the business we're in, Ian? The business *you're* in now? I know you're a newcomer to all of this, but you don't change plans, not like this. I've put out the word. I've spread it around. We have prospective buyers with their eyes on us from all around the world. They know where to look, and they know *when*, but they don't know what's coming. It's a surprise. It's going to bring them scrambling to our doors when they see what we have. But if they're watching and *nothing* happens? We'll be out of business. I've reached out to my contacts in Russia, Iran – *everywhere* – so *no*, this can't be pushed back, sweetheart."

"I don't think you understand what you're asking of me –"

"I don't think *you* understand, precious. This isn't a request. I've shown you where you're working, and you're going to get to it. This is what you signed up for. This is why you came to us." Lincoln holds his arms out wide. "And besides, it's not like I'm demanding mass production – not yet, at least. All we need for now is a couple of canisters. That's it. You think you can do that, sweetheart? And, before you answer, keep in mind that I have had a very stressful week, and I'm already close to the edge as is." He cocks his head, turning his ear toward Ian.

Ian knows he has to answer carefully. Knows there's only one right response. "Just a...just a couple of canisters?"

"That's right," Lincoln says, keeping his head cocked.

"I – I – I'll do my best."

Lincoln scrunches up his face. "Hmm," he says.

"I mean, all right, *yes*," Ian says. "Yes, I can get that done in time."

"Brilliant. I'm glad to hear that, Ian. You've made me very happy. I've got a couple of chaps to help you out. They'll do exactly as you say, to the letter."

Ian runs his hands down his face. He looks tired already, like he struggled to get back to sleep after Lincoln came to tell him about the boy's seeming knowledge of the formula. "I'm not trying to put it off," he says slowly, choosing his words. "But if the boy knows where the...demonstration...is happening...if he alerts his mother, if she alerts the authorities...what then?"

"That's not for you to worry about, sweetheart," Lincoln says. "That's my concern. You just need to make the GB2. You can start by writing the formula out on that nice new whiteboard we got you. Something for your newest assistants to work off. I know I made a big deal about writing it on the whiteboard back at the cabin, but this is a private place and we're all friends here."

"You want me to start now?"

"Time's a-wasting."

"I'm going to need coffee," Ian says. "And a lot of it."

"I can deal with that," Lincoln says. "Get your gear on, and I'll send your two helpers along." He turns, walking away from the makeshift lab. He claps his hands. "Arthur!" he calls. Arthur is in a room at the back of the building. He's cleared it out to use as a workout space. There are no weights, but he makes do with bodyweight exercises. He pokes his head out of the room when he hears Lincoln shouting for him. "Ian needs coffee!"

## 24

Tom feels better after sleeping. Doesn't feel so slow and sluggish. He's alert now, and he's thinking.

He's thinking about Fordham 1605. More specifically, he's thinking about the Fordham part. There's a Fordham neighbourhood in the Bronx in New York City. It's also the name of an unincorporated community in Pennsylvania. New York is closest. It could be the best place for him to go. He doesn't know what he's looking for, but if there's something planned for the neighbourhood he'll at least be closer. By that point, he might have enough information to pass on to the cops, to put them on alert, help stop the mysterious 'Lincoln', or whoever might be behind whatever is planned.

If he knew what was planned, that would help. He's thinking it must be some form of chemical attack. In the cabin they had sodium fluoride, as well as the canisters. The canisters weren't labelled as clearly as the bags of sodium fluoride, but there were chemical symbols on them, as well as warning labels. Not all of the canisters had the same symbol, which implies they held different contents. Chemistry was never one of his favourite classes while at school, but even if it had been he doubts he'd remember anything from it all these years later that would help him know exactly what they held.

"What're you thinking?" Ella says, watching him.

He's by the window, watching the road and the parking lot. He hasn't seen anything to be concerned about. He turns to Ella. She's sitting on the chair in the corner of the room. Kit is cross-legged at her feet, watching the television. They have the volume turned down low. "I'm thinking about the chemicals at the cabin. Sodium fluoride is harmless on its own, but mixed with other chemicals, it can be lethal."

"You think this relates to Fordham 1605?"

"Probably. They must be plotting an attack – a chemical attack, it seems. But on whom? Where? Why?" He shakes his head. "There's too many questions, and we have no way of getting answers, not here."

"Could we pass this information on to someone who might be able to use it?"

"It's too vague," Tom says. "Would it even be helping, really? Would they take it seriously?"

"So what are you thinking?"

He tells her about the Fordham neighbourhood in New York. "It's not far from Vermont, but it's a whole other state. There's chaos and confusion here, sure, but it's not going to extend down to NYC. And even if the FBI have been called in, how are they going to trace it to there? So far as we know, they don't know anything about Fordham. Hell, this is all just theory – Fordham could be a name, rather than a place. But right now, the place is all I have to go on."

"You want to go there?"

Tom nods. "But I need you and Kit to be somewhere safe first. If it *is* where they are, if it's where this all culminates, I can't take you into that. Can you think of somewhere else I can take you, somewhere safe, maybe *with* someone safe, someone you trust completely?"

"Why can't we stay here?"

"Not in a motel," Tom says, shaking his head. "We signed in with fake names, but they still might be able to track you down. They might have a hacker for all we know. They could get into the security system, see us arriving, see us coming right *here*."

Ella thinks.

"Your parents?" Tom says.

"They've lived in Florida the last two years."

"Eric's parents?"

"They moved away a few years after Eric's death. They wanted to hang around for Kit, but they said they couldn't. It was too difficult for them to stay. They're in Ohio now." She pauses, then adds, "My cousin's on vacation. She's in Europe for a few weeks. Her house isn't far from here. That could do, right?"

"Depends," Tom says. "What kind of house is it? Is it in the middle of nowhere or a neighbourhood?"

"They have neighbours," Ella says. "It's a nice place."

"Okay. It's better that there's people around." He glances at their bags. They're mostly still packed. He stands. "Let's go."

Ella blinks. "Right now?"

"We might not have time to waste."

## 25

"What's your cousin's name?" Tom says on the drive to the house.

"Lara."

"Is her surname also Wiley?" Tom says.

"It is. Her dad is my dad's brother. My uncle."

"Is she married?"

"Yeah, but she kept her own name. We Wileys are very modern women."

Tom smiles. He's watching the mirrors. Even when there's not the threat of being followed, it's force of habit. Right now, there *is* a threat. He doesn't see anyone following.

"She's got two kids, too," Ella says. "And Kit has been out to the house, so he might settle better there."

"He didn't settle at the safehouse?"

"He was fine. He drew. He wrote. But I don't know how long it would've lasted. At least here, Lara's youngest, her son, he's a similar age to Kit. They've played together – well, as much as Kit plays. But he's familiar with the house, and the rooms. He'll recognise the toys. It'll keep him settled for longer."

"Where in Europe is she?"

Ella thinks. "I think she's in France right now. She told me the whole itinerary, but if I'm honest I only half-listened. It's not like I needed to know *all* the details – I wasn't going. They're travelling all over. They flew to London to begin with, I remember that much. They're making their way from there."

"That must be an expensive trip."

"Her husband's mom died a few months back. She left him a large inheritance. She made him promise to do something with it – something for themselves, for their family. They'd always wanted to go to Europe."

They reach the house. The street is similar to where the safehouse was. A suburb with identical homes. Ella gives directions. He pulls onto the driveway. Before they set off, Tom made sure she knew how to get into the house. She said she knew where the spare key was hidden. They don't have to loiter out the front, or attempt to break in. Ella goes straight to the decorative rock it's hidden under and unlocks the front door.

Tom enters first. He carries his Beretta, though he keeps it concealed. He keeps his hand close to it as he makes his way through the house, room by room. It's clear.

At the back of the house, there's an office. A desk under the window, framed family portraits the only decoration. There's a laptop, closed. Tom opens it. He pushes the power button. It comes to life. It doesn't need a password. He picks it up and carries it through the house, back to Ella and Kit. They're in the living room. Ella has put the television on to distract Kit. He sits cross-legged in front of it, like back at the motel. A cartoon is playing.

Ella eyes the laptop. "What are you doing?"

Tom places it on the sofa next to her. "I'm not doing anything with this," he says. "I want *you* to look up what sodium fluoride can be used for. I know a couple of uses already, but I want to know a broader scope, see if there's anything that might jog our memories about those canisters we saw. While you're doing that, I'm going to take a walk around the neighbourhood. I'll take the key with me. I'll lock you inside while I'm gone."

Ella nods and places the computer onto her lap while Tom leaves the house. He pauses on the doorstep, looking around, checking the other houses – their doors and their windows. No one else is out, not in the immediate vicinity. No one is watching him, either. He takes a slow stroll to the end of the driveway, looking left and right. Trees line the streets. It's a nice place, just like Ella said. Upon second glance, it's nicer than where the safehouse was. Affluent. He can see the difference in vehicles here – the cars are newer models, more expensive. They shine, too, like they've all been recently cleaned and buffed. The lawns are manicured. The houses look pristine. It looks like the kind of place that calls the cops if they spot someone lingering outside after dark. This is good. Extra security for Ella and Kit. Right now, it's still light. Tom is a stranger, but he shouldn't look too suspicious.

He circles the block a couple of times. He watches out for black Hyundais in particular. He doesn't see any. Doesn't see anyone in the parked cars, either. No one that could be sitting and watching. The neighbourhood looks clear.

He's aware, however, after what he saw at the safehouse,

that he's going up against professionals. He saw how they approached the house. How a second team held back, covering the first. How they approached so they wouldn't be seen from inside. He's seen them following cars, too. They're careful. They're not prone to mistakes. From what he heard in the cabin, the Underhill brothers weren't a part of this operation, not really. They were outside help, brought in because of their cousin. The brothers were potentially easy, considering what he might be going up against now.

What that means is, if they *were* following on the drive here, would he have seen them? Can he be certain? Especially if a vehicle change occurred. It's something for him to keep in mind. It means that going forward, he's going to have to be doubly careful. Doubly observant. He can't take anything for granted. The neighbourhood appears secure, but is it really?

He pauses before he re-enters the house, lingering on the doorstep again. He stands close to the wall, out of view. He watches the road. He looks up and down the street. A couple of cars pass, but they maintain their speed. They don't slow down to eye up the house. He sees the drivers, and they don't even turn their heads. Tom grits his teeth. It appears clear, but after his thoughts he's not convinced.

And now he's wondering, can he really leave Ella and Kit here? Is it truly safe for them? Is he *certain* that no one knows they're here?

He doesn't want to take them with him to New York City. Not because they'll get in his way or slow him down, but because he doesn't want to take them into danger.

He goes back inside the house. It's not a decision he has to make right now, but he'll have to make it soon. He doesn't plan on staying here long. He needs to move. Something big could be coming, and he has to find out what that is, and how to head it off. If they had a better idea, if they had more information, it would be so much easier to just call the cops, the feds, and hand it off to them. But even then, preventing a potential attack, that wouldn't necessarily deal with the people coming after them. Tom needs faces and names. He needs to know where to strike.

Ella is waiting for him. "It's like you said," she says. "Harmless on its own, but deadly if it's mixed with the wrong thing."

Tom goes to the window before engaging. He positions himself so he can see outside. Kit is close by on the floor. He doesn't register Tom. He stares straight ahead at the television. It looks like a new cartoon is playing. "What did you find?" Tom says.

"Well, if sodium fluoride is reacted with methylphosphonyl dichloride – that's the word used online: *reacted*. I don't know what that means exactly, but that's what it says. Anyway, if they're *reacted* together, it creates methylphosphonyl difluoride, and *that* is used in the production of sarin and soman gas. I'm not familiar with soman, but I've heard of sarin."

"The subway attack in Japan in the nineties," Tom says.

Ella nods. "That's probably how most people know about it, right? But it also says it's used in *other* chemical weapons, too. Stuff I've probably never heard of. Maybe you have."

Tom thinks of the canisters he saw in the cabin. "Do you have the symbol for methylphosphonyl dichloride?"

"I can get it," Ella says, beginning to type. Her brow furrows as she types slowly. "It's a damn hard word to spell." She sounds it out while she types, then hits enter. "Okay, I've got it." She turns the laptop toward Tom.

"Jesus," he says. There's a P in the centre, then lines come off it in seemingly all directions. There's an O. A couple of Cl's. The lines leading back to the P are all different, and probably mean something in themselves.

"Does it look familiar?" Ella says.

"I'm honestly not sure," Tom says. "Maybe. I recognise the P, but that doesn't mean anything. It could've been on some of the canisters at the cabin. I know they had different symbols."

"Well, it's enough to know for sure now that they *are* making a chemical weapon. A gas, by the looks of it."

"That's how it looks," Tom says. He sits back and tries to recall the details of the sarin attack in Tokyo. They targeted the subway. Over a dozen people died, and hundreds – maybe even thousands – of others were harmed.

"I also looked up potential targets in the Fordham neighbourhood," Ella says. "You were gone longer than I expected."

"And?"

"There's a Fordham University. I don't know if that's enough, but there *is* a Chemistry department. It's run by a Professor Richard McCulloch."

"It might be worth my talking to him," Tom says. "See what he makes of this."

"Well, speaking of, there's something else I need to tell you."

Tom looks at her.

"Last night, before I put Kit to bed, he was writing something out. I realised it looked familiar – it was the formula they had written on the whiteboard in the cabin."

Tom frowns. "You're sure?"

"No," Ella says. "But I *think* that's what it was. Some of it looked familiar. And he'd drawn the whiteboard and Ian, too. He hadn't written out the whole thing on the whiteboard – maybe a half? Just over a quarter?"

"Do you think he remembers the whole thing?"

"He might. I lost his notepad at the safehouse. I'm sure I can find some paper here someplace. If he writes it all out, I can send you a picture. You can show it to the professor, see if he can decipher it."

Tom nods.

Ella looks at him. "When are you going?" she says. She doesn't sound eager for him to leave, but she understands why he has to.

"Not just yet," Tom says. He doesn't want to spook her with his thoughts from outside. "Soon. First, I need to be sure that you're safe here."

## 26

Lincoln is close to Ian's makeshift lab, but he's not looking through the window, watching what's happening inside. He's on a chair close by, lost in his thoughts. Around him, his men hurry around, busying themselves. Occasionally, Arthur barks at them. Lincoln is separate from them. Lost in his own world. Lost in memories of his brother. Four years younger, yet first to die.

Lincoln wasn't there for the firefight. Everything has been so hectic lately, so busy, so much to do and not enough time. If Lincoln had been present things would have gone differently, he's sure of it. But that's a what-if that will plague him forever. That's something he's just going to have to live with.

He was busy for *them* – for himself and his brother. With this one demonstration, and subsequent sale, they'd be set for life. Money would never be an issue again. Sell the formula – hell, sell Ian – and they're travelling the world for the rest of their days. They talked about how they'd chase the sun. No matter the time of year, they'd always be somewhere *hot*, where the sun never stopped shining, the beer never stopped flowing, and the women were beautiful. It was grey in Walworth – grey and wet and the people were miserable, and Lincoln and Stan swore to each other that would never be their lives. They'd make it out and become something, and they'd never have to go back again.

But now Stan is dead, and Lincoln is going to have to travel alone, and all he wants more than anything else is to take Stan *back* to Walworth. If he had his remains, it's what would feel right. It's where he belongs. Lincoln would want to know where he is. Would want to know that he could return to him, visit him whenever he wanted.

This grief is a distraction. In his quiet moments, it plagues him. He's had so few quiet moments lately. When this is over, what then? Will thoughts of Stan refuse to leave?

No, because while Lincoln cannot bury or scatter his brother, he *can* avenge him. That will be satisfaction enough for Lincoln. The detective will die. It's all figured in as part of the demonstration. Lincoln is not careless. He won't rush off and do anything that could jeopardise their plans, but he *will* put things right.

Detective George Ross. The man who killed his brother. Lincoln has done his research. He asked questions. He greased palms. There were other cops present, but the detective was the one who shot Stan dead. Two bullets in the back. Stan was either attempting to flee, or running from cover in search of a better vantage point from which to return fire. Lincoln likes to think it was the latter.

He also likes to imagine Stan had survived, and he'd torn the detective in two with his assault rifle.

But that's not what happened. The first bullet punctured his left lung. The second bullet came immediately after, and penetrated his heart, killing him instantly. There were two other men there with Stan that night. They were able to escape. They reported back to Lincoln what had happened. Lincoln kept his composure, though all the while he stared at the two men and knew he would trade them both in an instant to have his brother back.

He looks down at his phone. He knows everything about Detective George Ross. He knows his height, his weight, his health history. He knows his birthday, his parents' names, and where he grew up in New Jersey. And, most importantly, he knows his current address. He has plans for this address.

And Lincoln knows what he looks like.

Lincoln unlocks the phone and flicks through his pictures. He brings up the image of Detective George Ross. It's from his police ID. He's staring straight into the camera. He has a wide face – aged and jowly, dotted with stubble and looking older than forty-four. His hair was once dark, but it has faded and thinned out, and most of his scalp is visible through what little remains on top.

Lincoln has become very familiar with this face. He doesn't *need* to look at it – he can recall every detail from memory. This face haunts his dreams. It flashes behind his eyelids every time he blinks. The face is always fresh in his mind, but he stares at the picture because of how it makes him feel. It makes him angry. It makes his blood boil. But it also reminds him that he doesn't have to wait for much longer. That soon the owner of this face will be no more. They will cease to exist. The man who killed his brother will die by his hand.

The phone rings, snapping Lincoln out of his thoughts. It's Dean. He doesn't answer straight away, though he knows it could be important. He can't. He has to swallow. Has to breathe deep. Has to compose himself.

"Hello, Dean."

"They've stopped driving," Dean says. "I'll send you the co-ordinates."

"Where are they?"

"They're still in Vermont. They've come to a house – it looked like it was empty, but the woman knew where a key was hidden."

"Do we know who the house belongs to?"

"I haven't had time to check yet. I thought I should call you first."

"And is our new friend still with them?"

Dean makes a sound at the back of his throat like he's annoyed. "Can't get rid of the son of a bitch. And he's *careful*, Lincoln. He's keeping watch. He's patrolled the block a few times already. I had to make myself scarce."

"Do we have a name for him yet?"

"I've made some calls, tried to find out who the car is registered to. No luck. I even called the dealership where it was bought – in *Texas* – to see if they had anything on file. They said they remembered the guy, but only because he insisted on paying cash. They said that's rare these days, only reason they remembered him, but if they ever knew his name they've forgotten it now. It's not the kind of thing they keep on file."

"Hmm. Do you think he saw you on his little patrols?"

"No – I've been careful all the way here. Whatever this guy's story is, I'm not taking any risks with him. That's why I'm calling. I managed to get close enough once he went inside to put a tracker on his car, but I'm not engaging him solo. I know what he did to Jake and his cousins, and I saw first-hand what he did at the safehouse. There ain't a chance in hell I'm gonna tackle him on my own."

"Afraid of a challenge, Dean?" Lincoln smirks to himself.

"I'm not getting myself killed just to try and prove something. I know my limitations, and this guy's *it*. I'm man enough to admit I need numbers on this one, and lots of them."

"A bullet will kill him, same as it will everyone else."

"Yeah, well, I want a lot of guns firing a lot of bullets from a lot of different directions, just to be sure."

"I'll talk to Neil," Lincoln says. "He should have regrouped with the others by now. Send him a pin, and I'll send him to your location."

"Okay," Dean says, and he sounds relieved. "Okay, that's great. I'll keep an eye on things here."

"Make sure this is the end of it, Dean. This has to be the finish line for our runaways. I don't care about noise or cleanliness anymore – just get in there and make it *fast*. Don't give them a chance to hit back. End it."

"Yes, sir."

Lincoln hangs up. He stands, flicking off the picture of Detective George Ross's face and searching for Neil's number. It doesn't take him long to find it. While it dials, he turns and looks in on the lab. Ian and his two helpers are hard at work. They wear yellow hazmat suits. Clear visors show their faces. Lincoln can see how Ian is perpetually frowning. He oversees his new assistants, admonishing them if they're not careful enough for his liking, telling them to slow down when they're going too fast. He glances up. He sees Lincoln watching. Lincoln waves. Ian looks away.

## 27

Tom hasn't seen anything. No Hyundais, and no suspicious loiterers. He's swept the block again, and still nothing. If there's no one around, if no one knows they're here, then the house is the safest place to leave Ella and Kit. He can't justify taking them to New York.

"I'd better go," Tom says to Ella. "I'm going to have to borrow your cousin's laptop. It could be useful to me out there."

"Sure," Ella says. "Just try and bring it back in one piece, though I'm not gonna hold it against you if you can't. Lara on the other hand…" She grins at him.

Kit has heard them talking. For the first time since they arrived, he turns away from the television. He looks up at Tom and his mother.

"While I'm gone, just stay in the house," Tom says. "Don't go anywhere, don't call anyone. Avoid being seen. If you see anything or anyone that alarms you, call me. I'll be far away, but I can talk you through what to do."

Ella nods along. "We'll be careful," she says.

"I'll be as fast as I can," Tom says. He turns and heads for the door. Ella follows him. Surprising them both, Kit gets to his feet and walks with them. Tom looks down at him before he opens the door. "Take care of your mom, okay?"

Kit blinks. He begins to fidget. He looks agitated. He shifts his weight from foot to foot and looks up at Ella, then from her to Tom and back again. Tom hasn't seen him move so much, hasn't seen him so animated before.

Ella looks concerned. She reaches down and picks Kit up. She strokes the hair at the back of his head.

"What is it?" Tom says.

"I..." Ella says, but she doesn't finish.

Tom looks at her.

She sighs. "I don't think he wants you to go," she says. "You've saved us twice. He feels safe with you around. I mean, I do too, but I understand what you have to do. Kit sees you the same way I do – you're a protector."

"What should I do?" Tom says.

"It's okay," Ella says. "It'll be fine. *We'll* be fine. He'll calm down eventually. He'll settle. Being here, in a familiar place, it'll help. You should go."

"I'll be in touch," Tom says.

Ella nods. Kit is staring at him.

Tom leaves the house. He closes the door behind him. He hears Ella and Kit move away from the door, heading back through to the living room, probably. Tom feels a twisting in his stomach. He feels bad leaving, but he has to. This has to be done. It's the only way to end things. The only way to make sure Ella and Kit will be all right, and that they can return home safely.

He gets into the Toyota and starts the engine. He doesn't reverse. Doesn't pull off the driveway straight away. He pauses, looking at the house. Again, he thinks about the men he saw in action. How they were professional. How they were *careful*. He remembers what he thought to himself, when he first circled the block. He needs to be more careful. He needs to be extra vigilant. There's no space for mistakes with these people.

He stops the engine and gets out of the car. He stands next to the open door and looks up and down the road. He looks at the houses opposite. Checks their windows. There's still nothing to see. It's always been the same. He hasn't seen anything all the while they've been here. It's been a few hours now. He can't afford to waste time.

Yet still, something niggles at him. He can't let it go. An error is the difference between life and death. If anything were to happen to Ella and Kit, he wouldn't be able to live with himself. There can be no errors, not from him. Everything has to be perfect.

He circles the car, still eyeing the street. Then, he looks at the car. He stares at it for a moment, seeing his reflection in the black paint. He gets down onto his stomach and looks under the car.

There's a small, flashing red light. Tom reaches out and tears it from the undercarriage. A tracker. He doesn't know how long it could have been here. Doesn't know how they could know this is his car.

But he was right. He was right to be concerned.

He takes the tracker to the road and drops it down a storm drain. He goes back into the house and he gets Ella and Kit. They both look up at him, surprised to see him return so soon.

"Grab your things," Tom says. "It's not safe for you here. I'll explain in the car."

## 28

A black Hyundai appears in the distance behind them. Tom spots it. It keeps its distance. It's being careful. It didn't come speeding up as he left the neighbourhood. It took its time before it's gotten even this close.

"They're behind us," Tom says. There's no point keeping this information from Ella. She needs to know. She needs to be prepared.

She swallows and looks at her own mirror. "Where?"

"Black Hyundai." Tom reads off the plate.

"I don't see it."

"Then just trust me," Tom says. "It's there."

Ella sits up. She looks at Kit. She turns back around and takes a deep breath. "Just the one?"

"Just the one that I can see."

"How many people are inside?"

"I can't tell from here."

It's a five-hour drive to New York City from where they were in Vermont. This journey is going to take them longer.

Tom turns off I-87 after spotting the Hyundai. He takes backroads. Quieter roads. The Hyundai keeps its distance, but it follows. He takes winding roads through small towns. He stops for gas, just to see what the Hyundai does. It holds back. It disappears. Tom fills the tank and looks back down the road the way they came, but there's no sign of their follower. By this point, he's sure it's just the one vehicle. He hasn't seen any others following behind the Hyundai, not consistently, anyway. Vehicles that *were* there were only present briefly. They've turned off, continued on their way.

"Are they still out there?" Ella asks when he gets back in the car.

Tom pulls off the gas station forecourt. The Hyundai is nowhere to be seen. "I don't see them," he says.

"Could there be another tracker?"

Tom shakes his head. "I searched the car. I was thorough."

As they leave the town, the Hyundai reappears. Tom nods at the mirror. "They're back."

"Jesus," Ella says.

Tom gets back onto the I-87. The Hyundai stays with them. He wonders if they've grown suspicious. If they've figured out that Tom has spotted them. If they have, they don't do anything stupid. They stick to their initial plan. They keep their distance, allowing other vehicles to get between them. They don't speed up. They don't do anything careless.

It's rush hour, and the highway is busy. They all crossed into New York state a while back. They pass by the outskirts of Albany, the Hudson River off to their left.

Ella looks back at Kit, checking in on him. Tom glances at him in the mirror. He stares out the window. Ella turns back around. She bites her lip. "I suppose it's too much to hope they've turned off for the city?"

"They're still with us," Tom says.

"What are we going to do?"

"I need to find a way to lose them. It's busy here. I don't think they'll attempt anything. When we get past Albany, the road should clear up a little, once we get out into the country. I'll be able to speed up. I'll try and get rid of them there. After that, if we create some space and some time, we'll swap vehicles."

"Will we have enough time to sit in a dealership?"

"It's not going to be by the book," Tom says.

"Oh," Ella says. "Well, if it comes to that, I think I should make you aware that it would be my first time. I'll be no good to you in that regard."

"Just leave it to me," Tom says, but he's distracted. Something is happening behind them. They're nearly clear of Albany. From an on-ramp, another car joins the highway. Tom doesn't think anything of it at first, until it hits its hazard warning lights, just once. The Hyundai flashes back at them, just once. The new vehicle – a dark blue Chevrolet Silverado – slows down and falls into line behind the Hyundai.

Tom grunts.

Out the corner of his eye, he sees how Ella looks at him. "What?" she says. "I don't like that sound. *What?*"

"There's another one," he says.

She's scared. She was already scared, but the bad news keeps mounting. He sees how tightly she grips the door handle. She reaches out to him, the back of her hand on his thigh, palm facing up. Tom slips his hand into hers, trying to comfort her.

"Be honest with me," she says. "Are we going to be all right?"

Tom needs to watch the road. He needs to watch the mirrors. He can't look at her, as much as he'd like to. Instead, he squeezes her hand. "Yes," he says. "I made a promise, to you and to Kit. I always keep my promises."

She takes her hand back. She knows he's going to need both of his.

Tom maintains his speed. Stays casual. Like nothing is wrong. The two vehicles following do the same. They keep their distance. Like him, they're waiting for an opening. They're not going to strike here. They're stuck in a state of equilibrium, the three vehicles stuck in their positions upon the road, no progress and no regression.

The countryside is coming up. Tom sees fields and trees on either side of the road. The traffic is thinning, too. This is their opportunity. He presses down on the accelerator.

They take off. The Hyundai and the Chevy aren't expecting it. Tom pushes the Toyota hard. He cuts across lanes, overtaking traffic, putting more and more vehicles behind them. For a moment, he loses their pursuers in the mirrors. There's no sign of them. He doesn't slow. He knows they're back there. Knows they won't give up.

Sure enough, the Hyundai and the Chevrolet reappear. They match his speed. If they had earlier suspicions about his knowledge, they're now confirmed.

Despite this, they continue to keep their distance. They don't try to close the gap, not yet. Tom takes his eyes off the mirrors. He focuses on what lies ahead. He needs to lose them. Looking behind isn't going to help him do that. He sees signs for an off-ramp. He overtakes a long-haul truck and pulls into the lane for the ramp. Slowing only a little, he grips the steering wheel tight as he turns off the highway. With luck, the truck concealed what he did. He doesn't hang around to check. He keeps going.

"Did we lose them?" Ella says.

"I don't know," Tom says. He builds their speed back up. He can't afford to slow.

There's a strip mall in the distance. As they get closer, he sees an outdoor store, a few restaurants, a glass-fronted studio that's for either karate or dance. There's a thrift store and a couple of fashion outlets.

The Hyundai and the Chevrolet come back into view. They're coming fast. They're trying to close the gap now. They have no doubts – they've been seen. The time for subtlety is over.

The strip mall is busy. The parking lot is active. Tom heads for it.

## 29

Ian is getting agitated. His temper is short, and flaring.

Lincoln watches through the glass. Sees how Ian berates the two men assisting him. Lincoln turns his head to better hear.

"This is *important*," Ian says, voice rising. The inside of his clear visor mists with his breath. "You're being *careless*. How many times do I have to tell you? This is dangerous. *All* of this is so fucking dangerous!"

When it's time for the demonstration, Lincoln and the others won't be wearing hazmat suits. That would make things too obvious. They'll have APRs. If he turns his head to the right, he can see them stacked on a table in the centre of the abandoned building's floorspace, awaiting their use. He remembers unboxing them, and the wave of memories the sight of them brought back. He remembered his grandfather's gas mask, from World War Two. He was part of the ARP – Air Raid Precautions – during the Blitz. While he was in his twenties and able to join the army, he hadn't been drafted because of the tuberculosis that had ravaged his lungs as a child. The ARP probably wasn't the best place for a young man in his condition, but he'd wanted to help. He'd needed to feel like he was contributing to the war effort in some way.

He kept his gas mask. It lived atop the china cabinet in the dining room. Their grandmother hated it being there, but their grandfather was proud of it and what it represented. He refused to move it. He wanted it displayed, just like the china plates and statuettes beneath it. On the weekends when Lincoln and Stan would stay with their grandparents, they'd get the mask down and take turns wearing it while they played war.

The sight of the APRs brought this overwhelming memory back to Lincoln, making his breath catch in the back of his throat, making his heart skip a beat. He saw Stan through the constricted eyes of the gas mask, running ahead of him in the back garden, carrying a long stick that he pretended was a rifle, every so often turning and 'shooting' back over Lincoln's shoulder, providing him with cover. Even in their imaginary battles they never fought against each other. They always fought *together*.

"Don't knock anything over!" Ian says. "This is no place for clumsiness!" One of his assistants, carrying a tube from one workspace to the next, has jostled a Bunsen burner.

Ian looks up. He sees Lincoln watching. Ian motions for the other two to keep doing what they're doing, then he makes his way to the door. He steps outside and peels back the hood of the hazmat suit. He sucks down cool air. His face is flushed. His hair is slicked down with sweat, and beads of it run down his temples and cheeks. "They're *careless*," he says.

"You'll have to make it work," Lincoln says. "Although it

looks to me as though they're doing their best, Ian. They're keeping their heads down and they're getting on with their work. They're doing what you tell them to. Could it be that you're upset, and you're taking it out on them?"

Ian blows air through his nose. "I'm not making any secret of that," he says. "I *am* upset. This is too much to do in too little time. You can't *rush* this kind of work. It's not safe."

"Yes, yes, you've made that very clear already, Ian. But what do you expect me to suddenly say? *Oh my, Ian, you're so right. You'd best slow down after all.*" Lincoln looks at him. "We both know that's not going to happen. I've given you a job to do, and I expect you to see it through."

Ian's shoulders sag. He runs his hands back through his hair, causing it to stick up in wild directions.

"But just think of it this way – you do all this work now, and you're going to reap the benefits before you know it."

"Uh-huh – how hard are you going to drive me when the orders start coming in?"

"Now, now, Ian, there's no need to be so moody. I've told you, we're selling to the highest bidder, not every Tom, Dick, and Harry who comes calling, impressed by what they saw. And by that point, we can hire you some helpers. Some *proper* helpers. Chemists, like yourself. The midnight oil *will* be burned, but it won't all be by you." Lincoln looks through the window, at the rack where the one completed canister is currently stored. "And look at that," he says, pointing. "You're halfway done already. Frankly, I'm not sure what all these complaints are about."

"We're tired, Lincoln," Ian says. "It's been hours. We've been working non-stop."

"You'll be able to rest soon enough." Lincoln is firm. He's not backing down on this. They can't. There's not enough time. There's never enough time. "But it's imperative that your work is finished first. You know this. I don't want to have to keep repeating myself."

Ian looks at him. He wants to say more but he's stopping himself. He turns away, looking around the rest of the abandoned building. He sees how the handful of other men present are busying themselves. They dismantle and clean their weapons. They work out. They keep themselves occupied, preparing for what is coming. No one is just sitting around, doing nothing.

Ian sighs. "We need more coffee," he says. "And something to eat, too."

"Fine," Lincoln says. "If that'll keep you happy. My old dad used to always say, a happy worker is a productive worker." He smiles at Ian. He doesn't care if he's happy or not. He wants the second canister completed.

"I'll be happy enough –"

"*Fuck!*"

The curse is loud, drawing both of their attention. It comes from within the makeshift lab. They both turn to the sound. One of the men within is on fire. A Bunsen burner has toppled. Chemicals have spilled. The other man is trying to put the first out, patting at his suit.

Ian's eyes bulge. "Shit!" he says. "He must have chemicals on him. These suits are supposed to be flame retardant!" He shoots Lincoln a look, gesturing into the lab with an arm. "This is what I'm talking about! They're careless!"

There's no time for arguing. The chemicals in the lab are highly flammable. They're explosive.

Both men run into the lab. Ian doesn't have time to pull the hood of his suit back over his head. Lincoln takes a deep breath and holds it while he grabs the completed canister of

GB2. He hurries back out of the lab. The other men in the building have seen what's happening. They're rushing over.

"No!" Lincoln says, holding up the hand not holding the cold canister. "Get back! It could blow!"

They do as he says, backing off and finding cover. Lincoln wants to join them, but before he flees he looks into the lab.

Ian has pushed the burning man aside. He's toppled and fallen onto the other man, and they're both trying to get back up. Ian isn't concerned about them. He's concerned about what else could catch fire. "You shouldn't have panicked, you asshole!" Ian is shouting, sweat pouring down his face. "The suit would have protected you!" Ian is trying to get the chemicals clear. He grabs containers and canisters and throws them toward the open door. Lincoln waves Arthur over and hands him the completed GB2 canister, then starts dragging the other chemicals clear.

The fallen Bunsen burner touches off a spilled chemical on the worktop. Lincoln doesn't know what it is, but it spreads fast. It spreads to the containers that Ian hasn't managed to get clear. Ian follows the trail of the fast-moving flame. The other two men see it, too. Their eyes are wide. They can't move fast enough. They can't escape.

Lincoln is by the door. He slams it shut. "Everyone down!" He dives to the side, away from the door and the windows. He plugs his ears with his fingers.

There's an explosion. It's small – smaller than it would've been if Ian hadn't managed to get the bulk of the flammable chemicals out – but it's enough to ensure no survivors. To be certain, Lincoln scrambles to his feet and goes to the shattered window, his boots crunching over shards of shattered glass as he goes. A fire is blazing in the room. He sees the charred corpses of the three men. He sees the whiteboard that had the formula written upon it. It's not intact anymore. It shattered in the explosion. The formula is gone.

Behind him, he hears Arthur calling to the others. "Get the fire extinguishers! *Now*! We need to put this out before it can spread! Before anyone can see it!"

His men hurry past him with the fire extinguishers, spraying them into the lab through the broken window. They aim for the flaming chemicals. They aim for the bodies. Lincoln takes a step back, almost stumbling. Arthur is beside him suddenly, holding out an arm to steady him. In his other he holds the canister of GB2. Their *only* canister of GB2.

"They're dead," Arthur says. "There's no way they could've survived that."

"I saw their bodies," Lincoln says, staring straight ahead. He points to the canister without turning. "You're going to have to put that somewhere safe. It's all we have."

# 30

Tom slips the Toyota into the first available space he sees. He's already unbuckling himself as he kills the engine, and is out of the car and reaching into the back for Kit. Kit allows him to pick him up without protest. Tom doesn't carry him far – just to the other side of the car, to Ella. He puts him on the ground and Ella puts his bag onto his back. She already has her own and Tom's backpacks. She has her cousin's laptop, too, packed in with her clothes. They shoulder the bags. Ella takes Kit's hand and holds it tightly.

They start moving, Tom leading the way, heading for the closest store – a clothing outlet. Tom looks toward the entrance to the strip mall. He sees the Hyundai and the Chevy pulling in. They've slowed down. He can see the men inside scanning the parking lot. There's only one man in the Hyundai. There are four in the Chevy. Five total.

"Get down," Tom says as they slip between parked vehicles. They don't stop. They crouch low and keep moving. Tom looks back through the windows. He sees the

Hyundai and the Chevy speed up. They pass by them. Tom looks through the windows to his left, following their progress.

"Come on," he says, standing again. They hurry across the road. He glances back and sees that their pursuers have parked. The five men have gotten out of the vehicles. They're armed, but he's not surprised at this. He sees the bulge of their holsters under their jackets. Handguns. One of them wears a duster, and he keeps an arm pressed to his side. This is more concerning. Could be something more powerful. Likely an assault rifle, like at the safe house.

Tom, Ella, and Kit reach the outlet store. Kit's legs pump furiously to keep up with their pace. He doesn't complain. His face barely changes, but Tom can hear him breathing harder. As they slip inside the store, Tom hears a voice across the parking lot cry out, "*There!*"

He doesn't look back. He doesn't need to. The call was about them.

The three walk swiftly through the store, Tom still leading the way. Ella keeps hold of Kit, making sure he keeps up. Tom heads to the back, to the exit. Glancing over his shoulder, he sees that three of the men have entered the store. One of them is the man with the duster. There's no sign of the other two. Either they've split and one is guarding the front while another heads down the alley between stores and attempts to cut them off, or else both of them are coming to the back. Either way, it's not ideal. Tom's Beretta is tucked into the back of his waistband, close to his right hand. It's fully loaded.

"Excuse me," one of the store assistants calls out in a cheery voice as Tom nears the rear exit. "You can't go out that way – that's a fire door."

Tom ignores her. Tom pushes it open. He hurries Ella and Kit through with him.

"Excuse me, sir –" Tom slams the door shut, cutting her off.

They pass the alleyway between the outlet store and the karate/dance studio. Tom sees two men hurrying down it. Tom and the others clear the alley, get behind the studio. "Pick up Kit. We need to run."

They pick up speed. They pass the studio, and the next outlet store. He spots an open door for the next building. He can hear noise inside, and smell food wafting out – one of the restaurants. Behind, he hears the door of the first outlet store opening and closing, and the increasingly frustrated protesting cries of the ignored store assistant.

Tom's destination is the outdoor store. They're outnumbered and there's potentially an assault rife in the mix, but there's a good chance the outdoor store sells guns. Assault rifles are banned in New York, but there might be something with a little more firepower, something that could even the playing field.

They slip through the open rear door of the restaurant and find themselves in a busy, bustling kitchen. The food smells Mexican. A mix of chefs, busboys, and dishwashers turn and look at them as they burst inside.

"Uh, you're not supposed to be back here," one of the busboys, a teenager with a wispy moustache, says.

Before Tom can respond, Ella does it for him. She tells the kitchen staff the truth. "There are men chasing us," she says. "They're armed, and they're coming this way!"

At first, there's no reaction from the kitchen staff. A couple of them exchange glances. They frown. Then, one of the busboys steps forward. He's Mexican, and only a little older than the teen with the wispy moustache. He's looking at Ella and Kit when he speaks. He sees how tired and dishevelled they are. "When you come out of the kitchen, there's a fire exit to the right," he says. "We can try and slow them down, and we'll call the cops when you're clear."

But before Tom and Ella can start moving again, the first of their pursuers reaches the open door. His gun is drawn. A Glock. "Freeze!" he shouts.

"Holy shit!" the teen with the moustache cries.

At the sight of the gun, the kitchen turns to chaos. The Mexican busboy pushes Ella and Kit down, into cover, behind a stainless-steel counter. Tom dives the opposite direction. The chaser opens fire. The Mexican busboy takes two in the ribs. He groans as he falls, spinning midair and flopping onto the tiles on his back. Blood blooms brightly through his whites.

Tom looks up. There's a magnetised knife rack on the wall. He hears the man approaching. Hears his footsteps coming quickly, but cautiously, through the kitchen. Through the front, where the kitchen staff fled, he hears the cries and shrieks of panicked diners.

Tom doesn't hear any of the other men in the kitchen with the shooter. They must have done the same as at the outlet store – some to the front and some to the side, covering every exit. The approaching footsteps are nearly on top of Tom. Tom snatches a cleaver from the magnetised strip. The footsteps spin his way at his movement. Tom is swinging the cleaver out from his hiding place. He buries the blade deep in the man's right thigh. The man screams. Tom bats the gun from his hand, making sure no one has followed him in through the exit. It's clear. Tom pushes the man back. Despite the cleaver in his leg, he manages to keep his feet. He claws at Tom's face. Tom backs him up onto a prep station. There's another knife next to a chopping board. A boning knife. The man sees it. He tries to reach for it. Tom kicks at the cleaver still in his leg. Feels it bite into the bone. The man's hands instinctively reach for it. He's screaming again. A lot of blood is running out of him. It soaks the bottom of his pant leg and pools in his boot.

While he's distracted by his agony, Tom grabs the boning knife. He places his left hand on the man's face and pushes him back on the counter, stretching out his neck. A juicy vein throbs. Tom punctures it with the knife, driving it all the way in. He pulls it straight back out. Blood sprays. The stainless-steel worktops drip with blood. The man falls to the ground.

Tom turns to Ella and Kit. Ella is peering over the top of their cover. She has a hand over Kit's eyes.

"Come on," Tom says, waving them over. "Stay close."

He doesn't head through the front of the restaurant. If the others haven't followed, the front will be covered. The fire exit will be covered. Tom heard a lot of turmoil in the front as the kitchen staff fled. The customers could have fled with them. If this is the case, the men might already be in the restaurant, making their way through to the kitchen.

Tom pulls out his Beretta and keeps it low. He goes to the back door, the same way they came in, waving for Ella and Kit to stay behind him and out of the way. He looks out the back, scanning the area. There's a flash of movement to his right. He wheels on it, Beretta raised. There's gunfire. Tom drops to a knee and fires back. Just one man, so far as he can see. Holding back to cover the rear door while the other went inside.

The man outside is fast, but Tom is faster. Tom fires

twice, both bullets hitting the man in the chest. The man's own bullets hit the wall close to Tom, above him from his kneeling position. Tom sweeps the area, gun raised, but sees no one else out here. Still no sign of the man with the assault rifle, and so he still remains a big problem.

Tom stands and motions for Ella and Kit to follow. "Stay close," he says.

They're not far from the outdoor store. Just a few buildings down. Tom peers down the alley, toward the fire escape. There's a man there guarding it, as he expected, but his head is turned, looking their way, toward the gunfire he's just heard. Tom fires at him. The man throws himself through the fire escape, setting off an alarm. Tom keeps him pinned as Ella and Kit get clear of the opening. He waits for them to create some distance and then he catches up to them. He leads the way. They stay close.

## 31

The fire is out. Lincoln surveys the scene.

He takes a deep breath. He smells cooked meat. The three dead men, burned alive, their bodies blackened, their hazmat suits melded to them, through them. The smell makes his mouth water. He closes his eyes.

The lab is destroyed. Everything that was in it, too. The walls are blackened and dripping from the fire extinguishers. Lincoln needs a moment to centre himself. He thinks of Ian, of his complaints. How he said they were overworked.

Lincoln doesn't blame himself. He did what he had to do. And they weren't overworked – they were *careless*. Ian was too busy complaining when he should have been *focussing*. If he hadn't left the lab to talk to Lincoln, then this wouldn't have happened at all. Ian's own bellyaching has cost him his life.

Lincoln opens his eyes when he realises someone is beside him. He looks. It's Arthur. "Is the GB2 in a safe place?"

Arthur nods.

"That's a good boy," he says.

Arthur doesn't say anything straight away, though it's clear there's something on his mind. Lincoln can guess what it is. It's on his mind, too. "Was anyone else hurt?" Lincoln asks before they have to tackle their main concern.

"No," Arthur says. "Everyone else is fine." Again, he hesitates. He clears his throat. "What…"

Lincoln holds up a hand. He takes another deep breath, ignoring the smell of cooked, burnt flesh. "Do you know," he says, turning to Arthur and forcing himself to smile. "Ian was starting to annoy me. Just a bit."

Arthur's eyes flicker toward the three corpses. It's hard to tell which is Ian anymore. "Uh…"

"I mean, don't get me wrong, I didn't want him to *die*," Lincoln says. "Not yet, anyway. Not while we need him. But I can't help but feel like this is a little bit deserved."

Arthur frowns.

Lincoln laughs. "We have to look on the bright side, don't we, Artie? If we don't laugh, we'll cry. That's what my dear old mum used to always say. Of course, she was a right miserable cow, so what did she know about it?" He chuckles.

"Lincoln," Arthur says, looking concerned. "What are we going to *do*?"

"We'll muddle through," Lincoln says.

"Okay, but – but what's the plan? I know Ian had written out the formula, but it's destroyed. There's only one other person who knows it."

"I'm aware of this," Lincoln says.

"The professor," Arthur says. "I know the plan was to kill him as part of the demonstration, but I don't think that's an option anymore. We should bring him in instead. Force him to make it."

"Mm," Lincoln says. He steps out of the lab, away from the carnage. He snaps his fingers at a couple of men nearby. "We need this cleaned up," he says, thumbing back into the lab. "Nice and tidy, there's some good boys." The two jump into action, doing as he says.

Arthur follows close behind. "Lincoln?" he says. "The professor...?"

Lincoln nods. "Yes, fine," he says. "Take me to the canister. Show me this safe place."

Arthur directs him into a back room. The canister of GB2 is laid flat in the corner. It's in a box filled with foam peanuts for protection.

Lincoln kneels next to the box. "Good," he says. "This is good." He strokes the tip of his finger along the side of the canister. It's cool to the touch, like it hasn't been anywhere near an all-encompassing lab fire. "The professor," he says, stroking the canister still. The one canister upon which all of their hopes and dreams rely. Upon which their reputation relies. Potentially their lives, too, if they fail to follow through and their demonstration is deemed a waste of time. Some of the people he's contacted, he knows they lack patience. Knows they won't take too kindly if they think he's trying to mock them. Lincoln has already lost his brother for this. He's not willing to sacrifice himself, too. He looks up at Arthur. "From everything Ian told us about this professor, he sounds like a man of morals. Dr Frankenstein, horrified at the monster he's created. Do you think we can *make* him talk?"

"I do," Arthur says. "Because we're monsters too."

Lincoln smiles at this, and it feels genuine upon his face. "Yes," he says. "I suppose we are." He straightens, though it's difficult to part from the GB2. He wants to be near it at all times, to ensure its safety. "He's probably got a family. We can always use them for leverage. It's not like we have any qualms about that sort of thing, now, is it?"

"Qualms don't make money," Arthur says.

"Very true," Lincoln says. "Very true." He thinks about the team led by Neil and Dean he currently has running down a mother and child, as well as their mysterious accomplice. Ella and Kit Wiley. No qualms there. None at all. It's not like it's the first time Lincoln has had to order the deaths of women and children. He's numb to it now. Doesn't lose any sleep over these kinds of things. And of course, their demonstration is going to kill many people – men, women, and children. He barely gives it a second thought.

But then a thought *does* occur to him. He frowns, holding up a hand for Arthur. "Wait," he says.

Arthur looks at him expectantly.

"The boy," he says, remembering what Neil told him he found in the safe house. The drawings and scribblings the boy was making.

*The formula.*

He saw the formula at the Underhill cabin. He *knows* the formula.

"We need to hedge our bets," Lincoln says.

Arthur cocks his head, not understanding.

"The *boy*," Lincoln says, pushing past him, pulling out his cell phone and quickly searching for Dean's number. "The boy knows the formula!" he says to Arthur while the call rings out. "Between him and the professor, we'll get an answer!"

Dean answers. He's breathing hard, like he's running. "Sir," he says. "We're engaged."

"Keep the boy alive!" Lincoln says as fast as he can. "The boy – Kit – we need him. Under no circumstances – and I mean *none* – is he to be harmed. Woe betides anyone who does. Make sure that's known."

Dean pauses. "Sir? How are we supposed to –"

Lincoln hears gunfire, drowning out Dean's words.

"This son of a bitch has killed two of us already," he's saying when the noise clears. "Neil is dead – cut him up with kitchen knives. This ain't just some regular guy. He's dangerous as all hell."

"Then kill him," Lincoln says. "And kill the mother – but *not* the boy. Do *not* kill the boy. Bring him to me."

## 32

Tom, Ella, and Kit get into the outdoor store. They enter from the rear, Tom kicking open the locked back door. They race through an empty office, past the security office and its glowing monitors, past the storage area, and find themselves on the shop floor.

They keep moving while Tom scans the store. The three remaining men coming after them have probably split, entering through different points again, same as they have at every other building Tom and the others have run through. Near the ceiling, he sees security cameras. There are a lot of them, covering all of the shop floor. There's a lot of valuable merchandise here. He searches for the gun sales point. He spots a sign with an arrow, leading through to another part of the building.

"This way," he says, holding onto Ella's arm with his left hand. In turn, she keeps her grip on Kit's hand.

The store is active. He sees half a dozen people in the blue shirt uniform of the business. Most of them are preoccupied with customers, pointing things out, giving recommendations. There are another dozen people inside, roaming, looking. There's a couple of people paying. It's busy.

Tom looks back. He looks toward the entrance. He sees the man with the duster and the concealed assault rifle come through the automatic door. From the back, the same way Tom and the others entered, he sees the other two men run through, screeching to a halt as they scan the area.

Their eyes settle upon Tom, Ella, and Kit. They're through with being careful. Their weapons are already in their hands. They start shooting.

The store fills with the sounds of gunfire and screams. Tom drags Ella and Kit down with him, but they don't lie flat. They crouch and hurry on between the stands of puffer jackets and the displays of tents. Tom doesn't hear the assault rifle yet. He hears two handguns.

Up ahead, he sees one of the employees spin as they attempt to flee, winged by a bullet. Tom stops when he gets closer, but the bullet tore through the man's neck, through his carotid artery, and he's already dead. Blood has sprayed upon the jackets close by, and it pools upon the ground beneath them. Tom waves for Ella and Kit to go around so they don't slip in it. Tom stands quickly, fires a few times toward their pursuers, to spook them as well as give him a chance to observe their locations.

The two men with handguns *are* spooked, and they dive for cover, but the third, at the front of the store, is ready. He's shouldered the assault rifle – an SR16 – already and he's waiting. When Tom pops up, he opens fire.

Tom throws himself flat to the ground, the rifle tearing apart the stands around him. He can hear people screaming and crying out as they get caught by stray rounds.

Tom doesn't stay where he is. Lying flat won't accomplish anything. He keeps moving, hurrying across the ground on his elbows and knees. He catches up to Ella and Kit. They continue on, heading to the gun sales point. Around them, the screaming is dying down, replaced by groans and sobs. There's no one still standing, except for maybe the three attackers. Everyone else is either dead, or cowering.

The lack of screams and gunshots means Tom can better hear their pursuers. They're following still, hurrying through the racks and down the rows, trying to catch up. They know they don't have much time. Subtlety has been thrown out the window. They've opened fire. They've killed bystanders. This isn't the first business they've attacked. The cops would have already been called after the restaurant. And now it's only a matter of time before the cops arrive and the three get caught in another shootout.

Tom can't hang around for the cops. He has no idea how long it might take them to get here, and they're not going to come charging straight in. They're going to surround the building. Appraise the situation. That's a lot more minutes left alone in here, outnumbered and outgunned. As per usual, they're on their own. They're the only ones who can save themselves.

Tom spots the gun sales point. This area is for more advanced campers, and for hunters. There is netting and canvas. Fishing poles and hunting equipment. Knives and hatchets. Gas stoves. Even a rack of ghillie suits.

From behind the gun sales point, an employee rises, hearing approach. He's shouldering a shotgun – a Remington. Tom sees how he swings the barrel off to the right behind them, aiming for the attackers. He fires once, but it's all he can manage. He's promptly cut down by the assault rifle.

Knowing their location, Tom stands and fires the Beretta, sending the three men scattering. They aren't close. They're spread out, covering ground. They duck into cover. Tom sends Ella and Kit in another direction to find cover, then he races for the gun stand, diving behind it. Bullets from the SR16 pound into and through the models hanging on display above him.

The employee's eyes are open, but he's dead. Tom takes the shotgun from him, assuming it to already be fully loaded. He checks it. It's a Model 870. He knows it can hold up to eight rounds – seven in the internal tube magazine plus one in the chamber. He checks it. It means taking all of the shells out but he has to be sure. Assumptions aren't enough. He can't get caught short. He counts six shells. They're 12/70 7mm buckshot. It was worth checking. He quickly reloads, then starts moving again. There's a lull in the assault rifle fire. They know where he is and they're trying to get closer. They're waiting for him to stand, to try something. Tom gets around the back of the sales point. He dives out from behind the counter.

The assault rifle and the handguns open up. Tom runs across the store, away from Ella and Kit, firing two rounds from the shotgun as he goes. Both of them are aimed at the man with the SR16. He's the main threat, and thus Tom's priority. Thanks to the buckshot, Tom's aim doesn't have to be accurate. The man with the rifle realises this, and he panics as he's fired upon. He tries to get to cover as the buckshot spreads. The pellets pepper him in the neck, arm, and shoulder. He goes down, dropping the SR16.

The other two men are spread out either side of the man

who had the assault rifle. The man on Tom's right is closest now. Tom dives down, rolls through, comes up on a knee. The man almost runs into him. Tom fires point blank into his chest. The blast takes the man off his feet and throws him back into a tent, flattening it. He lies very still, a gaping hole in his torso.

Tom stands and turns to his left, searching for the one survivor. He spots him. He's running for the dropped SR16. Tom fires. The man dives. Tom runs for him. As he nears, he spots him trying to get the SR16 free. Its strap is tangled in the fallen man's body. His weight is pressed down on top of it. The man trying to get it senses Tom's approach. He lets go of the rifle and tries to raise his handgun.

He's too slow. Tom fires the shotgun. The blast catches the man in the face, almost blowing his head off his shoulders, tearing his face to ribbons.

Tom stands where he is and sweeps the area, shotgun stock nestled into his shoulder. It's clear. He drops the shotgun and calls for Ella and Kit.

They emerge from the back of the store. "Head out front and find a car," Tom says. "Not our car – we need new wheels. They know the Toyota. Find something different, something close to the parking lot exit."

"Shouldn't we wait for the cops?" Ella says.

"There could be more of these men coming," Tom says. "They might get here before the cops, and they might all have assault rifles. Just go and find a car."

"Then what?"

"Then wait for me. I'll do the rest."

"What are you doing now?"

"Just go," Tom says, running in the other direction. There's no time to explain. He heads to the door at the back where they first came through, marked 'Staff Only'. He kicks it down and goes back to the office they passed with the security footage playing on screens. There's no one else back here. The footage is running through a laptop open on a desk beneath the screens. Tom sees a USB sticking out the side of it. He ejects it, then pockets it. It has the men's faces. He needs to know who they are, who they work with, who they work *for* – if it's 'Lincoln' or someone else. Their faces could bring answers. They could reveal who Lincoln *is*.

He leaves the back. The front of the store remains clear. It smells of death and carnage. Familiar sights and sounds for Tom. He runs outside, in search of Ella and Kit. It doesn't take him long to spot them. They've found a car.

## 33

Lincoln paces.

It's proving to be a long night. A *stressful* night. He checks his cell, but he hasn't heard anything back. Too much time is passing. He doesn't like it. They were already engaged – it should be over by now.

Arthur joins him. "This isn't looking good," he says.

Lincoln doesn't need to be told this. He's already very much aware. Instead of saying this, he just grunts. "Mm."

"I guess they *could* be on their way here..." Arthur says. "Maybe things got hot and they had to book it..."

"It's a possibility," Lincoln says. "But we have to be realistic. Look online, scour the airwaves. We know roughly where they were – see if there are any reports coming out of that area."

Arthur nods, then goes off to do as he's told.

Lincoln blows air, finding his eyes drawn once again to the burnt-out lab. The bodies are gone now, but the smell of their charred flesh remains. He runs his hands down his face and he waits. He's tried calling Dean already. Tried the other men with him. Nothing. Lincoln knows what this means.

It doesn't take long for Arthur to come back to him, and from the look on his face things went how they've worried.

"They're dead," Arthur says.

Lincoln grits his teeth. "What happened?"

Arthur tells him. The shootout at the strip mall. The dead civilians. All five shooters are dead. The man who killed them has disappeared from the area, along with the woman and child he was travelling with.

Lincoln takes a deep breath. "Well," he says, struggling to put a cheerful face on this. "At least the boy's still alive. There's still hope for us yet."

Arthur doesn't say anything.

"You know," Lincoln says, "at the minute, it feels like if it wasn't for the bad news I wouldn't be getting any news at all. I don't suppose we know who this man is yet?"

Arthur shakes his head.

"He's killed a lot of my men."

"I know that," Arthur says.

"Still got about a dozen left."

"By my count, too."

"That should be more than enough."

"What's the plan?"

"That's a question for later," Lincoln says. He turns his back on Arthur, walking away. "I need to digest all of this. I need some time to think."

## 34

The car Ella and Kit found is a white Nissan. Tom found them waiting for him by it. He made sure no one was around, watching. It was a quiet part of the parking lot. Everyone else at the strip mall was gathered near to the outdoor store now that the shooting had stopped. They watched to see who might emerge. To them, Tom just looked like another fleeing customer who'd managed to get out.

In the distance, coming down the road and lighting up the dark sky, cops approached. Their sirens were faint but getting louder as they drew closer. In all of the noise and confusion, Tom broke into the Nissan. He hotwired it while Ella strapped Kit into the back. She dove into the front with Tom as the engine roared to life. They drove away from the strip mall.

They've been driving for over an hour now. It's dark. It's getting late. Tom watches the mirrors. They're not being followed. Not anymore.

"I think we're clear," Tom says.

"Yeah?" Ella says. She blows out air, relieved. She looks at him. "Where did you go back there? When you sent us out to find the car."

"I got the security footage," Tom says. "We have your cousin's laptop – we put it into that and search their faces. Finally find out who we're going up against." Tom looks ahead, checking the signs at the sides of the road. "We'll put a little more distance behind us and then find a motel for the night, check in and do our search, then get some rest. Keep your eyes open for a place we can stop."

"Have you spent much time in New York?" Ella says.

"State or city?"

"Either."

"I've passed through both a few times. I don't know them particularly well."

"Same," Ella says. "I wish I could give you better directions."

"We'll find one. A motel always turns up."

After twenty minutes, sure enough, they spot a sign for a motel at the next turn-off and ten miles down the road. Tom heads that way. By the time they pull into the lot and park around the back, Kit is asleep. Tom gets keys for a room. He carries in their bags while Ella carries in Kit.

Tom doesn't settle in straight away. He can't. He has to do the first thing he does whenever he checks into a motel and he's being pursued – he checks the area over. He stands at the front of the building for a while watching the road, pretending he's on a phone call so as not to look suspicious. The motel is the only building on this stretch. It's easy to see if anyone else is hanging around. There are no vehicles parked on the side of the road, hiding out in the dark. No one lurking in the shadows around the building, or hanging around in their vehicle in the parking lot. It's clear. *They're* clear, for now.

He returns to the motel room. Kit is asleep, turned onto his side toward the wall. Ella has changed into a white vest. She sits at the laptop. She has it open, on, and charging. "I've connected to the Wi-Fi," Ella says.

"There's no one out there," Tom says, taking the USB from his pocket and sitting at the laptop. "It's a quiet road. A quiet motel. There aren't many vehicles in the parking lot."

"You think we're safe?"

"For the night at least." Tom uploads the footage into the laptop. He skims through, finding the best shots he can of the three men who were coming after them in the outdoor store. He's only able to get decent shots for two of them. He searches the images. While it loads, he looks at Ella. She sits beside him, her right hand rubbing at the top of her left arm. She rests her mouth and chin on her shoulder, watching him as he works, waiting to see what answers the footage might give them.

The faces bring back hits. The top result is from Interpol. Ella notices this too. She sits up. "What does that mean?" she says, pointing at the link. "What's a red notice?"

"It means these men are wanted internationally," Tom says. "It means Interpol are actively searching for them."

"Who *are* they?" Ella says, frowning hard. "What is going *on* here?"

Only one way to find out. Tom clicks the link.

Tom sees their names. One of them, the man whose face he took off with the shotgun, was called Dean. While there's red notices for both of them, they don't seem to be the top of the totem. They're known associates. Intrigued, Tom explores further. He finds whom they answer to. A pair of brothers, one of whom has a familiar name. Lincoln and Stanley Collyer. The red notice is primarily for them.

There are pictures of the brothers, side by side. They're in Navy uniform. They look alike, though Stan is slightly heavier. Lincoln has a narrow face and a thin face and pronounced cheekbones. His nose looks like it's had a couple of breaks. His jaw is strong and clean-shaven in the picture. His hair is dark and cut short.

There's a note next to Stan's picture and his name. It says 'recently deceased.' Tom keeps this in mind as he reads on about the brothers.

The Collyers are from London, England. Lincoln is older by four years. At sixteen he joined the Royal Navy straight after high school. Stan was eighteen when he did the same. By then, Lincoln had already been serving six years. He spent four years with the Royal Navy, then joined the Royal Marines. He was a Royal Marine for another four years before joining the SBS.

Ella must be up to the same part of the report as Tom. "What's the SBS?" she says.

"British Special Boat Service," Tom says, trawling through his memories of various acronyms from across worldwide military branches.

"What does that mean?"

"Are you familiar with the SAS? Special Air Service."

She thinks, her eyes scrunching. "I think so...maybe."

"The SBS are the seabound equivalent. They deal with water-based threats to the UK. Maritime counter-terrorism, amphibious warfare, things like that. And they're highly trained. They're tough. This is concerning."

"Were you in the Army, Tom?"

He nods, once.

"Were you anything specialist like this?"

"I was a private. A grunt. And then I was CIA."

Her eyes go wide at this. "CIA? How come you haven't mentioned that?"

"It wasn't pertinent."

"So, like, you were a secret agent? A spy?"

Tom shakes his head. "Nothing so elegant. I was more like a blunt weapon – a hammer. I was in a black ops team. We ran overseas operations – extractions, assassinations, primarily in the Middle East, but not always."

"Oh my God..." Ella says, looking at him in a new light. "Okay, but that means *you're* pretty tough too, right? That all sounds hardcore."

"I never underestimate an opponent."

Tom continues reading. Lincoln was with the SBS for six years. Stan remained with the Navy for five years. He never went into anything else. It was an eventful time. He didn't have a particularly shining record. He received regular reprimands for unruly behaviour – fighting, excessive drinking, insubordination. Finally, he was court martialled after one fight too many and discharged from the Navy. After that, he seemed to get into petty crime in and around London.

Then, abruptly, Lincoln left the SBS. He disappeared on a mission and wasn't seen again for two years. At the same time, his brother also disappeared. When both resurfaced, they were running guns in Africa. They transitioned from the British armed forced into weapons smuggling. They've been doing this for the last ten years. It brought them to the attention of Interpol, as well as various other national and international agencies.

Tom reads up on Stan Collyer's death. A shootout with cops in New York City. He was gunned down by a detective called George Ross. Tom files the name away. He could be someone worth talking to when they get to the city. The shootout occurred only a couple of weeks ago, at the beginning of the month. May.

A thought occurs to Tom. "Wait," he says.

Ella looks at him while he thinks.

"What was it Kit said, about Fordham 1605 – *he says it wrong*. Does that sound right?"

"He says it wrong or he writes it wrong, something like that," Ella says. "Also, *he's not from here* – that was part of it too, I think. What? What is it?" She looks between Tom and the laptop screen, trying to decipher what he's realised.

"The brothers... Lincoln, the name we've heard before, the one still alive – he's British," Tom says. "They write the date differently over there. The European way. They put the day and then the month."

Ella frowns. "So?"

"Fordham 1605. It's not just a location – it's a *date*. May sixteenth."

Ella's eyes widen. They look at each other. Ella looks toward the date in the bottom right corner of the laptop.

Tom has already worked it out. "Whatever's happening in Fordham," he says, "it's happening the day after tomorrow."

## 35

Lincoln stands outside, taking in the cool night air. He looks across the water, toward the lights of New York City. He watches them twinkle on the surface of the Hudson. He whistles gently. It's a nonsense tune, but it's jaunty and it helps him think.

Arthur comes out to find him. He doesn't say anything. He stands next to Lincoln at the railing, looking at the city lights with him.

"I think, in time, I might come to miss Dean," Lincoln says. "I always liked him. I wasn't so fond of Neil. He didn't have much of a sense of humour."

Arthur looks at him. Still, he doesn't speak.

"I know what you're wondering," Lincoln says. "You want to know what the plan is. What we're going to do next."

"We're all wondering that, Lincoln."

Lincoln nods. "Fair, fair. You were in the Army, weren't you, Arthur?"

"Yes, sir."

"Does the US Army have a slogan? A motto?"

Arthur nods. "This We'll Defend."

Lincoln thinks it over, nodding. "I like it," he says. "In the SBS, we said By Strength And Guile. It's not as well known as the other one, is it? *Who Dares Wins*. Feels like everyone knows that one, but I always liked ours. *By Strength And Guile*. Two qualities that can get you out of a lot of jams. And *this*, Arthur, this is one almighty jam."

Arthur waits.

"We need the boy," Lincoln says, turning away from the city lights and toward his trusted right-hand. "Now, bear with me while I think out loud. We have plans in place for the professor, too, but I think we'll have more luck with the boy. Now, these three – mother, son, and mystery accomplice – they seem to be running. They're in New York state now. Are they coming this way? Are they trying to find answers themselves rather than leaving it in the hands of the authorities? The boy was writing Fordham and the date over and over again. If they *are* coming here, they could run right into our hands. But that doesn't narrow the search enough. So, the boy can wait. As long as he's alive, we can catch up to him later. We know their identities at least, and we know where they live. If things get quiet enough for them, they'll go home. We'll grab them there. If we have the formula we can always find some chemists who'll be willing to take a hefty payday in order to brew us up a fresh batch of the GB2." He turns back to the lights, thinking. "We have to carry through with the original plan, albeit with some minor amendments where the professor is concerned. There are too many eyes on us to deviate from it now. We have the one canister. It'll be enough to demonstrate what it can do. The money will come in. We can rebuild from there. We'll find the boy." He turns to Arthur. "*That's* the plan," he says. "We stay the course. We get the professor. We find the boy. We carry out the demonstration. Not necessarily in that order, but by strength and guile, we'll win the day."

Arthur nods. He's smiling. "I'll let the others know."

"Tell them to maintain a high level of preparation. It's not long now."

## 36

It's early morning. Tom drives the Nissan. He's had to stop for gas, but now they're on their way, heading south toward New York City. Their plan remains the same – go to Fordham, to the University, and speak to the professor there. See if he can make sense out of what they know of the chemicals. Or, ideally, if they can get Kit to write out the formula that he saw in the cabin.

"Can you get him to write it out?" Tom asked Ella last night while they talked through their plans for today.

"I can ask," Ella says. "I can try to coax. There's no guarantee, but he likes to draw. He likes to write things down. You've seen him. If we give him some paper and set him in the right direction, like maybe asking him to draw Ian in the cabin, then we should be okay."

Now that they believe they know the meaning behind Fordham 1605, the stakes have become time sensitive. Of course, they still don't know what the stakes truly are. They have to treat it as something catastrophic, no matter how big or small it may turn out to be. They have to treat this as an emergency situation, and they're on a countdown.

Ella is on the phone. She's calling the police in New York City. She's put it on speaker so Tom can listen in.

"We need to report that a man named Lincoln Collyer is somewhere in the city," Ella says. "And that he's potentially planning some kind of an attack."

The police operator on the other end doesn't sound disinterested, but she doesn't sound as helpful as she could be, either. "An attack? What kind of an attack?"

"We're not sure," Ella says. "If you look him up you'll be able to see who I'm talking about – he's a British mercenary, a gun runner, and he has a group working for him. All we know is that he has something planned in New York City – possibly in the Fordham neighbourhood specifically. Please, if you look him up you'll see that he and his men are wanted by Interpol. There's a red notice for him."

"Which part, *exactly*, of Fordham?"

"We don't know."

"But you're certain it's Fordham?"

Ella bites her lip. "We're not certain. Look, we don't know for sure what's going to happen, but there could be an attack – like, a bomb, or a chemical attack, or *something* – and people could get hurt."

"How do you know this?"

"Because I was kidnapped by these people, back in Vermont –"

"Have you contacted the police in Vermont?"

"Yes, of course. This man, Lincoln, his men *killed* the deputies that were protecting me."

The operator is silent. Tom thinks he can hear the tapping of keys. She's potentially looking this up. "Ma'am," she says after a moment, "you keep saying 'we'? Who is 'we'?"

"My name's Ella Wiley," Ella says. "I have my son with me, and a man who's helping us."

"Who is the man?"

"It doesn't matter. What matters is that something is going to happen in New York City, and we think it's going to happen tomorrow, and the man behind it is probably in the city right now. You need to find him before he can do anything. You need to...to – I don't know, to shut down the city, to cordon off the roads, *something*."

"Ma'am, we can't shut down the city based on a rumour," the operator says. "We need more specifics."

"I've told you everything I know."

The operator falls silent. Tom hears the tapping of keys again. "I'll pass this information along, but without a precise location we can't expect much to come of it. It's a big city, Miss Wiley. You're asking us to find a needle in a haystack. Where are you now? If you're near to us you can come down to the station and we can –"

Ella hangs up. "That was frustrating," she says to Tom.

"You did what you could," Tom says. "We've made them aware, and if they have any sense they'll increase the police presence in Fordham. But other than that, we remain on our own."

"Feels like that's the way it's been since this started."

"That's how it always feels," Tom says. "It's like the Army. The only people you can rely on are yourself, and those right there beside you in the thick of it."

They drive on. They're not far from New York City now. Another hour, traffic depending, and they'll be at Fordham.

## 37

It's easy enough for them to find Fordham University. It takes up most of the neighbourhood. They find a place to park off the campus and then walk the rest of the way, crossing the green to the main building. They pass a few dozen students outside. Some of them are lounging on the grass, reading or hanging out. A few of them are throwing a Frisbee, spread out in a triangle. Tom asks directions to the chemistry department and a young lady in reflective shades and a wide-brimmed straw hat points out which building it is.

"Do you know if anyone's in there right now?"

The young lady shrugs.

Tom and the others go to it. Ella holds Kit's hand. He keeps pace with them, but he looks around, up at the big stone buildings they pass by. They get into the chemistry department. It sounds quiet. They go down the brightly lit corridor, their boots scuffing and sometimes squeaking on the buffed floor. They move room to room, looking in each one. They see a full class of students in white lab coats and protective eyewear hunched over beakers and tubes at workstations.

Tom checks a directory on the wall, searching for Professor Richard McCulloch's room. They continue down the corridor until they come to an empty lecture hall. Through the glass in the door Tom sees movement inside, a lone figure in front of the board, sitting at a desk and making notes. Tom knocks, then steps inside without waiting for a response. Ella and Kit follow close behind.

The man looks up at them. He has a friendly face, but he seems surprised to see them, looking each of them over, particularly studying Kit. "Little young, isn't he?" the man says, smiling. "Or is he just advanced?" The man has long white hair that sticks out wildly at the back and partially at the sides, and a white beard that's been allowed to grow. He looks a little like Santa Claus, though much slimmer. He's tall, too. Taller than Tom by about six inches.

"We're sorry to disturb you," Tom says. "Mr...?"

"Professor," the man says. "Professor Richard McCulloch."

"Just the man we're looking for," Tom says. "We're sorry to disturb you, Professor McCulloch, but we have a question, and we were hoping you – or someone in this building – might be able to help us with it."

Richard puts his pen down and steps out from behind his desk. "What kind of a question?" he says, clearly intrigued.

Tom and Ella exchange looks. Tom turns back to him. "It's a long story," he says. "Maybe we should all take a seat."

They do so, and Tom tells Richard what has happened, from the beginning. It's a wild story. Tom half expects the professor to kick them out, to ask them what kind of practical joke they're trying to play, demand to know why they're wasting his time.

Except, none of those things happen. Instead, Richard's face darkens. His eyes narrow. He looks between the three of them. He stands abruptly while Tom is still talking, nearing the end of the tale, but he doesn't try to leave. He stays close, pacing, tugging at the hair under his bottom lip. When Tom finishes speaking, ending at last night's strip mall escape, Richard is silent. Tom intended to continue, to tell the professor of Fordham 1605 and the chemical formula that Ella said Kit began to write out, but there is something about Richard's demeanour that causes him to stop, to wait, to gauge the man's reaction. Tom watches him, waiting for him to say something. He hears a dry click from the back of Richard's throat when he swallows.

Finally, he turns to them. "You said there was a man at the cabin," he says. "A man who got away. You said he seemed to be in charge of the chemicals. Did you hear his name?"

"Ian," Tom says.

Richard closes his eyes tight. His mouth sets in a thin line. "Ian Farrow?"

Tom never heard Ian's surname. He looks at Ella in case she did. "I don't know," she says.

Richard holds up a finger. "Just give me one moment," he says, turning away. "I'll be right back."

He leaves the room. Tom gets to his feet. He goes to the door of the lecture room, standing close to it to keep watch down the corridor, hand resting close to his Beretta.

"Are you worried about him?" Ella says.

"We might have come here to talk to him, but we don't know him," Tom says. "And he had a strange reaction to everything we just told him. To Ian in particular." After a moment, Tom hears footsteps coming quickly down the corridor. Only one pair. He spots Richard hurrying along. There's something in his hand – a picture. It flaps while he walks. Tom returns to Ella and takes a seat as if he never got up.

Richard returns, a little out of breath. Wherever he went, he was fast about it. He comes closer and holds up the picture. It looks like a staff photograph – the chemistry department faculty lined up in front of one of the buildings, wearing their white lab coats, beaming into the camera. There are just over a dozen people in the picture, male and female. Richard points to one of the faces. A man. He's standing next to Richard. "Was this him?"

Ella's eyes narrow. "That's him," she says, her voice quiet, almost breathless.

Tom looks up at Richard. He nods, once. "How do you know him?"

Richard takes a step back, deflated. He puts the photograph down on his desk, then braces himself against it for a moment with both hands. He breathes deeply and then turns back to them. "He was my assistant," Richard says. "We worked together for three years. I think I know exactly what this is about." He takes a seat at the desk, his body turned toward them. His face has blanched. His body has hunched, collapsing in on itself. He looks older. "It's about GB2."

"What's GB2?" Tom says.

"It was an experiment gone wrong," Richard says.

Tom and Ella wait. Kit sits close to Ella. He looks around the room. Occasionally his eyes will settle on Richard, and he watches him, but he quickly loses interest.

Richard looks between them. "So it was just coincidence?" he says. "That the three of you were dragged into this? That you were all just in the wrong place at the wrong time?"

Ella nods.

"And it was just a coincidence that you came here? That you came to *me*, specifically?"

Tom tells him about Fordham 1605, how it led them here, to the university, to him. Of how it must have been something Kit overheard, and he's written it down, over and over. Tells him, too, of how he believes it's a date. Tomorrow's date, to be precise.

"But you didn't know Ian had worked here?" Richard says. "That he'd worked with me?"

"We didn't even know his last name."

Richard sits, frowning. "This Fordham 1605 – you don't know for *sure* what it means?"

"No. Same as we don't know what GB2 is. But it sounds like you might have some ideas, and we're waiting on answers."

"Have you contacted the authorities?"

"We already told you we have," Ella says. "I called them on the way here. They need specifics. They need details. Locations. If you'll talk to us, tell us what you know, *you* could help us with that."

"I don't know where Ian is now," Richard says. "I don't know where he's been for the last seven months, since he quit."

"Why'd he quit?" Tom says.

"Because I wouldn't make GB2."

"What *is* GB2?"

"It's a chemical weapon," Richard says. "A gas. I assume you're familiar with sarin?"

"Yes," Tom says. "And I'm also aware that its military designation is GB."

Richard nods. "Exactly. GB2 is practically identical to sarin, but without any of its corrosive qualities. But if inhaled, it has a 99% fatality rate. And then, it leaves no trace in the lungs. A perfect weapon for assassinations, wouldn't you say? A perfect way to circumnavigate the laws of war that prohibit the use of chemical weapons. With GB2, there's no evidence that a chemical weapon was ever used in the first place, unless you witness it firsthand. When first released, the gas is a grey colour. Within a few minutes it quickly dissipates, leaving no trace behind that it was ever there."

"How do you know this?" Tom says.

Richard grits his teeth. "Because I created it," he says. "Accidentally. Right here in this building."

"How do you create something like that accidentally?"

"With great hubris," Richard says. "I suppose I maybe let Ian get into my ear, but I have to shoulder the full responsibility."

"What do you mean?"

"Ian got a kick out of putting together chemicals he shouldn't have. We have a good stock here. We could make sarin gas. We could make soman. It amused him. It amused me, too, I suppose. It was careless. But I knew how to dispose of them properly, safely. Ian would talk about how great it would be if we could create something new, something we could take to the military and make our fortune with. It was just talk, just fantasy. But I entertained it, and I shouldn't have. We'd make sarin gas together and he'd say, 'what if we add this, what if we add that, what if we take out this,' etc. And one time I got carried away, and GB2 was the end result.

I have to admit, I was excited at the time. Excited at what we'd done, that we'd created something *new*. But then we tested it on lab mice." He bites down on his bottom lip, sucking on it. When he lets go, Tom sees that it's pale. "When I saw what it did to the mice… After I cut them open and realised what it could do to a *human*, I saw what I'd done. I saw how stupid, how *vain* I'd been. I destroyed what I had created. I got rid of all of my work on GB2.

"Ian was furious. He said that after all of our talk of weaponry advancements, we'd finally made one and I'd destroyed it. I tried to reason with him. Tried to explain the chaos we could have caused, the lives we would risk – the blood that would be on our hands. And I explained to him, there are bans on chemical weapons for a reason. Our government wouldn't have bought it. He said we should have gone to the black market with it. There would be plenty of people out there who would pay more money than we could imagine for such a weapon and its capabilities. He quit. I begged him not to do what he was suggesting. He wouldn't listen. I tried calling him but he blocked my number. I went to his apartment but he was gone. I haven't seen him since. A part of me has dreaded this day. I think I always knew it was coming."

"And Ian's the only other person who knows the formula for GB2?" Tom says.

Richard nods.

"Not anymore," Ella says. She has an arm around Kit. She squeezes him.

Richard's face drops. "He knows it?"

"He saw it on their whiteboard."

"But you said that was days ago. How can he remember? It's a complicated formula."

"Kit isn't like other children," Ella says. "He doesn't speak much, but he *remembers* things."

"The people coming after you, do they know about this?"

"We don't know," Tom says. "But they've attacked a couple of places where we've been now. Chances are they could've found some of Kit's writings, his drawings. If so, they might've figured it out."

"It's a dangerous knowledge to have," Richard says. "Especially if Ian is looking to sell it. He may not want anyone else to have this information."

Tom thinks. *Fordham 1605.* Fordham, tomorrow. Right here. "If that's so, he may be looking to eliminate the people he *knows* are aware of the formula," Tom says. "He and Lincoln both. You say GB2 leaves no trace, but that's only so good if there's not a person who can step forward and identify what caused the death. That someone is you, professor. Other than Kit, you're the only other person alive who knows what GB2 is and how it works. If they have something planned for tomorrow, for Fordham, it could be you. You could be a target. This whole university could be a target."

Richard is pale still. He looks sick with the thought of what Tom is suggesting.

Tom looks at Ella. "*This* could be Fordham 1605. This building. This man. Right here, tomorrow."

"Will they use the GB2?" Ella says. "We know they've been stockpiling the chemicals for it – Ian could have already made it."

"Maybe," Tom says, turning back to Richard. "They use the gas, and no one knows what killed you, or else they suspect something went wrong in the lab."

They sit in silence, digesting this possibility.

"We're going to talk with a detective who might be more

inclined to listen to us and help," Tom says. "You should come with us. It'll be safer for you."

"I can't run around the city with you," Richard says. "I'm an old man. I can't keep up. I'll go to my house and I'll stay there. I won't come in tomorrow. If I'm not here, then maybe they won't follow through on what they have planned."

"But Ian probably knows where you live, right?" Ella says.

"It's fine," Tom says. "Richard is right. He can't keep up and we can't afford to be slowed down. Go home. We're going to talk with the detective. So long as he's willing to listen and believe us, then we'll get him to send some cops to your house to make sure no one tries anything."

"Cops were supposed to be watching out for me," Ella says. "It didn't go so well."

"I know that," Tom says. "And we'll tell *him* that, too."

"And if he doesn't listen?" Richard says.

Tom turns to him. "Then we'll come back to you, and we'll stick together. Give me your address, and I'm going to give you my number. If anything happens while we're with the detective, you call me."

"Anything... Like what?" Richard says.

"You'll know it when you see it," Tom says. "But let's hope it doesn't come to that."

## 38

Lincoln sleeps late. He needs his rest, especially after all of yesterday's stress. Tomorrow is a big day. They all need to be ready for it.

While he eats in the room they've transformed into a makeshift canteen, he calls Arthur to him. "You're awake," Arthur says, taking a seat opposite.

"Have you slept?" Lincoln says, spooning honeyed porridge into his mouth.

"I got a few hours."

"We all need to be at our best for tomorrow. I don't want you running yourself ragged."

"I'm fine. I know my limitations, and I know how far I can push myself."

Lincoln has been in the gym with Arthur, and he knows that Arthur can push himself very far indeed. "How are the men?"

"They're good. A little demoralised at the colleagues they've lost these last few days, but it's nothing the salve of a big payday can't fix. I have news for you, though."

Lincoln rolls his eyes. "If it's anything like the news I've been getting recently, I'm not so sure I want to hear it, sweetheart."

"This could be considered good news."

Lincoln raises an eyebrow. He spoons in more porridge and waits to hear what it is.

"The men watching the professor, they saw something that ought to please you."

"Do tell," Lincoln says.

"The woman, the kid, and the man," Arthur says. "They went to the university. They went to see him."

Lincoln absorbs this, porridge forgotten. "Oh really? Ella, little Kit, and the mystery bastard, here in New York City, eh?"

"The men were torn as to whether they should pursue. They decided against it. Said that McCulloch didn't go with them, and he was their priority."

"But they've made contact now. They're in the city. I doubt they're going to go far now. This is good. I know the city is a big place, but this is very good for us. We have an idea of where they are now. Tell everyone else to keep their eyes peeled."

"Already done," Arthur says.

Lincoln winks at him. "I knew I could rely on you, sweetheart."

"I'm concerned about what they might have said to the professor, though."

"I've got the same concerns, but it's too late for them now. We make our big move tomorrow, and nothing can stop us."

"We don't know how much they know," Arthur says.

"If they knew enough, the professor wouldn't have been left behind. We grab him tonight. We hold onto him until he's willing to talk. We don't *need* him for tomorrow. Originally he was supposed to be one of the bodies, just another statistic among all the others, but it's not going to matter if he's not there. Once we have him, we can find ways to persuade him. We know where his kids are and all the rest of it."

"Ian was adamant that he wouldn't talk to us."

Lincoln waves a hand. "Ian was just concerned we'd find someone to replace him. He was thinking about his own bottom line. Everyone talks if you give them the right kind of persuasion. Money or torture – if one doesn't work, the other will. That's what I've always found. And besides, there's always the boy."

"How do you torture a nonverbal autistic kid? How do you persuade them with money?"

Lincoln shrugs. "Whatever the third way is, we'll figure it out."

"I want to raise a concern," Arthur says, suddenly solemn.

Lincoln pushes his bowl away, done with. "Well," he says. "This sounds serious."

Arthur looks at him.

"I'm all ears, sweetheart."

"The detective," Arthur says. "I'm worried that it's personal."

Lincoln stares back at him. "Of course it's personal," he says. "He killed Stan. My *brother*. Your friend. It *is* personal, but it's all part of the plan, too."

"I'm worried that you've persuaded yourself that's true."

"Hitting the detective creates a distraction. You know what cops are like – they've got that brotherhood mentality. Even if they don't like each other, if one of them gets hurt they have to avenge it. They'll all be so preoccupied with the detective and his building, they won't be watching out for us. I've told you all this. I've made it very clear. And it's not like it's going to be a *small* occasion, Arthur. You know this. The whole city will know he's dead." Lincoln grins.

"But it's still a vendetta. You're insisting on being there. It stops being professional when that happens."

"I'm not going to miss it," Lincoln says. "I wasn't there for Stan. I'm going to be there for the son of a bitch that gunned him down."

"You're not going to let him go."

"I can't," Lincoln says, leaning across the table, baring his teeth, feeling his calm momentarily slip away. He pulls himself back, breathing deeply. "You're right," he says, softer this time, back to his usual temperament. "I can't. And I shouldn't. But I *am* being sensible. We've all got our places to be tomorrow, and that is mine. And I'm not coming back here, Arthur. After tomorrow, once this is done, there's no need for me to stay in New York City."

"There's no guarantee we'll have found the boy by then."

"But you understand what I mean. Once the demonstration is over, and we have the boy and the professor is dead, we don't need to be here anymore. We go and we make GB2 and we get rich and fat off the profits. If I don't see the detective die tomorrow, when do I get another chance? Stan can't rest easy until I do this for him. *I* can't rest easy. But don't fret, Arthur. Like I said, I'm being sensible about it all. I *am* being professional. I've figured it into the plan. This works out for us. It's all a part of it. I wouldn't jeopardise what we have coming."

Arthur doesn't say anything.

"You trust me, don't you, sweetheart?"

Arthur has to nod his head at this. "You know I do. I'm just worried that your judgement is clouded."

"Then I hope I've set your mind at rest. We've got eyes on the detective, yes?"

Arthur nods. "He's at home."

"Good. It'll all go as it's supposed to, Arthur. Trust me. Trust me like you always have."

## 39

It didn't take long for Tom and Ella to find out which station Detective George Ross works out of. They go to it, but it's his day off.

"Do you know where we can find him?" Tom asks the desk clerk. "Or how we can get in touch with him?"

"We don't give out personal information," the clerk says, which is what Tom expected. "Is this pertaining to an ongoing investigation?"

"Yes," Tom says.

"I can arrange for you to speak with an on-duty detective, and –"

"Forget it," Tom says, turning away.

"Hey!" the clerk calls, but Tom ignores him.

Ella and Kit are waiting outside. "I take it from your face that it didn't go well?" Ella says.

"He's not working today. They wouldn't give his address, or a contact number."

"So what now? You said it yourself – he's our best way to bring the cops into this."

"We'll find him," Tom says, walking down the steps and heading back to the Nissan. Ella and Kit walk with him. "I don't reckon his address will be listed, so we'll not be able to look him up online, but I have a friend. She does this kind of thing all the time. I'll give her a call and she'll be able to track him down for us."

As they reach the car, they spot two people in dark suits and, despite the warmth, long overcoats, hanging around it. A man and a woman. The two look up as Tom, Ella, and Kit approach. The two turn their bodies toward them. The woman steps forward. She speaks. "Mr. Rollins?" she says. She's Polynesian, with a New York accent. Her long black hair is tied back in a ponytail.

Tom holds back, touching Ella's elbow so she knows to do the same. He eyes the two. His Beretta is on him, tucked into the waist of his jeans. He can see, under their coats, that they're both armed. They make no indication that they're going to reach for their weapons. Regardless, Tom puts his hand close to the Beretta, ready for whoever these people are, and whatever comes next.

"Looks like him," the man says.

The woman nods. "And you must be Ella and Kit Wiley," she says. She points a thumb over her shoulder, back toward the Nissan. "And this vehicle doesn't belong to any of you."

"Who are you?" Ella says.

The woman holds up her empty hands, signalling that they're not looking for trouble. "I'm Joanie Samu and this is Duane Foley," the woman says. "We're with Interpol."

## 40

After checking their ID, Tom and Ella agree to speak with Joanie and Duane. They go to a nearby diner and take a booth in the back where they have privacy. Ella orders food for Kit while the adults drink coffee, except for Tom. He drinks water.

"So you're agents with Interpol?" Ella says. "Looking for Lincoln, right?"

"Yes and no," Joanie says. "Interpol doesn't have agents. That's a Hollywood fallacy, I'm afraid. Duane and I are part of a response team, sent here to assist in a potential major incident. We heard your phone call."

"So you're taking us seriously?" Ella says.

"We're very aware of Lincoln Collyer and his operation," Duane says.

"We were sent the recording of your call and we came straight here from the National Central Bureau in Washington DC," Joanie says. She sips the coffee. "We've been on the road all morning. We were on our way into the station when we saw you entering it ahead of us."

"If all you had to go off was a phone call," Tom says, "how did you know it was us?"

"We did our homework on the way here, Rollins. We know about the attacks in Vermont. We know about the cabin. And we know that *you* were seen in the area."

"We're aware of you, Rollins," Duane says. "We know about San Francisco. About Dallas. You've been a busy man the last few years."

Ella glances at Tom, wondering what they're talking about.

Tom shrugs. "How many of you are there in your response team?"

"There's just the two of us right now," Joanie says. "But once we've assessed the situation, and if we can gain further information as to what is planned and where it's due to occur, we have a team of ten more ready to go."

"Are they in DC?"

Joanie nods. "But they'll be flying up here if needed."

"If you're not agents, what do you do?" Ella says. "What are you here for?"

"We offer investigative assistance," Joanie says. "We facilitate international police cooperation and information sharing. How much do you know about Lincoln Collyer? There's *plenty* of international information to share on him."

"We know enough," Tom says. "We know about the red notice."

"Then that explains why neither of you seemed surprised to hear who we're with," Duane says. "But don't you think it's dangerous having the kid with you?" He tilts his chin toward Kit.

"He's not leaving my side," Ella says, eyes narrowing,

defensive. "He – both of us – we've been in more danger when we've been apart from Tom."

Duane defers and takes a drink.

"What else do you know about Lincoln and his organisation?" Joanie asks, getting them back on track.

Tom sips his water. He and Ella exchange glances.

"What more do you know about what they have planned?" Joanie says, pressing.

"We should tell them about Richard," Ella says, leaning close to Tom, lowering her voice.

"Who's Richard?" Duane says. His demeanour is blunter than Joanie's. Tom notices how she shoots her partner an impatient look, silently warning him to pull back, to not press so hard.

Tom tells them about Professor Richard McCulloch. He tells them about Ian Farrow, too. He tells them about GB2, and he sees how their eyes go wide, how their lips press together into thin lines.

"Jesus," Duane says when Tom is finished. "Collyer is escalating. He's run guns and he's done mercenary work – hell, he's wanted for four known murders on three continents, but *this*..."

"We don't know for sure he's planning on a gas attack," Tom says. "But that's where everything is pointing."

"We've been trying to warn people," Ella says. "To get the cops to listen, but they won't do anything unless we can give them answers we don't have."

"We're trying to track down Detective George Ross," Tom says. "He's had a run-in with the Collyer brothers before. He may be more open to listening, and more likely to galvanise the rest of the force."

Joanie looks impressed. "You *have* done your research," she says.

"We've talked with Detective Ross," Duane says. "After the killing of Stan Collyer. That's who we were on our way to speak with again, when we spotted you."

"You won't find him at the station," Tom says. "It's his day off."

Joanie smiles. "We have his home address."

"Then we're coming with," Tom says. It's a flat statement. He stares down Joanie and Duane with a level gaze that lets them both know he's not open to discussion.

"All right," Joanie says. "You can tell him about GB2 directly. It might be best if he hears it from you."

## 41

Lincoln is cleaning his Sig Sauer when Arthur comes to find him. His cell phone is in his hand. "I've got Liskey on the line," he says.

Liskey is one of the men watching Detective George Ross's apartment building. Lincoln is instantly alert at the mention of his name. "What does he want?"

Arthur holds the phone out to him. "To talk to you."

Lincoln takes it. "What's happening?"

"We've got activity here," Liskey says. "Some new arrivals you're gonna want to hear about."

"Don't leave me in suspense, Liskey. I'm not interested in a guessing game."

"It's the three," Liskey says, getting straight to it. "Ella, Kit, and the guy. But there's two others with them. A male and a female."

"Anyone you recognise?"

"No. They look like cops."

"An escort, maybe?" Lincoln says, thinking out loud. It seems Ella and the man are putting the work in. They've been to see Richard, and now they're on their way to see the man who killed his brother. This isn't a coincidence. They're looking for answers. They're looking for *him*.

He looks up at Arthur. "Do you know about this?"

Arthur nods. "He's told me already."

Lincoln speaks back into the phone. "I'm on my way. Keep an eye on things, of course. If anything happens – anyone comes or goes – call me direct."

"Got it," Liskey says.

Lincoln hands the phone back to Arthur. He quickly reassembles his gun and loads it. "I'm going out there," he says.

"I heard."

Lincoln gets to his feet. He smiles at Arthur. "You're in charge, sweetheart. You know what's happening. You know what to do. I'm not going to rush into anything, I promise. I might be out there a while. If that happens, get the ball rolling. Liskey already has everything else I need out there. You know the timings. I'm counting on you."

Arthur nods. This isn't too much of a deviation from the script. Lincoln was always going to go out to the detective's building. This is just happening earlier than anticipated. Arthur doesn't attempt to argue it. He knows there's no point. Instead, he goes with it. "Then I'll probably see you tomorrow."

"You certainly will, sweetheart," Lincoln says, grabbing his jacket. "And when you do, I'll have a bloody big smile on my face."

## 42

Joanie and Duane are driving a black Cadillac. Tom gets Ella to drive the Nissan, following them. He watches the mirrors.

"You don't trust them?" Ella says.

"It's not them," Tom says. "We're in a city now. This isn't like the drive we took down here, with all of those wide, open spaces. If someone tries something, if an ambush is coming, I need to be ready for it."

Detective George Ross lives in the Bronx, not far from Fordham University. He lives to the north. If it wasn't for the traffic, it wouldn't take the small convoy long to get to him. As it is, they sit in a traffic jam for twenty minutes. It's hard to tell what's causing the hold-up. Tom doesn't like it. It makes him antsy. They're sitting ducks.

He turns in his seat, looking out of the back window, checking the buildings around them – their windows, and their roofs. He doesn't see anyone up there. Nothing suspicious, anyway. He looks down and sees Kit looking back at him. Tom doesn't turn straight back around. They look at each other in silence for a moment. "How you doing, Kit?" Tom says. "You okay?"

Kit doesn't respond.

"Everything all right?" Ella says.

"Yeah," Tom says, turning back. "We're fine."

The traffic starts moving again, waved through by a cop, and they see the cause of the hold-up: a minor crash between two yellow cabs. No one has been hurt, but there's a pair of destroyed fenders, and the damaged vehicles are blocking the road.

Joanie and Duane pull up in front of an apartment block. Ella parks behind them. They get out of their respective vehicles and rejoin each other on the sidewalk. Tom looks up and down it, checking the area and the nearby people. It's busy. There are plenty of walkers around. Most of them are passing harmlessly by, but they could be disguising anyone observing, plotting.

"Little jumpy, aren't you?" Duane says.

"Maybe you should be more," Tom says.

Joanie goes to the front of the building and hits the intercom for Detective Ross's apartment. "I spotted his car," Joanie says while she waits for a response. "Unless he's gone for a walk – which after meeting him I'd say is unlikely – he should be home."

A gruff voice comes over the intercom. "Yeah?"

"George, this is Joanie Samu from Interpol."

There's a brief pause, then George says, "Has he resurfaced?"

"Potentially," Joanie says.

"I'll buzz you in. You know where I am."

The group enters the building and takes the elevator up to George's apartment. Stepping out of it, Joanie and Duane lead the way down the corridor. Tom puts Ella and Kit directly behind them and he follows at the rear where he can see best.

Detective George Ross opens his door before they reach it. He was probably watching their approach through the peephole. He's eyeing Ella, Kit, and Tom. He turns to Joanie and Duane.

"They with you?" he says.

"They are," Joanie says.

"Civilians? Why?"

"You should hear what they have to say, Detective Ross," Duane says.

The detective waves a hand. "Just call me George," he says. "I'm off-duty." He turns, beckoning them all to follow him into the apartment.

George Ross, Tom remembers from what he's read online, is forty-eight years old, but he looks much older than he did in the picture. He could pass for sixty, easily. He's short, about five-seven, and round. Built like a barrel. His cheeks are unshaven and dotted with white stubble, and he's bald on top. The hair he has around the sides and back is wild and sticking out. Dark at the tips, but mostly grey. He has a squat nose that looks as if it's been broken a few times.

The reasons for his aged appearance soon become apparent once they're fully inside his apartment. Tom closes the door behind him and looks around. There are dozens of empty beer bottles and crushed cans next to the kitchen sink, along with a stack of Chinese take-out containers. The trash is overflowing with pizza boxes. George does not live a healthy lifestyle. The smell of alcohol and BO hangs in the air.

George appears to be aware of the smell. He opens a couple of windows, allowing some fresh air to get into the room. He looks down at Kit and smiles at him. "And who's this?" he says, lightening his tone.

"This is Kit," Ella says. "He doesn't really talk."

George doesn't look up at Ella. He continues to smile at Kit. "Do you like candy, Kit?" George takes a hard toffee from his pocket and holds it up.

"He likes candy just fine," Ella says. "But whether he'll take it from you is another matter."

"I'll give this to your mom, Kit, and if you want it, you can get it from her." George straightens, handing the piece of candy to Ella. "Is he autistic?"

"He might be," Ella says. "We don't know for sure yet." She takes the toffee and holds it out for Kit. Kit takes it, unwraps it, and puts it in his mouth. He pockets the wrapper.

George smiles down at him. "I had a sister was autistic," he says. "Non-verbal. Hyper-sensitive. Couldn't really take her anywhere. But she always loved those toffees. Think it's why I got the taste for them. It's when I started carrying them around, too. If ever she started getting riled up, I'd give her a toffee and she'd calm right down."

"Kit doesn't really get riled up," Ella says. "Not often, anyway. He's usually on a pretty even keel, no matter what. Where's your sister now?"

"She lives Upstate, with my other sister. After our parents died, it was either that or she had to go into a home. My sisters were always close, though. Myra, the non-autistic one, she was the only one it ever felt like Michelle would ever listen to. It was like they had their own secret language, and that was how they communicated. Like ASL, but they made it up themselves." George grins at the memories. "Why don't you all take a seat. Sounds like we've got a lot to talk about."

There are two old, beaten-up sofas and a chair. Ella and Kit take one of the sofas and Joanie and Duane go to the other. Tom doesn't sit. He goes to a window and looks down. He sees a lot of cars. He sees the tops of a lot of heads. It's too busy here to know if anyone is a threat. He doesn't like it.

"You don't want a seat?" George says.

"I'd rather stand," Tom says, turning away from the window and leaning against the wall next to it, folding his arms.

"Suit yourself," George says, lowering himself into the chair. He looks at Joanie. "I assume this must be about Lincoln Collyer again for you to come direct to me on my day off."

"I'm afraid so," Joanie says.

"Is he in the city?"

"He could be. We should maybe introduce our guests and then Rollins can bring you up to speed on what Lincoln has been up to recently."

They make quick introductions. It doesn't take long – he already knows Kit, and the two from Interpol. That only leaves Tom and Ella. For the second time today, Tom tells the story that led them here.

George listens. His face never changes. He takes it all in stride. Halfway through the telling, he takes out a toffee, winks at Kit, then pops it in his mouth and sucks on it while Tom tells the rest. "Huh," he says when Tom finishes. "A lot of things from that night I had my run-in with Stan Collyer make a lot more sense now."

"That was only a couple of weeks ago, right?" Ella says.

George nods. "Feels like longer. I went through all the psych evaluations, talked to the shrink – all the standard stuff after a shooting. Felt like it lasted forever. But yeah, just a couple of weeks."

"What happened?" Tom says.

George blows air. It's clear he's told this story many times already, including to people already in this room. "We'd been investigating this apartment building – eyewitnesses had seen suspicious activity, like things being snuck inside in the dead of night. Alarming things, too – guns, first and foremost, but stuff that looked like it could maybe be used for making bombs. There's official quotes from neighbours in the report. I can't remember them off the top of my head, but they were along those lines. I'm paraphrasing.

"The main thing is, they were enough for us to be concerned about. We staked out the building. Watched the apartment. You know New York well? I notice neither of you have the accent. Anyway, all you need to know is, it was a rundown area. People minded their business around there, so for them to report anything at all it had to be a big deal. Something to spook them, right? So we watch, and we see four guys regularly coming and going. One of the neighbours says most of them are American, but one of them has a British accent. That's interesting, but it doesn't give us much to work with, you know?

"So we're watching this place for about three weeks. We don't see anything. They're just hanging out in there. They looked about as bored as we were. But then finally, we get eyes on the weapons. Assault rifles – AR15s, AR16s, M4s, SR16s, and a few others, too. We don't see anything that looks like it could be used to make bombs, but this is enough for us to move in on. Assault rifles are banned in New York."

"We're aware," Ella says.

George nods. "If they're looking to sell them – and this was a large quantity of assault rifles; they were gonna shift them in bulk – well, that's illegal. We had enough reason to get inside, toss the place, see what else we could find. See about these potential bombs they could be making. This is two weeks ago, now. We're almost up to date.

"That night, we moved in, and they must have seen us coming. They were more vigilant than they looked through the windows. We get into a gunfight. A couple of them manage to get away, but the others are bagged. I put down the Brit personally. And soon after that is when I meet these two." He indicates Joanie and Duane. "And they come and tell me about Lincoln and Stan Collyer. Stan's the one I killed, but you already know that. They come and tell me Lincoln probably ain't gonna take too kindly to what I done. I'm gonna have to watch my back." George snorts. He holds out his hands. "I'm a New York cop. A detective. I'm *always* watching my back."

"What else did you find in the apartment?" Tom says.

"There were containers there, all right," George says. "And they were concerning. Large containers. I can't pronounce it."

"Methylphosphonyl difluoride," Joanie says.

"Yeah," George says. "*That*. They're with the CDC now."

"The buy in Vermont," Tom says, speaking mostly to Ella. "They needed to resupply what they'd lost in New York."

"That's how it sounded to me when you told it," George says. "And now you're telling me they were never making bombs – they were getting ready to make chemical weapons.

To make *gas*. Jesus Christ..." He glances at Kit, then at Ella. "Excuse my language."

"I wish taking the Lord's name in vain was the worst thing Kit has been exposed to this week," Ella says.

George sets his mouth grimly. He nods sympathetically. "Poor kid," he says. "All right," he says, turning back to Joanie and Duane, to Tom. "I ain't seen him. They haven't been hanging around, they haven't come knocking at my door. What're we thinking?"

"Right now all we can do is be on the defensive," Tom says. "We can't even be sure if what we're theorising about Fordham is right, but it's all we have to go off."

"And it was Kit who heard this?" George says.

"He keeps writing it down," Ella says. "And he said that the men talking said it wrong. *'He says it wrong.'* That has to be about Lincoln. The Englishman. The European way of writing a date."

George nods. "All right. Well, we can't take any chances."

"Your station isn't on the same wavelength," Tom says. "We need you to persuade them otherwise. To take this threat seriously."

"I'll make some calls," George says. "It might take some persuasion, but after what we found in that apartment, I reckon I can get through to them."

"Professor McCulloch is going to need protection," Tom says.

George pushes himself up out of his chair, pulling out his cell phone. "So long as the chief will listen, I'll get extra patrols in the Fordham area. Get people out to the university. Get bodies on the professor, too. Do you know where he is now?"

"I have his address," Tom says. He's already explained why Richard isn't with them.

Joanie gets to her feet, motioning for Duane to follow her. "We shouldn't wait around," she says. "We'll go to Professor McCulloch, watch out for him. We'll place a call while we're out there and call in the rest of our response team. Bulk up the numbers we have in the area."

"Time's ticking," George says. "Let's get on with it."

## 43

Liskey points at the man and woman in the suits and overcoats leaving the apartment building.

"They're the two," he says. "They came here with Ella and the others."

Lincoln is sat in the back of the car, between Liskey and the front passenger. He watches between them. He looks toward the front of the building. No one is following them out. "It looks like she and the others are staying here," he says. He watches the two suits as they get into their Cadillac. "I want to know who they are and where they're going. They could be another obstacle in the way of tomorrow."

"You want me to follow?" Liskey says, reaching for the key in the ignition.

"*No*," Lincoln says, clamping a hand on his shoulder to keep him from starting the engine. "You stay here. Continue surveillance on the building. Report to me if anything happens." Lincoln reaches for his door. His BMW is parked behind. He has his keys out ready. "I'll follow them. You call Arthur and let him know what's happening. I don't have time." Lincoln slips out of the car and walks slowly to his BMW. He glances back, as if he's checking the road. The Cadillac hasn't left yet.

Lincoln gets into his BMW. He's casual about it. Doesn't want to make what he's doing obvious.

The BMW is pointing in the opposite direction to the Cadillac. There's a steady stream of traffic coming along the road. The Cadillac pulls out and merges with it. Lincoln starts his engine. He allows a few cars to pass by while he waits for a gap. One finally appears. It's narrow, but he's able to swing out into it in a U-turn. He's fast enough about it that no one blares their horn at him. He's surprised. He'd been braced for it, ready to ignore it. In New York City, he feels like he hears horns blaring all the time. He wasn't concerned if the two in the Cadillac had heard it, either. They probably know the city well enough to know it's a common occurrence, too. Nothing for them to get sensitive about.

Lincoln has eyes on them. There are three vehicles between them. It's slow moving along the road. He's far enough back that they can't see him with ease. He follows the suited strangers, another potential problem that will need dealt with before tomorrow.

## 44

George is on the phone for a while. He takes the cell through to his bedroom and Tom can hear his voice rising occasionally.

"It sounds heated," Ella says.

"At least he's taking us seriously," Tom says.

She nods at this. She yawns, stretching her arms above her head. "Do you think this could be it for us? Is it over now?"

"I guess we'll find out tomorrow," Tom says.

Ella is on the sofa. Kit sits close to her. He stares out the nearest window. Ella puts an arm around him, stroking his cheek.

"Is he bored?" Tom says.

"I can never tell," Ella says.

George finishes his call and comes back through from his bedroom. They look at him expectantly. "All right," George says. "They were willing to listen. Eventually. They're gonna increase patrols in the area, starting now, carrying them all the way through to the day after tomorrow. Overtime has been authorised and leave has been cancelled. People are being called in. The FBI have been contacted. I made them aware that Interpol are present and will be in touch, and they already have a response team en route. I told them this could be something big – something *serious*. That if we don't start preparing for it now, people could get hurt." He pauses a moment, then adds, "I also made mention it would be an embarrassment for the department if we'd received information and hadn't acted upon it, and then people died. Sometimes you have to play to their vanity. Sad but true."

"However you did it, we're glad you got them to listen," Tom says. "I assume you've been called in too?"

"Not tonight," George says. "I'm back in tomorrow anyway, and it's been kept that way after I told them about the situation here." George crosses to the kitchen. "Does anyone want coffee?"

"Coffee sounds good," Ella says.

"I'm fine," Tom says.

"What about the little one?" George says. "I got some soda in the refrigerator. You're welcome to that, too, Rollins."

"I'm sure Kit would love a soda," Ella says.

"I'll take a water if you've got one," Tom says.

"Ah, a clean-living man," George says. He hands Tom a bottle of water, then takes a soda to Kit. He returns to the kitchen to make the coffee. He looks at Tom while he pours water into the coffee maker, the empty, stained pot waiting beneath. "I could've guessed," he says. "You've got that look about you." He nods at the bottle of water. "Hardly ever drink the stuff myself. I only ever get it in for guests."

Looking at the haggard lines around George's eyes, Tom isn't surprised to hear this. George doesn't look like he keeps himself hydrated. It'll be one of the reasons he looks so much older than he is. Tom steps closer, joining him in the kitchen.

"I need to find somewhere safe for Ella and Kit to hide out," Tom says. "I'll stick with them there. You got any recommendations?"

George doesn't say anything straight away. He watches the coffee pouring through the filter and down into the warmed pot. "You said you'd never met these two before the other night?"

"That's right," Tom says.

"I like that you're looking out for them," George says. "That's real noble. A lot of people, they wouldn't get involved."

"I'm not a lot of people."

George smirks. "I know that. When you first walked in, you looked familiar to me."

Tom grits his teeth. "I get that a lot."

"I'll bet you do. When I was on the phone back there, I spoke to a buddy, got him to look into you. Y'know, I almost wasn't surprised when he started talking about San Francisco. That wasn't so long ago, and your face was *everywhere* around then. You were the country's most wanted man for all of twenty-four hours."

"I work fast when I have to clear my name."

George laughs. "You can stay here tonight," he says. "All of you. That way we've got two pairs of eyes watching Ella and Kit. We can take turns sleeping."

"Are you sure?"

"Wouldn't offer otherwise. I know my place is a dump, and if I'd known I was gonna have visitors I would've tidied up in advance, but it is what it is, and the bed itself is fine. Washed the sheets just last week. And maybe it's not the safest place to be, seeing as how I could be a target, but then we've got strength in numbers, right? How's that sound?"

"I think it sounds like our best option, George," Tom says. "For all of us, you included. Thank you."

"You go and run it by the lady, and if you've got any bags you go and grab them. I'll finish up this coffee."

## 45

It's getting late. It's dark outside. Tom sits by the window. The road and sidewalk below remain active.

"Does it ever get quiet around here?" he says, looking back at George.

George is on the sofa. He ordered pizza for them all. He's picking at a leftover slice. "It stays active," he says. "But you get used to it. The city that never sleeps, baby."

"Makes it hard to know if you're being watched."

Ella and Kit are in the bedroom. Tom looked in on them earlier, saw that they were both asleep. Exhausted after another long day, no doubt. He could see earlier, before they went to bed, that Ella was struggling to keep her eyes open. She yawned regularly. She kept stretching while she sat on the ground with Kit. He was drawing. He drew a picture of George. George made a big deal out of it. He's stuck it on his refrigerator.

"It's not ideal," George says, getting to his feet and stretching. "But this is all we can do. Watch and wait. Hopefully if they try and make a move we'll know it's them. We'll see them coming. You've been online, you've seen some of their faces, right?"

"Those men are dead," Tom says. "I know what Lincoln looks like, but he might not be among them."

"If someone's coming for me," George says, "I reckon it's gonna be the guy whose brother I killed. You think he's gonna be the kinda man who's gonna let someone else get his vengeance for him?"

"I don't know what kind of man he is," Tom says. "I don't like any of what I've heard so far. What I *do* know is, he's trained his men well. They're careful. They're professional. If they're going to try and get into this building and up to this apartment, they're not going to be sloppy about it."

They heard from Joanie and Duane a few hours ago. They'd reached Richard. They'd explained who they were to him and secured the area. Joanie is inside the house with him and Duane is outside in the car, watching the street. They've spoken to the rest of their response team. They're being briefed, gearing up, and they'll be flying up here soon. They should arrive in the early hours. Whatever Lincoln has planned, there's hopefully going to be enough bodies on the ground tomorrow to cut it off before it can even start.

"Seems strange to me," George says, "at this point, if they're still coming after you, Ella, and the kid. I mean, if they're targeting Fordham, you're already here, and potentially they're already here, too. If they go out of their way to find you, they're just making more work for themselves at this point."

"We don't know that they're coming for us," Tom says. "We don't know that they're coming for you, either. It's just better for us to be prepared for any eventuality. Last time we saw them was Upstate, at the strip mall. Haven't seen any sign of them here in the city so far. That doesn't mean I'm going to rest easy."

"I'm just saying, maybe we'll be fine tonight. Could be they don't even know you all are here. Lost you Upstate, like you said. They're just gonna press ahead with whatever they have planned for tomorrow. I'm confident we'll cut them off. There's gonna be a *lot* of us. We can all breathe easier and you can all go home without fear of reprisals." He pauses, chewing on the edge of a pizza crust. "Have you considered if you're maybe wrong about this? If Fordham 1605 isn't a location and a date, if it means something else?"

"I've considered it," Tom says.

"And?"

"I don't have anything else. It matches up to what Kit told us they said in the woods. Coming here was our best option. It led us to Richard, and it led us to you."

George finishes the pizza crust and joins him at the window. He doesn't look down. He looks out and across at the other buildings. "You wanna take first watch?"

Tom nods.

"I'll get some sleep, then. Wake me in a few hours. I've got an early start at the station. Gonna be on the streets all day, keeping an eye out for this limey bastard. You'll be able to snatch a few hours before I need to go."

"I could help tomorrow," Tom says. "It sounds like you're gonna have a lot of bodies, but one more could make all the difference."

"And I'd like to take you up on that offer, but even if nothing happens here tonight, I wouldn't be able to rest easy knowing Ella and Kit were alone here."

"Yeah," Tom says. "You're right." He glances at the door. "Speaking of bodies, I'm surprised none of them have been sent here, to watch out for you. Or to the professor, for that matter."

George grunts. "I think I put the scares into the department. Like I said, I threatened them with potential embarrassment. They don't want that. Everyone's out in the streets, shaking down CI's and asking questions, seeing what they can find. They want to cut this attack off before it ever has a chance to get going. Zero embarrassment, all the glory."

George heads back to the sofa. There's a blanket folded at one end and a pillow on top of it. He moves the pizza box to the ground and starts spreading out the blanket. "But it ain't long now," he says. "Tomorrow is just a few hours away, and I know there's people out there already – *good* people, and I'd vouch for each and every one of them – pounding the streets with their eyes peeled. One way or another, this is all gonna be over before we know it."

"I hope you're right, George."

"Of course I'm right," George says, lowering himself onto the sofa with a grunt, and covering himself with the blanket. "I've been doing this for twenty years. I've got the instincts." He taps the side of his head. "You're all here, now. We're watching each other's backs. We've got the city's cops out in force, we've got the feds coming to help out – hell, we've even got Interpol. The numbers are on our side. This is one disaster that's never gonna come to be. I can feel it."

In Tom's experience, the only way to avert a disaster is with a lot of sweat and blood, but he hopes that George is right. He turns back to the window. He watches the still-busy streets below.

## 46

Lincoln is not alone. He's with Zack and Marcus, the two men who have been watching Professor Richard McCulloch. They're down the road from his house, sitting in darkness. The two suited strangers from Detective George Ross's building led Lincoln here.

The Cadillac is parked outside, and the man is seated within, watching the street. Lincoln and the two men with him sit in silence. Lincoln parked his BMW around the corner when he realised where the two in the suits were stopping. He walked and joined up with Zack and Marcus. They've been here a few hours now. The woman is inside, with the professor. There's no sign that they're going to leave. It looks like she's spending the night.

"FBI, maybe?" Zack suggests. He's behind the steering wheel.

"CIA?" Marcus says. He's in the front passenger seat.

Lincoln ignores them both. From where they're parked, far away from the Cadillac, he can still see the windows of the house. A couple of the lights are still on.

"Maybe just detectives?" Zack says now.

"It doesn't matter who they are," Lincoln says, snapping, getting agitated. "What matters is that they're there. They came here from George's. They must know something. They must know about the GB2. They know too damn much."

Lincoln calls Arthur, tells him what's happening. He hasn't heard anything from the men watching George's building. The four in there must have remained put.

"You wanted to get the professor," Arthur says. "Are you going to let these two stand in your way? Shit, after tomorrow, what's two more bodies?"

"Send a couple more men," Lincoln says. "No risks. Not when we're so close. They know where to come. Tell them to be careful. To park around the corner and continue on foot."

"What kind of weaponry do you want them packing?"

"Bring heavy stuff," Lincoln says. "Enough to go around."

"Got it."

"We're going in?" Marcus says.

"Once the cavalry arrives," Lincoln says.

They wait in silence for the two men to come. They keep their eyes on the house and the Cadillac.

Lincoln has never met Richard. He only knows his face from photographs. Ian had plenty of stories about him. Said he was a great chemist who wasted his time teaching. Said he could have been so much more than he was, if only he had the aptitude for it. If he'd only had the *balls*. The fact he created GB2 is proof of that. The fact that he never attempted to make any financial gain from it proves Ian's point.

Ian was clear that Richard would never help them. He said he was too moral. Neither money nor threats could sway him. Lincoln is intrigued to find out how true this is. They don't need Richard for long. They can take him apart, inch by inch, until there's only enough left to write out the formula. And if they get the boy too, well, then they can race each other, see who'll write it down first. After that, neither of them will be needed anymore. Lincoln will learn from his mistakes. He'll keep a back-up record of the formula. He'll carry it on himself. They'll bring in new chemists, set them to cooking. The future is bright. The future is looking very, very lucrative. They just need to get through tonight, and tomorrow, and then the offers will come flooding in.

"Here they come," Zack says. "Our back-up."

Zack is looking into the side mirror. Lincoln turns around. He sees two of his men approaching the vehicle. One of them is carrying a holdall. Lincoln pushes open the door for them and then slides over. They get inside.

"Nice to see you, chaps," Lincoln says. "Did you bring what I requested?"

"SR16s," the man in the middle, closest to Lincoln, says.

"Enough for everyone?"

The man nods. "Plenty for a party."

"Good," Lincoln says. "Now listen. We're not going in guns blazing. If we rush them, that should give us control of the situation. It's been a tense few days. We've had some trouble. If any more trouble turns up, *that's* when we use these guns."

They nod along.

"There's a man in that car, and he's keeping watch, so we're going to have to be careful." Lincoln looks at the four men. They're all looking back at him, awaiting his instructions. "We're going to split up. The man in the car is our first priority. I'll deal with him."

Lincoln runs through the rest of the plan. He goes

through it twice, then has them repeat it back to him. No mistakes. They get in, fast and hard. When he's sure they're ready, they split. The two men who arrived last, they get out of the car first. They take two of the SR16s with them. They disappear around the corner. They're heading down the block, around the back of the house. They'll cover it from the rear, make sure no one can escape that way. Lincoln counts off a few minutes, giving them a chance to get close to position.

Zack has a boot knife. Lincoln takes it from him and then gets out of the car. Marcus leaves with him. Zack stays behind to watch the outside. Lincoln and Marcus walk toward the house on different sides of the street. Lincoln approaches from the left, on the driver's side. Marcus down on the right, slightly ahead. Lincoln holds back. Marcus reaches the Cadillac.

Lincoln has the boot knife out. He holds it low, concealing it, pressing the flat of the five-inch blade against his thigh. As Marcus nears the front of the Cadillac, he begins to stumble. He sways to his side, knocking against the side of the car. He drags himself along it. Lincoln sees the driver. He gives a start and stares, confused and annoyed. Marcus appears drunk to him. He stumbles on a few more steps, then falls to his knees in front of the Cadillac. He starts making retching sounds.

Lincoln watches the driver. He's clearly deliberating. Lincoln is close now. If the driver reaches for a radio, or his phone, Lincoln will make a move on the door and hope that it's unlocked. The driver doesn't do either, though. He opens the door, steps out, looking toward the fallen 'drunk' at the front of his vehicle.

It's easy for Lincoln to get behind him. He's fast, and he's quiet. The driver never even knows he's there, until the blade slips through his ribs and scrambles his heart. Lincoln doesn't make a sound. The man barely gasps. Lincoln pushes him back inside the car and quickly pats him down. He finds his wallet and checks his ID. Duane Foley. Interpol. Lincoln snorts. He tosses the wallet onto the body and closes the door.

Marcus has already got back to his feet and hurried back to their own car. He comes back with a couple of SR16s. He keeps hold of both of them for now. They go up to the house together.

Lincoln keeps the knife, in his left hand now, and in his right he holds his Sig Sauer. He signals to Marcus. "Call them at the back," he says. "Tell them thirty seconds." Marcus nods, taking a step back into the shadows and pulling out his cell phone. Lincoln waits until he's talking into the phone. He turns to the house and knocks on the door, a rapid-fire, frantic knock. "Hello, hello, is anyone home?" he says, putting on an American accent. "The guy in the car – he said he's not feeling good and I should knock on this door –"

A woman's voice calls through. "Who are you?"

"My name's Jimmy," Lincoln says. "I was just passing by and this guy fell out of the Cadillac. He looked real pale. He told me to come to this house, to tell you what was happening. He said he thinks it was his heart."

Lincoln can hear a phone ringing on the other side of the door. She's trying to call the man in the car. Lincoln grins. There won't be an answer. If she's trying to ring anyone else, it doesn't matter. She doesn't have enough time.

"*Shit*," he hears the woman say.

Before she can say, think, or do anything else, Lincoln

hears the voices of his men. They're inside. They've picked the lock at the back of the house and gotten inside.

"On the ground!" one of them says. "Both of you, on the ground, right *now!*"

Lincoln nods to Marcus beside him. He waves back at the car and Zack, to let him know things have gone according to plan. A moment later, the front door is unlocked.

## 47

Lincoln checks the woman's ID. Joanie Samu. Unsurprisingly, she's Interpol, too.

"This must be about that red notice, eh, sweetheart?" he says to Joanie.

She stares back at him, face set, eyes defiant. Lincoln, Marcus, Joanie and Richard are all in the dining room. The other two men are spread out, watching the front and the rear. Joanie and Richard are tied to chairs, angled toward Lincoln. He throws the ID to the side.

"Where's Ian?" Richard says. "Could he not come and perform his own dirty work?"

"Ah, so you all *have* been talking," Lincoln says, turning to the professor. "You met with Ella and Kit Wiley, yeah? And their mystery friend. Who was he? What was his name?"

Richard blinks. "I don't know," he says.

Lincoln cocks his head. "You don't *know*?"

"He wouldn't say. He was...secretive."

Lincoln isn't sure he believes this, but he doesn't press it right now. The mystery man's name has waited this long, it can wait a little longer. "All right. What did they have to say to you?"

"They told me all about *you*," Richard says. There's clear disdain in his voice. "About what you have planned."

"Is that so? And what do they think I have planned?"

"Don't speak to him," Joanie says to Richard.

Lincoln shoots her through the face. The impact throws her chair back. She hits the ground, eyes still open, head tilted to the side, and her blood leaks out and soaks into the carpet. There's spray on the wall behind where she was sat.

Lincoln pulls his face at Richard, like *whoops*. He turns to Marcus. "Do you think that was a bit loud?"

"Probably should've put a cushion over her face or something," Marcus says. "Tried to muffle it a little."

"It's New York, though, isn't it? It's full of crime. There's guns going off all the time. No one would bat an eyelid, right?"

"I don't know. This seems like a nice neighbourhood."

"Ah well," Lincoln says, turning back to Richard, who stares down at Joanie, looking like he might be sick. "That was on me, then. That was my mistake. I think we'll be all right, though, professor. Back here, in your dining room. The sound wouldn't have been that loud outside."

Richard doesn't look at him. His eyes are stuck on Joanie and the blood coming out of her skull.

"Thing is, sweetheart, I didn't have any use for her." He steps closer to Richard, pressing the hot barrel of the gun to Richard's cheek and forcing his head to turn so he's looking up at him. Richard winces. Lincoln takes the gun away. "But you could be useful. *Could* be. That all depends on how cooperative you are."

Richard frowns. "I don't understand," he says. "What do

you need me for? If you have Ian then you have the GB2. He knows how to make it just as well as I do."

"Well, you see, professor, therein lies the problem. Ian's not talking much these days. Not writing much, either. Not breathing, for that matter."

Understanding slowly dawns on the professor's face. "He's dead?" he says. "You killed him?"

"No, no, I didn't kill him. His own negligence did that."

Slowly, a dark grin spreads across Richard's face. "So you need me to make the GB2."

"We need the formula, sweetheart. You give us that, we'll be right out your hair. Your wild, wild hair."

Richard smirks. He's thinking that his knowledge makes him untouchable.

"Now, now, sweetheart," Lincoln says. "I know exactly what's going through that big brain of yours. You're thinking how you've got the knowledge we need. You're thinking you're the *only* person left in the whole wide world who can give us what we need. But you'd be mistaken, sweetheart. That's just not the case. You're one of two, and you're the first that we've come to see, that's all. So don't go getting smart on us. Don't go trying to be clever. You need to behave yourself and tell us what we need."

Richard doesn't say anything, but his smirk falters and fades away.

"You've already met the little nipper," Lincoln says.

Richard looks pained. "You know about that..."

"About little Kit? Of course we do. Nothing gets past us. So either you can play nice, or we can just go and see *him*. We know where he is. He's with my old pal, Detective George Ross. Yes, that's right, I can see that's a name you're familiar with. What's it going to be then, darling?"

Richard swallows. "What...what do you need from me? Exactly what? Just the formula?"

Lincoln smiles. "That's right," he says. "Just the formula. That's all we need from you, sweetheart."

Richard doesn't speak for a while. He stares at the ground. He watches the spreading pool of Joanie's blood soaking into his carpet, staining it a dark maroon. "I can't do it," he says without looking up. "The *deaths*..."

"Come on, now, professor," Lincoln says. "You need to get your head in the here and now. Think about your own well-being. Think about *Kit*. Poor little Kit. Bit of a spaz, I'm told, but he's one of them...what do you call them? Idiot savants, something like that. And he has something I need, right in that messed-up little brain of his, and nothing's going to stop me from getting it out. It wouldn't be the first time I've had to hurt a kid to get something I want. You keep that in mind, professor. You might think you're willing to be taken apart, to die, and to keep your mouth shut the whole while, but can you go to the grave knowing that the same thing is going to happen to that little boy?"

Richard looks up at him, horrified. "You're sick," he says. "You're a monster."

"I'm a businessman," Lincoln says. "And I'm trying to conduct business. Now, you tell me – is that business going to be with you, or with Kit?"

Richard sags, defeated. He doesn't speak for a long time. He stares down into his lap.

Lincoln waits, but his patience is wearing thin. He clears his throat but Richard doesn't look up. "*Well*?" he says. "Have you made a decision, or are you just wasting my time? Tick-tock, professor. Time's running out. And keep *this* in mind, professor – we know you have a family. We know about your daughter, and her children. How much more do I need to say? How much detail do you want me to give?" He recites the home address of Richard's daughter and her family.

Richard recoils like he's been slapped. He tries to take a deep breath, then he looks at Joanie's body. He stares at it for a long time. Finally, he looks up. When he speaks, his voice is small, gruff, and broken. "Okay," he says. "I'll do it. Just leave the boy and my family alone."

"You give us what we want, we've got no need for him." This isn't entirely true, but Richard doesn't need to know this. Ella, Kit, and the mystery man have caused him a colossal migraine. They've killed a lot of his men. And Kit still knows the formula. No one else can be aware of it. It's a buyer's market. Lincoln is looking to corner that market. "He'll be fine."

"I need to make a phone call first," Richard says.

Lincoln arches an eyebrow, watching him.

"I'll *make* the gas for you," Richard says, closing his eyes. "And I'll write out the formula for you – I'll write it out a thousand times if I have to, if it means you'll leave everyone else alone. But I can't make it here."

Lincoln claps his hands. "That's more like it, professor. *That's* what I like to hear. We'll set you up with a lovely new workspace. Everything you'll need."

Richard nods. "But my daughter is coming here in the morning." He glances at the clock on the wall. "In just a few hours, in fact. I need to call her. To put her off."

"Bit early for a phone call, Richard. Won't she be sleeping?"

"I'll leave a voicemail. Or I'll send her a message. I don't want her coming here, and neither do you. What if she walks in, finds this body, all this blood?"

"We'll be tidying up after ourselves."

"Then in that case I don't want her walking in and finding any of *you*. Just let me call her. I'll either talk to her or leave a message. Tell her something came up, work-related, and I'll be out of town for a few days. I'm going to have to pack a bag, too. You can't expect me to do that while tied up."

Lincoln considers this. He appraises Richard. He's an old man. His better years are clearly long behind him. He looks a bit like a long-haired Santa Claus, for crying out loud. It's doubtful he's going to try anything – to fight or to run. He doesn't look particularly capable of either.

"All right," Lincoln says, turning to Marcus on his right. "Cut him loose and accompany him through to the bedroom. Help him pack and watch him while he calls his daughter. Watch him *closely*. And if he starts typing out a message, you check what it says."

## 48

Tom is sleeping when he feels his phone begin to buzz.

He awakes with a jolt, pulling the cell from his pocket. He's on his back on the sofa. He looks to his right, toward the window, searching for George. He spies his outline, sitting and looking out. George lifts his head, listening, aware of the phone's brief vibration. It's already over. Tom looks at the screen.

It's a message. It comes from Richard McCulloch. A single word.

> Lincoln.

Tom sits straight up. He grabs for his boots and pulls them on. George watches his abrupt movements. He gets to his feet and comes closer. "What is it?" he says.

"Richard," Tom says. "I think Lincoln has him. I need to go."

"I should call Joanie," George says, reaching for his phone.

"No," Tom says, holding out a hand to stop him. "If Lincoln and his men are there, we can't spook them. They might hurt someone."

"I can make a call, get some men over there –"

"No," Tom says. "Listen to me – we don't have time to talk about this. Richard, Joanie, and Duane could be held hostage right now. If you call back-up, it's not going to be just one man, it's going to be a team. Maybe even SWAT, right? If Lincoln and his people see them coming, they'll start shooting. I've seen it happen. I can get there faster, and I'm on my own. They won't see me coming. I can get inside and put an end to this." Tom grabs his Beretta from where he placed it close by on the table. He gets to his feet and tucks it down his waistband. "You stay here with Ella and Kit," he says. "There's no time for discussion. I have to go now."

"What are you going to do?" George says.

"Just watch them," Tom says, meaning Ella and Kit, as he turns and heads for the door.

"Rollins," George says.

Tom doesn't answer. There's no time. He's already out the door.

## 49

Lincoln gets a call. It's Liskey. He answers it quickly. "Is George on the move?"

"Someone is," Liskey says. "The man – the one with Ella and Kit – he's just hurried out of the building and got into a white Nissan. He's pulled away *fast*."

Lincoln frowns. "Just him?"

"The others are still inside."

Before Lincoln can respond, there's a loud cry from the back bedroom. "*Shit!*"

He and the other two men turn toward it. The voice was not Richard's. It was Marcus's. Marcus, who was supposed to be watching Richard.

"Shit! Help!"

"Liskey, I'll call you back. Hold your position." Lincoln races through to the bedroom. One of the other men accompanies him. The other remains at the front, on guard.

The bedroom has an adjoining bathroom. The door is open and Lincoln can see Professor Richard McCulloch flat on his back on the tiles, blood pouring from a slash in the side of his neck.

"What's happened?" Lincoln says, stepping toward Richard but stopping in the doorway when he sees there's no point in getting any closer. There's nothing they can do for him. His white hair has been dyed red, and his pale skin has drained of all colour. He's already dead.

Lincoln looks up and down the body. Something gleams in the light, close to Richard's right hand. Lincoln leans in to better see. A razor blade. There's blood on it. Lincoln turns around, taking in the rest of the room. On the bed there's an open suitcase, half-packed with a few items of clothing.

Lincoln wheels on Marcus. "What happened?" he asks again, through his teeth this time.

Marcus swallows. He looks like a rabbit in the headlights. There are flecks of blood on his cheeks and around his mouth. He wipes them away with the back of his hand. "I watched him, like you said," he says. "He said he needed to get his heart medication. I followed him into the bathroom. He was going through the medicine cabinet and I was watching him. I was literally looking over his shoulder, into the cabinet, thinking I couldn't see any kind of medication when he stuck the razor into his neck. Right into the carotid. Knew exactly where he was aiming."

"You couldn't stop him?"

"It all happened too fast."

Lincoln looks down at the corpse. Richard is useless to him now.

The man who accompanied Lincoln into the room at the sound of the cries is looking at a cell phone. "How closely did you watch him call his daughter?" he says.

Marcus looks at him. "He showed me the contact he was

dialling," he says, poking at a splash of blood under his right eye. "I watched him make the call. I heard him leave the message putting her off."

"Did you see the message he typed out?" the other man says.

Lincoln crosses the room, grabbing at the cell phone and checking it for himself.

"He never sent a message," Marcus says. "He left a voicemail."

"You never *saw* him send a message," the other man, closer to Lincoln, says.

Lincoln reads it. It's just one word. His name. Sent to a man called Tom Rollins.

"This must be him," Lincoln says. "The mystery man. *Tom Rollins.*" He says the name out loud, trying it out. He wheels on the two men. "Look up a Tom Rollins – see if you can find his face. Find out if he's our man."

The two pull out their phones and get to work, doing as he says. Lincoln leaves the bedroom and the cloying stink of blood in the air. He calls Arthur. "We have a name," he says. "Tom Rollins. And it sounds like he might be coming this way."

"The mystery man?" Arthur says.

"None other."

Marcus hurries through from the bedroom and holds his phone screen up to Lincoln's face, desperate to redeem himself. Lincoln frowns. "I haven't seen him," he says, though he commits the face to memory in case it *is* their man. "Send it to Liskey. Get confirmation." Lincoln talks to Arthur again. He tells him what has happened with Richard, and how Liskey has told him that the man – potentially

Rollins – has left Detective Ross's apartment building and hurried away in a car.

"And you think he's coming to you?" Arthur says.

"It certainly looks that way, doesn't it? Unfortunately for him, I'm not going to be here." Lincoln chuckles. "Bring the times forward, Arthur. We're going to have to strike earlier in the day."

"Will it be enough? Will it be busy enough?"

"It's Grand Central Station – it's always busy. By the time we get there it'll be almost rush hour. I'm going back to Detective Ross now, deal with that loose thread, and I'll get the boy. I'm going to leave men here to deal with Rollins. I'll meet you at the station."

"We're on our way."

Lincoln turns to the men in the house.

"I've heard back from Liskey," Marcus says. "It's him. He says he has longer hair and a beard now, but it's our guy. It's Rollins."

Lincoln smiles. "Good. We know his name, but we won't need to remember it for long. Marcus, you and the other chap, you stay here. Rollins is on his way. When he arrives, ambush him and kill him. I don't care if it's noisy – it's another distraction for the NYPD. Just get it done." He turns to the other man standing guard at the front. "You come with me. We'll go get Zack and head back to the detective's building. Let's go – today's the day!"

## 50

The message was so abrupt, so to the point, that Tom figures Richard must have been surrounded. He sent the name sweating, under duress, doing his best to make it fast and get it over with before they could realise what he was doing. With this in mind, Tom doesn't go straight to the house. He parks down the block and continues on foot. He keeps the Beretta concealed for now.

From the end of the street he can see the Cadillac. There's no one inside. He looks the rest of the area over. It's not like the streets below George's apartment. It's quiet here. It's still early – a little too early for people to be setting off for work. He runs his eyes over the parked cars lining the road. They're all empty. A couple of cars pass by on the road but Tom stays out of view of them. The people within don't look like they're patrolling or searching. They look straight ahead, concentrating on their journeys.

Tom slips down the sidewalk, getting closer to the house, looking it over. The curtains on the front windows are open. He can't see anyone through them. He goes down the side of the house and heads toward the back, wondering if he's too late, if Lincoln has already gone. He wonders how many men Lincoln had with him. He has to consider that Lincoln may have discovered the sent message, too. They could still be in there, lying in wait for him. He has to be ready for that.

He scales the fence, watching the windows. These are uncovered, too. Again, he doesn't see anyone inside. He presses himself up against the wall closest to the rear door and pulls out his Beretta. He brings out his KA-BAR, too, holding it in his left hand. He keeps both weapons close, holding them low for now.

At the back door, he finds that the lock has already been broken. The door is open. Stepping lightly, Tom gets inside. He's in the kitchen. He looks around, Beretta raised. The area is clear. He checks the floor for anything that could cause noise, but sees nothing and steps through to the living room. Standing in the doorway, he sweeps the room with the Beretta, pointing it into every corner. Nothing. Nothing to *see*. The smell, however, is familiar. It's blood. It's death.

Tom moves to where the smell is strongest. He finds it in the dining room. Two bodies. Two faces he recognises. Joanie and Duane. They lie next to each other, blood soaking and staining the carpet around them. Joanie's eyes are open, staring blankly up at Tom.

Tom stands very still, listening to the house. Listening for movement. He hears creaks. They could be the house settling, or else they could be subtle movements.

He keeps moving, going through to the bedroom. The smell of blood and death is strong here, too. He spots a half-packed suitcase open on the bed. Next to it, he sees a cell phone. It's face up.

Then, he spots Richard's body lying prone in the

adjoining bathroom doorway. Sees how the blood has poured out of him, too. Tom takes a closer look. He sees the razor blade close to his hand. Richard has done this to himself. But why? Why didn't Lincoln and the others just kill him themselves? That's probably why they came here, right? To eliminate the original creator of GB2, the only other man who knows how to make it. Unless they did, and they made it look like a suicide, but then how did Richard find time to message Tom? Why is there a half-packed suitcase open on the bed?

Tom thinks about this, but only briefly. He's not convinced he's the only living person in the house. His attention goes back to the phone. The same phone that messaged him. If it's lying there, they must know that Richard contacted him. What else do they know? Do they know where he came from? Do they know where Ella and Kit are?

He leans against the doorframe, peering out, looking left and right along the hall. To his left, at the end, there's another bedroom. A spare. There's a bathroom, too. The only rooms Tom hasn't checked. He doesn't need to check them now. He doesn't need to waste the time. All he has to be aware of is that if there's someone else in this house, that's likely where they are. He steps out of the bedroom, Beretta pointed down the hall, covering it. He backs up, heading back through the house. He needs to get outside, get clear, get back to the Nissan. There, he can call Ella, warn her and George. He can head back to them.

Gunfire erupts from the end of the hall and Tom dives for cover in the dining room. It was automatic fire. The bullets tear up the ground and the walls where Tom was previously stood. He lands close to Joanie and Duane's bodies. Tom rolls to the side, away from them, and gets up, pressing himself to the wall.

Tom is pinned in the dining room. The only way through into the living room is covered by the automatic rifle. Tom looks around. He grabs a dining room chair. He hurls it into the path of fire, momentarily drawing its attention. As the chair is shot to pieces, Tom leans around the wall and fires at its source.

A man cries out. The shooting stops. Gun raised, Tom races toward him. He's in the bathroom at the end. He's on his back, groaning. He's dropped the assault rifle. He sees Tom and tries to grab his handgun. Tom puts two bullets into his chest, stilling him. He spins, covering the hall. Since he's close, he kicks open the door into the spare bedroom. It's clear.

He moves on. The shooting was loud and has no doubt got the attention of the neighbours. The cops will be called. They'll come here, surround the place. Tom needs to be fast. He can't afford to get held up here. He keeps the gun raised as he moves through the house.

He's attacked again in the back yard. The man emerges and wraps his arms around Tom from the side, pinning them to his sides. Tom doesn't know where he came from. He wasn't here when he scaled the fence.

But that doesn't matter. The man squeezes, trying to drive the air out of his lungs. Tom struggles against him, trying to break his hands open. The man's grip is firm. He's strong. Tom tries to throw his head back but the man avoids his blows.

It's getting hard for Tom to breathe. His lungs are compressing. He can't refill them. His weapons are pressed to his side. He looks down. He can see the man's right boot.

It's bracing itself, almost directly under the barrel of the Beretta. Tom moves the gun a little to the right. He squeezes the trigger. The bullet blows through the boot with ease. There's a burst of blood. The man's grip instantly loosens. Before he can let go entirely, before he can cry out, Tom pushes himself back, slamming the man into the wall. His arms drop from Tom's sides. Tom spins, KA-BAR slashing, and cuts the man's throat. He shoves him away, leaving him to bleed out. He jumps over the fence, checking that the area is clear, that there are no armed men coming for him.

It's clear. Tom runs for the Nissan, pulling out his phone.

## 51

Ella is awake. She's roused and dressed Kit. She was alarmed when she entered the living room and saw that Tom was gone. George explained to her what happened.

"What about you?" Ella says. "Don't you need to leave soon?"

George shakes his head. "I've called the station. I've told them I'm with two important witnesses and that I can't leave them. There's plenty of people out there and we all have our parts to play. Right now, you and Kit are mine."

Ella sits on the sofa, keeping Kit close. She chews her lip as she stares out the window, watching as dawn breaks and the sun rises.

"How long's he been gone?" she says.

George is in the kitchen, making coffee. He pours a cup for himself, and then one for her. As he hands it over, he says, "An hour. But it's not like he was going five minutes down the road. And it's early, but the city is always busy. He could've had traffic to contend with."

Ella holds the coffee, but she doesn't drink from it.

George looks down at Kit. He's watching the television. It plays the news. "I don't have any cereal or anything," George says. "We've got some cold pizza left from last night."

"He's fine for now," Ella says.

There's a knock at the door.

Ella and George freeze. They look at each other. George wears his holster. It carries his Glock. He pulls it out. "I'm not expecting anyone," he says, his voice low. "And I haven't buzzed anyone into the building. Put Kit in the bathtub and then come back here."

Ella does as he says. She carries Kit through to the bathroom and lays him flat in the empty bath. "Stay right there, okay?" she says, pressing a finger to her lips. "And don't make a sound." Kit looks back at her, face blank, but Ella isn't concerned about the latter. It's so rare for him to make noise. On her way back, she realises she can hear her cell phone buzzing in the bedroom. She has to ignore it for now.

She goes back into the living room. George mouths to her, *Answer the door.* He takes a knee, the Glock raised, covering the area.

Ella goes to the door. She removes the chain and turns the lock. She looks back at George. He nods. Ella pulls the door wide, stepping out of the frame, giving George a clear view.

Nothing happens.

She looks at George. He hasn't moved, but he's frowning. Ella peers around the open door. Outside, it's clear. There's no one there.

Slowly, George rises to his feet. He waves for Ella to step aside. He comes toward the door. He's stepping out into the hall. He's going to investigate. Before he crosses the threshold, Ella spots something outside the apartment windows. A pair of ropes unfurl from above. Ella frowns, not understanding. "What's that?"

As George turns, two dark shapes rappel into view, and smash through the windows. They're armed with automatic rifles. George sees them, too. He raises the Glock.

Ella hears two gunshots close by. They're not from George. She sees blood spray from the front of his knees and his legs buckle beneath him. He cries out, dropping his gun as his arms fly out in front of himself to keep from landing on his face.

Ella spins to see who has shot him. A familiar face. She saw him online. Lincoln Collyer. In the flesh.

He strikes Ella across the face with the barrel of his gun. She goes down, tasting her own blood. Through bleary eyes, she sees Lincoln place a boot on George's ribs and force him onto his back. In her ringing ears, she hears his English accent.

"Well, well, Georgie, sweetheart," Lincoln says, smiling down at the detective. "Here we are, finally face to face." He pulls himself away from George to turn to the man who has followed him into the apartment. This man carries a bag. He sets it down beside the door. Lincoln gestures to the two who came through the windows, too. "Find the boy," he says. "Bring him to me."

The three spread out, though it's not a big apartment. It won't take them long to find Kit.

Ella forces herself up, finding a shallow reserve of strength knowing that they're here looking for her son. Knowing that he's in danger. "No!" she says, grabbing at the legs of the nearest man.

He reaches down and grabs a handful of her hair. He

yanks her up to her feet. Lincoln calls out to her. "You could always just tell us where he is, darling," he says. "Speed the whole process along."

Ella spits her blood toward Lincoln.

"How uncouth," he says, though he's grinning.

The man holding her hair forces her head back, slamming it into the doorframe. He throws her through the open door, into the bedroom. While she's prone on the ground, he looks the room over.

"Got him!" a voice calls from the bathroom.

Ella hears someone clapping. Lincoln, probably. She hears the man who pushed her through here leaving the room. She forces herself up, her head spinning. She sees them dragging Kit through to the living room.

"He's a well-behaved boy, isn't he?" Lincoln says. "Take him down to the car. Liskey, you stay here with me." Liskey is the man who threw Ella down. He's the man who carried the bag into the apartment.

The two men who came through the window escort Kit out of the apartment. They each have a hand clamped down on his shoulders.

Ella uses the bed to drag herself up. She needs to go after them. They might shoot her dead, but she can't just let them take her son.

Her eyes settle on her cell phone. It's on the bedside table. Next to it are George's car keys. She looks back. She sees Lincoln and Liskey in the living room, both of them looking down at George's prone, broken body. Ella grabs her phone. There are four missed calls from Tom. She pockets the phone for now, and the keys. On the other side of the window is the fire escape. She takes a deep breath to steady herself, to keep her from stumbling and swaying, alerting the men that she's doing something.

She can't let them get away. She can't let them take Kit. At the window, she glances back. Neither man is paying attention to her. They're focussed on George. She's forgotten, momentarily. No doubt they're planning on dealing with her soon. She can hear their voices – mostly George and Lincoln. She wishes she could go to George. Wishes she could help him, but she's unarmed, and she has to think about her son.

She gets the window open as quietly as she can, just enough for her to fit through, and she slides out onto the fire escape.

## 52

Lincoln pushes Detective George Ross onto his back, and he flops on the floor like a landed fish. He's clearly in pain, but he refuses to show it. He won't give Lincoln the satisfaction.

Lincoln almost admires this. He grins down at the detective. "You're a lot fatter than I expected," he says.

"Fuck you," George says, though he struggles to get the words out. He gasps for breath. His legs are badly damaged. The left points in the wrong direction.

Lincoln took a great deal of satisfaction in kneecapping him. The left patella is completely shattered. He admires his handiwork, soaking it in, knowing that he doesn't have long to enjoy this.

"If you – if you hurt that boy," George says, grimacing. He coughs, and a spasm of pain racks him. He groans before he's able to continue. "If you hurt that boy, I swear to God –"

"Oh, Georgie," Lincoln says, clucking his tongue. "What do you really think you can do? You're not in a position to do *anything*." Liskey is grinning. Lincoln wriggles his eyebrows at him. "And Georgie, honestly, sweetheart, how do you think this scene ends?"

George coughs.

Lincoln sighs. "I really wish we could have had longer together. I had such grand plans for us. But you know what they say – life is what happens when you're making plans, and this week has been a prime example of that adage. But I do have to take the time to say that after dreaming of this moment for so long, I really am disappointed to come face to face with the man who killed my baby brother. You're really not very impressive, Detective Ross."

"I was impressive enough to gun that son of a bitch down."

"In the *back*," Lincoln says. "There's nothing noble about *that*, Georgie. Nothing noble at all." Lincoln spits on him, feeling aggravated.

George laughs through his pain. "Sure thing, you limey fuck," George says. "I'll pass on your regards when I see your brother in Hell. Now just get this over with."

Lincoln stares down at him. He squeezes the handle of the Sig Sauer tight. George laughs again. Lincoln shoots him through the face, then twice through the heart.

It doesn't bring him any relief. He knew it wouldn't. There's only a little satisfaction in what he's done, but it *needed* to be done. For Stan. For what this fat Yank did to him.

He takes a step back and exhales through his nose. It was part of the plan, too. Part of today. Part of the distraction.

"All right," he says, turning to Liskey. "Eliminate the woman and then plant the explosives."

Liskey turns on his heel and goes through to the bedroom where he disposed of her. While looking down at

George's corpse, he hears Liskey halt abruptly in the bedroom's doorway. Lincoln turns to the sound.

"She's gone," Liskey says. "The window is open. She must have got out onto the fire escape."

Liskey makes like he's about to run out after her. Lincoln calls out to stop him. "Just leave her for now. We've got the boy – that's what's important. We can deal with her down the line. Plant the bombs. I'll meet you at the car."

## 53

The city is getting busier. Tom doesn't like it. It's hard for him to build up any speed, and he's in a hurry.

He doesn't like, either, that Ella hasn't answered her phone. It worries him. He cuts corners and swerves into traffic wherever he finds an opening. People blare their horns and flip him off, already so angry early in the day, but he ignores them and pushes on.

He's close enough now, only a couple of blocks from George's building, that if he has to he can dump the Nissan and continue on foot. It might be faster for him to run. He's giving this serious consideration when his phone rings. It's Ella.

Before Tom can say anything, she's shrieking into the phone. "They have Kit!" she says. "They came to the apartment and they got Kit!"

Tom feels his scalp tighten. "Where are they now? Where are you? Ella? Ella! I need you to speak to me."

"I'm on the fire escape," she says. "I'm making my way

down." Tom can hear how breathless she is. Can hear the clanging of her sneakers hurrying down the metal steps. "I can see them – I can see the car they're getting into. It's a black BMW."

"Where's George?"

"They blew his knees out. I think he's probably dead by now. I've heard gunshots. Where are you?"

"I'm not far," Tom says. "Ella, don't do anything – don't get yourself killed. These people are dangerous. How many have you seen?"

"I've seen four, including Lincoln, but I think there's another in the car, the driver." She sucks down air. "Tom, I can't wait. They have my son."

"I'm nearly there, Ella."

"I can't *wait*." Ella hangs up.

Tom puts the phone away. Ella is going to run into danger and get herself hurt. He can understand, though. He doesn't have children, but he can imagine that it must be impossible to stand by and not try to help.

The drive is taking too long. Tom can't stay in his lane. He slams a hand down on the horn and pulls out into the oncoming traffic. Taxis and SUVs swerve to get out of his way, to avoid crashing. They hit their own horns. Tom weaves through them. He has to get back to the building.

## 54

Ella reaches the bottom of the fire escape. She hits the ground and hurries to the corner of the building, keeping the black BMW in sight. Kit is inside. She can't see him, but she knows he'll be in the back, wedged between the men.

She doesn't have a weapon. She has no way to confront them, but the sidewalk is picking up foot traffic, and there are plenty of cars. If she goes to the BMW, if she's able to sneak up on them and get close enough, she could catch them by surprise. Pull open the back door and yank her son out, and if they try anything she can scream "Kidnap." Surely someone would step in, try to help her? And after all the gunfire upstairs, in George's apartment, there must already be some cops on their way. His neighbours must have called in the noise.

It's not a great plan, but it's the only one she has. It's all she can do. She needs to get her son back. She can't let them get away.

She makes her way closer to it, moving from building to

dumpster to parked cars, staying low so they won't see her approach. But, as she gets closer, a gunshot rings out. The people around her scream and scatter. Ella looks back and sees that the bullet was meant for her. She dives into cover behind a dumpster.

The shooter was Lincoln. He's emerged from the building, accompanied by the man who stayed with him. He's not carrying the bag he originally brought into the apartment. There's no sign of George, and Ella knows he's dead. She grits her teeth at this thought. As much as the knowledge hurts her, she can't dwell on it. She can mourn him later. Remember how good and considerate he was with Kit later.

There's a few more gunshots. She feels them hitting the dumpster. Ella needs to keep moving. She pushes the dumpster away from the wall and slips down behind it, escaping down an alleyway. They might come after her, looking to finish the job. She can't stay behind cover like a sitting duck.

She keeps running. She hears a couple more gunshots ring out behind her, and senses the bullets passing close by her body, hitting walls and bags of trash.

Ella reaches the end of the alley and scales the chain-link fence there, throwing herself over the top, avoiding the barbed wire. She lands on the other side and looks back to see Lincoln walking away, heading to the BMW. Ella runs, heading around George's building. She feels his keys digging into her thigh. She pulls them out, not knowing what he drives. The key has a Ford logo. She starts hitting the unlock button, looking at every parked Ford she passes, searching for the one that will flash its lights at her.

## 55

Tom reaches George's neighbourhood. He can see his building down the road. Behind him, cars are still blaring their horns. A couple of people have swerved at him, annoyed at his risky manoeuvres. Tom ignores them all. He sees a clearing on the sidewalk where it's wide enough for the Nissan and he mounts it, racing down until he can get back onto the road.

Suddenly, up ahead, people start running, fleeing. Tom can hear gunshots. As he gets closer, he recognises Lincoln. He's firing into the alleyway that runs down the side of George's building. He stops and strides toward a BMW. He gets into the front. The BMW turns in the middle of the road. A man in the back sticks the barrel of his SR16 out of the window to get the other cars to back up. He fires off a loose salvo, and Tom sees the nearest vehicles slam into reverse and back up, colliding with each other in their desperation to get away from the rifle.

As the BMW turns, Tom can see into the back. He sees Kit. It takes Tom a moment to realise it's him. He's struggling.

A couple of the men in the back are fighting to control him. One of them forces him to sit down in his lap, an arm clamped across his chest, another over his mouth. Kit continues to shake violently.

Tom looks around. There's no sign of Ella or George. Tom wonders who Lincoln was shooting at in the alleyway. It must have been Ella. He wonders if she got away.

The BMW has turned around. The man in the back fires again, clearing them a path. They speed through the gap, away from the building.

They're being reckless, Tom thinks. Here, and back at Richard's house, too. They're making a lot of noise. Today is the sixteenth of May, the day they've planned for. Have they stopped caring about all subterfuge? Are they planning on making a lot more noise?

Tom follows the BMW, pursuing it through the gap in traffic they have created. Suddenly, there's an explosion. Tom feels the concussive force of it bear down on the Nissan and force him forward. He looks back in the mirror. He can't see anything, but then debris begins to rain down in the streets. He looks back and up, at George's building.

The explosion has come from George's floor. Potentially from his apartment. Glass and brickwork hit the road and the sidewalk. Tom sees a woman's head crushed by a lump of concrete. He sees windshields shatter, and a roof cave in. He swerves in the road, avoiding the wreckage falling like comets.

With the smoke clearing, Tom can see that the explosion *has* occurred in George's apartment. It's blown out the windows and the walls. The explosives were likely planted right up against the exterior walls. They weren't planted to cause structural damage to the building, to cause the few floors above George's to teeter and break off, but they're going to be unstable regardless. The people in there need to get out.

Was this what they planned for the sixteenth of May? An elaborate vengeance against the detective who killed Lincoln's brother? The explosion seems excessive. If they have Kit, then surely they'd already entered the apartment. And what about the GB2?

Is there more to come?

Tom wants to stop, to get out and help, but they have Kit. The BMW is driving fast. Tom needs to drive faster. He slams his foot to the accelerator and catches them up, closing the gap before the traffic can completely gridlock and they're able to escape him.

## 56

"Get us to Fordham Station," Lincoln says. Zack is driving. "Double-time. Let's go!"

He wipes his mouth with the back of his hand. He breathes deeply, seeing how the traffic is stalling to a halt in the oncoming lane. Cops will be coming. Emergency services of every stripe. They'll be coming *here*, away from where they need to be.

Lincoln turns. The boy is struggling in Liskey's lap. He tries to bite at Liskey's hand but Liskey manages to snatch it away from him. The boy is snarling soundlessly. He twists on Liskey's lap, trying to wriggle free. The man in the middle is watching, unsure how he can help.

"Get him under control," Lincoln says.

"What do you think I'm doing?" Liskey says. "Should I choke him out?"

"No – I need him conscious." Lincoln turns back around and searches the glove compartment. He has a notepad and a pen here, brought along especially for the boy. He hands them back to the man in the middle. "Here – get him to write. See if he'll write out the formula."

The man takes the notepad and pen, but he blinks. He looks down at Kit's hands, pinned to his sides. He looks back at Lincoln. "*How?*" he says.

Lincoln stares at him. He stares at Liskey, and then at Kit. "Do I have to think of everything?" he says. He starts clicking his fingers in front of Kit's face, trying to get his attention, to get him to focus. It doesn't work. "Kit! *Kit!* Look at me. *Look* at me." Lincoln shakes his head, struggling to communicate with the child. The drive is bumpy. The driver is swerving. He mounts the sidewalk briefly. They're all being thrown side to side, up and down.

Lincoln has had enough. "*Kit!*" He slaps the boy's face.

The boy stops struggling. He stops snarling. His face goes blank. He turns toward Lincoln without looking directly at him. He doesn't cry, despite the bright red welt on his cheek. The lack of tears surprises Lincoln. Unnerves him a little.

"Kit, look at me."

The boy does not, but he doesn't resume struggling, either.

"Kit, do you want to see your mother?" Lincoln says, trying a new tack. "What do you call her – *mom*? Do you want to see your mom?"

Kit's eyes flicker and briefly meet his.

"Yes, that's right – you want your mother, don't you? Your mom?"

Kit says nothing. He sits very still.

"If you behave yourself, if you're a good little boy, we'll take you to her. Do you understand?" Lincoln looks at the other men in the back. "Do you think he understands?"

"Isn't there supposed to be something wrong with him?" Liskey says.

"That's what we've heard," Lincoln says. "How do I know if any of this is getting through?"

"He's stopped struggling, at least," the man in the middle says. He's still holding the notepad and pen. Lincoln takes them from him.

"That's right, he's stopped struggling," Lincoln says, deciding it's best to continue with the soft approach. "He's behaving. He's being a good boy, just like we asked. Would you like to draw, Kit? Would you like to write something down – maybe something you saw in the cabin a few nights ago? You remember Ian, don't you? You could write down what you saw on the whiteboard. Do you remember that? It was called a *formula*. All the letters and symbols – do you remember?" Lincoln holds the notepad and pen out to him but Kit doesn't take them. Lincoln isn't deterred. "We know you remember it. We've seen you start to write it out before. If you do this for us, we can take you back to your mom. Wouldn't you like that? I bet she'd be very happy to see you again."

Kit's eyes slowly settle on the notepad.

"That's right," Lincoln says. "Write down what you saw on the whiteboard in the cabin – all those letters and symbols. Write it down for us, and we can take you back to your mom. I'm sure she misses you. We'll take you straight to her. We've spoken, her and I. I know exactly where to find her. We've arranged to meet. Go on, take the paper. Write it down." Out the corner of his mouth, he says, "Let go of his arms, Liskey. Leave his hands free."

Liskey does as he's told. Kit doesn't reach for the paper. Not straight away. He continues to stare at it. Lincoln thinks he understands. He thinks he's got through. He just needs to keep up the soft approach. Just needs to be gentle with him, to promise and cajole him. Just needs to continue speaking to him of his mother. To keep making promises he has no intention of keeping.

Before Lincoln can speak again, before Kit can take the notepad, Lincoln realises a car is gaining on them. He spots it out the corner of his eye, through the rear window. A white Nissan. It's coming *fast*.

"Brace yourself!" Lincoln cries out, spinning in his chair and holding onto his seatbelt. "Hold the boy tight!"

The Nissan rams them from behind, causing them to lurch forward. It's a hard, crunching impact. Zack almost loses control. He battles to right the wheel, to keep them going straight. "*Jesus!*" he says through his teeth.

"What the hell was that?" Liskey says.

The man behind Lincoln, the man who caused the other vehicles to move with his SR16, is trying to turn, to see out the back. "It's not a cop," he says. "It's just a Nissan – someone coming after us after the detective's building?"

"Rollins is driving a white Nissan," Lincoln says. "It must be him. How far out from the station are we?"

"Just a couple of minutes – end of this block."

Lincoln pulls out his cell phone. He calls Arthur. Arthur answers on the first ring. "We're inbound," Lincoln says. "Are you in position?"

"We're at the station," Arthur says. "We have the canister. We're on the platform and we're good to go. A train is due in just a few minutes."

"We're coming in hot," Lincoln says. The Nissan rams them again. It's not as hard this time. Zack is aware of their pursuer now and was able to accelerate out of the worst of the bump.

"Who?"

"Don't know for sure, but potentially Rollins. We'll deal with him. I should get with you in time for the next train. I'll have the boy with me. We haven't had time to get him to give us the formula yet, but I think we're close. I think I've managed to get through to him, but it might take some time. I'll try to get him to do it on the train. If it pulls in and I'm not there, get on without me. I'll find another carriage and meet you onboard. Have you got spare masks?"

"Enough for you and everyone with you."

"Good. I'll be with you ASAP." Lincoln turns to the man behind him. "Can you shoot him?"

"Yes, *sir*," the man says, sounding gleeful, like he's been waiting to be given this option. "I'll have to blow out the back window. Everyone prepare for that."

He starts to turn, bringing up the SR16. The back window shatters. Lincoln feels something hot and wet splash the back of his head. He feels something hit the back of his chair. He turns. The man in the Nissan is armed. He's shot through his own windshield and through the BMW's back window. He's killed the shooter before he could raise his own rifle, putting a bullet right through his head.

And now Lincoln knows for sure. He recognises the driver of the Nissan. His face is fresh in his mind, only recently seen for the first time. His hair is longer and he has a beard, but it's *him*. It's Rollins.

## 57

The BMW screeches to a halt, going sideways as it pulls hard on its handbrake. Tom pulls back, bracing and preparing for what they could be planning with this manoeuvre. He grabs the handbrake and does the same, turning the car sideways to offer him protection from them. He knows they have assault rifles. He was able to get one of them before they could get him.

Sure enough, two of the men get out with SR16s, opening fire on the Nissan. Tom scrambles out of his door as their bullets smash through the windows on the passenger side. He hits the road and stays low, throwing himself behind a Jeep parked at the side of the road. He doesn't fire back straight away. He looks through the rear window, taking in the situation.

Three of the men are out of the BMW now, each of them armed with an SR16. He can see that they're carrying spare magazines, too, and handguns. They're equipped for a long standoff. They lay down suppressing fire upon the Nissan. They must think he's still behind it.

Tom sees movement at the other side of the vehicle. Lincoln. He has Kit. He's carrying him. He's running toward a nearby building. Tom sees that it's a subway station – Fordham Station. They disappear inside.

Tom leaves the Jeep and gets closer, hiding behind a newsstand. There's no one inside. The other people in the area have fled as soon as the shooting started. The three at the BMW have ceased firing. They've destroyed the Nissan. Two of them hold back, rifles raised, covering the area, and one of them cautiously comes forward. Tom lines up his shot. He fires twice, both shots hitting the point man through the skull. He goes down. Tom fires upon the other two before they can turn their rifles on him. They move, get themselves behind cover. They shelter behind the BMW and fire back, hitting the newsstand.

Tom hears the rumbling of a train pulling into the station, and knows he's running out of time. He's pinned down, but he needs to get into the station. Needs to catch up to Lincoln and Kit before they can get into the train – before the train can *leave*. Lincoln must be planning to escape on it. There's nowhere else for him to go in there.

He fires back, but it feels fruitless. They're set in. They're covered. They're carrying heavier weaponry than he is. Tom is stuck. He can't leave his position.

## 58

Lincoln drags Kit into the station with him. He lifts him over the barrier and then jumps over it himself. No one calls after him, no one tries to stop him. The shooting out in the street behind has got everyone's attention.

Lincoln grabs Kit and drags him along, keeps him moving fast. The boy starts to trip over his own feet. Lincoln grabs the back of his shirt and stops him from falling. Some of the people on the platform glance at him, at the way he's manhandling the boy, but their attention is torn more by the gunfire in the street. They turn toward it. Lincoln can see the worry and the growing panic on their faces. Can see how they're becoming twitchy, worrying that the firefight might come closer, might come toward them.

A train is pulling into the station. Lincoln scans the platform, looking for Arthur and his men. Arthur has three men with him. These men, other than those outside the station keeping Rollins at bay, are the last remnants of Lincoln's organisation. It has been a difficult and unexpected week.

But he can always rebuild. Especially in a few hours, after the world has seen what they have, what is available. Once the money comes rolling in, he can always rebuild. It'll be necessary for a short while. Rebuild, so he has men and protection. And *then*, once he's made his money from GB2, that's when he'll chase the sun.

Lincoln can't see Arthur. He drags Kit onto the platform, toward the train. One hand on the boy, he uses his other to call Arthur on his cell. "Are you onboard?"

"We're in," Arthur says.

"Liskey and the others are outside dealing with Rollins," Lincoln says. "I have the boy. We're going to get into the last carriage in just a moment." The platform is clear now. Only Lincoln and Kit remain on it. The car's doors are still open. It isn't ready to move yet. Lincoln looks toward the station, makes sure Rollins doesn't get through and attempt to pursue. He can still hear gunfire. "Wait until we're just outside of Grand Central Station before you crack the canister. Since we've only got the one canister, we want most of it to be released into Grand Central. The platforms will be packed out, people waiting to get into this train. That's where it'll do the most damage. *That's* our target."

Arthur doesn't say anything. He grunts in the affirmative. He already knows this.

"I don't see anyone coming," Lincoln says. "I'm getting onboard now. Get back here and bring us a couple of masks."

"I won't be long."

Lincoln looks toward the station again. No one is coming. The platform is clear. He takes the boy into the train.

## 59

Tom hasn't heard the train pulling out of the station yet, but it's hard for him to hear much of anything with the gunfire laid down by the two remaining men at the BMW. He attempts to fire back, but they're in cover, and their fingers are tight on their triggers. They're destroying the newsstand.

Tom gets to the ground and crawls toward the parked cars. They spot his movement and start shooting up the cars. Glass shatters and coats the ground. He has to crawl through it. He grits his teeth. They keep him pinned. There's nowhere he can go. The train is going to pull out soon, if it hasn't already. Tom is going to lose Kit, and he can't even stand up without risking getting shot.

He hears the roar of an engine being pushed to its limit. Tom looks to his right, down the road. Since the gunfight started, there hasn't been any traffic on the road. People have turned off, have kept their distance, avoiding the danger. But now, he sees a Ford racing down, charging toward the BMW.

Tom can't fully see the driver. They're ducking low. As

they speed by, he spots a flash of blonde hair. He thinks it could be Ella. And then she's gone by, out of view, charging for the BMW.

The men there see her coming. They turn their guns upon the Ford.

They're too late. The Ford plows into them. Tom sees it crash directly into one of the men, crushing him between the Ford and the BMW. The rear end of the BMW is pushed back. Blood sprays from the man's mouth as his insides are mangled. The other man is thrown to the side in the impact, the Ford clipping his hip. He hits the ground.

Tom is already on his feet, running to the scene of the crash. The man hit by the Ford is slumped over the hood, either dying or already dead. The other man clutches at his hip, trying to drag himself along the road. The bone is likely shattered, maybe the whole leg. He sees Tom coming, Beretta raised, and he frantically grabs for his SR16. Tom shoots him through the head.

He goes to the Ford. Ella is conscious, but she's dazed. Blood runs down her face from her left eyebrow and the top of her forehead. Her blonde hair is streaked red. She blinks up at Tom. "Kit," she says. "Where's Kit?" She forces her eyes wide, looks around. When there's no sign of him, she turns quickly back to Tom. "Get him! I'm fine – get Kit!"

Tom turns and runs into the station. As he draws nearer, he can hear the train beginning to pull out. He reaches the platform. The train is rolling away. It's slow now, but it will soon speed up.

Tom pumps his arms and his legs, pushing himself. He holds his breath, like a sprinter in a race, hoping to make himself faster. He's running out of platform. The train is getting away from him.

With one final push, he leaps from the platform. He hits the back of the rear car, slamming into it with his full body and almost bouncing off. He manages to grab onto a railing and holds on as tight as he can.

The train picks up speed.

## 60

The route from Fordham Station to Grand Central Station is a direct line. It takes twenty-two minutes. Lincoln is aware of this fact as he manages to find a seat with Kit despite how packed the car is. Most people are standing. They're too jittery to sit. People who wouldn't ordinarily speak to other strangers while on their commute are talking animatedly about the gunfire they heard. They look back toward the platform and the station. They're moving now. The danger for them is over. They're leaving it behind.

Just over twenty minutes, Lincoln thinks, and mission accomplished. Just over twenty minutes and he can leave this godforsaken city. Leave it a little better off than he found it, he thinks, and grins to himself.

Suddenly, there are gasps, alarmed cries, shrieks coming from the back of the car. Lincoln hears a hard thud. He sits up, trying to see through the bodies blocking his view. He makes out snippets of what people are saying.

"– just jumped on the train, from the platform!"

"Jesus – somebody call the cops!"

Lincoln can't see anything, can't see what they're talking about, but he has a sinking feeling that he knows who it is. He looks at Kit. Kit is looking toward the rear of the car, too. Lincoln pulls out the notepad and pen and waves them in front of Kit's face, using them to get his attention.

"Kit, *Kit* – look at these. Do you want to draw? Remember what we were talking about in the car?"

He senses commotion behind him now, coming from the front of the car. Hears an increase in wind pressure as the door is opened and someone steps through, pushing people aside, this new arrival's head on a swivel while he checks the faces. It's Arthur. He's easy to spot. He's a good head and shoulders above everyone else. Lincoln whistles to get his attention and then waves him over. Arthur gets close, leaning in to hand Lincoln two masks. Lincoln takes them from him and conceals them within his jacket, not wanting to alarm anyone onboard, though no one is paying them any attention. They're all distracted by the man who has jumped onto the outside of the train.

Arthur looks around, can sense that something has happened. "What's going on?"

Lincoln motions him to come closer so he doesn't have to raise his voice. "I think Rollins is on the train."

Arthur's head snaps back, as if looking for him.

"Not *in* the train," Lincoln says. "*On* it. I didn't see what happened, but it sounded like he jumped from the platform."

"Jesus," Arthur says.

"He's still out there. If we're lucky, he'll fall off the side and get crushed on the tracks, but we can't bank on that. Where are the others?"

"Just the next car back," Arthur says. "They came with me. I told them to stay put there for now."

"What kind of weaponry have you got?"

"Handguns, mainly. But we've also got a Rattler and an M203 grenade launcher, minus the rifle. Small stuff, easily hidden, just in case we need to fight our way out of Grand Central."

"And the canister?"

Arthur opens his jacket just a little and Lincoln sees the familiar stainless-steel gleam of the canister containing the GB2. It's looped onto Arthur's belt.

"Good. Get the others and bring them back here with us. It won't be long until we reach the station, but we need to keep Rollins at bay until then."

Kit is looking up at him. He's had some reaction to Rollins' name. Lincoln grits his teeth but he keeps himself from getting too harsh. "Come on then, Kit. How about you write down that formula we were talking about, eh?"

Arthur looks down at Kit as if seeing him for the first time. "Does Rollins know you're here?"

"I don't see how he would know which carriage we're in," Lincoln says. "He wasn't at the platform when I came aboard. I was looking out for him. There was no sign."

Arthur lifts his chin toward Kit. "If he writes it down, then what? Keep the mask from him?"

"Not yet. We'll have to get away, make sure it's right. *Then* we'll see..."

Arthur nods. He turns to go back through to the other car and get the three men waiting there. He has to push people out of his way to get through. The other passengers are still looking toward the back of the train and out of the windows, trying to figure out where Rollins has gone.

Lincoln can hear people on their cell phones, calling the police, telling them about the gunfight outside Fordham Station and about the man who's jumped onto the train. It sounds like they *will* have a fight to get out of Grand Central. It sounds like cops could be swarming the damn place.

Kit is still looking up at him. "Tom," he says.

Lincoln blinks at him. "I thought you were supposed to be mute."

Kit doesn't say anything to this.

## 61

Tom holds onto the train, the wind whipping at his face and his clothes, chilling him to the bone despite the shining sun.

He's on the roof of the train. With his aching muscles he managed to drag himself up, away from the windows where he could be seen and exposed as an easy target. He doesn't know where Lincoln is inside, which car he's in. He doesn't know if he's completely alone, either, or if some of his men have met him here.

They go underground, into darkness. The wind turns into a roar and Tom is deafened. The only light comes from the windows below, throwing shadows against the tunnel walls. Occasionally, there is a security light in the ceiling or in the wall. Tom keeps low and moves by feel, reaching out ahead and pulling himself along. There aren't many handholds. He moves by grip and leg strength. He heads toward the front of the car. He needs to get inside the train. Needs to find Lincoln and Kit.

He has his Beretta and his KA-BAR. The gun is tucked

into his waistband and the knife is in its sheaf. The Beretta's magazine only has a handful of bullets remaining. He has no idea what he's going up against. These will have to be enough.

Head down, he reaches ahead and pulls, continuing on his seemingly endless journey. He feels the train curve to the left ever so slightly. It's not a hard turn. It charges straight ahead. It feels like the route is mostly a straight line. The train sways viciously, as if consciously trying to buck him off. Tom holds on as tight as he can, shimmying forward, feeling the cold steel through his shirt, chilling his stomach and his chest, and scraping roughly against him.

Then, his hand finds purchase. He doesn't raise his head to look. There's no point. There's not enough light to see by, and he doesn't want to risk catching his head on the roof of the tunnel or something hanging down from it.

But he's made it. He's at the end. He's reached the front of the car.

## 62

Lincoln tries to be patient. He watches Kit scribble, but he writes *Fordham 1605* over and over.

"Come on, Kit, that's no good," Lincoln says, biting his tongue to keep from snapping. "That's not what we talked about. We already *know* that. We're in it. Don't you remember what we talked about in the car?"

Kit looks back at him blankly.

The other people around are still talking about Rollins. Lincoln hears them asking each other where he went, what could have happened to him. Wondering if he's still out there, still clinging onto the side or maybe on the roof where they can't see him. Some of them question if he's fallen off, if he's been churned up on the tracks, and if they'd have even noticed if it happened.

"It's not like this is a car," one man says to another. "It's not like when you hit something with your wheel and you feel the whole vehicle go up and over. It'd probably just cut him in half and we'd never even know it happened."

The other man grimaces. "*He'd* sure feel it."

Lincoln smiles at this prospect. They can always hope.

Arthur has returned with the other three men. They stand close to Lincoln and Kit, shielding them with their bodies, holding onto the rails overhead. They survey the area, alert and on guard. Sometimes Arthur glances back at them, down at the notepad to see if Kit has written what they need. Lincoln shakes his head at him.

Lincoln sighs. "Just write it out, Kit," he says, keeping his voice low and as gentle as he can make it. "Come on, now, that's a good boy. Remember what you saw in the cabin, what was written on the whiteboard. You remember the cabin, don't you? You write that down for me, and I'll take you back to your mom. That's our deal, remember?"

Kit stops writing *Fordham 1605* and looks up at him, eyes narrowed. It's hard to read his face. Hard to know what could be going through his mind. Lincoln stares at him, waiting for something to happen. He glances at the time. It's still ten minutes until they reach Grand Central. Time is ticking away.

Kit speaks. Says the same thing as before. "Tom."

"All right, yes, if you write it down we'll take you to Rollins, too. How's that sound? Just write it down. Come on, now."

Kit looks down at the page. He stares at it. He doesn't attempt to write.

Another five minutes pass. Lincoln sits back and runs his hands down his face. He felt so close back in the car, right before Rollins rammed them. Now it's like pulling teeth. If he'd paid enough attention of his own, if he understood chemistry better, he wouldn't have to worry about this. It wouldn't be an issue.

He thinks for a moment, closing his eyes, recalling all the

times he saw Ian write out the formula. There weren't many times, and it might as well have been in Chinese so far as Lincoln was concerned, but he does his best to conjure some of the formula. The very beginning of it. The letters and symbols there. A thought occurs to him. For Kit. Yet another tack.

He takes the notepad from Kit, and the pen, and he turns it to a fresh page. Kit watches him. Lincoln pretends like he's not there. He puts on a little show for the boy. He scratches his head. He taps his front teeth with the end of the pen. Then, he presses it to the paper. He writes out the first few symbols he can remember, not caring if they're exactly right. Then he stops, he frowns, he scratches his head again. He rubs his jaw. He stares at what he's written, unfinished. Out the corner of his eye, he sees Kit is still watching him. He's looking at the paper.

Slowly, not wanting to rush it, he turns to Kit. He shows him the notepad. He offers it and the pen to him, and raises his eyebrows.

Kit understands. He takes the pad and the pen. Underneath what Lincoln has written, he starts over. Lincoln's eyes go wide. The boy has taken the bait. He's writing out the formula for GB2. It doesn't make sense to Lincoln, but it certainly looks familiar.

Arthur turns to him. "It's nearly go time."

Lincoln smiles up at him. "Look at this, sweetheart," he says. "He's only gone and bloody done it."

# 63

Tom drags himself forward and drops into the narrow gap between cars. He braces himself, catching his breath. He looks through the door in front of him, into the second car from the rear. He scans the bodies in there, scans the faces he can see. He can't see Lincoln, or Kit. He can't see any children at all.

Before he enters this car and starts working his way forward, he turns and looks into the rear car. Scans the faces again. There are more of them there. A lot of people are standing. They block his view. It's hard to see past them.

Then he spots a man. A tall, broad man. The biggest man in the car. Tom doesn't recognise him, but there's something about his demeanour. There are three men beside him, all of them standing. The way they carry themselves, the way they look around, eyes narrowed, alert, it sets off alarm bells. Tom doesn't ignore these bells. These men are on watch. They're on guard. The men speak to each other, faces lowered, mouths barely moving. Then, they start to do something.

A body sways where it stands in front of the door,

blocking Tom's view. He tries to see around the body, over its shoulders. It sways again, and the tall man returns to view. All four men. They reach inside their jackets. They pull out gas masks.

Tom has seen enough. He pulls out his Beretta and forces the door open. The people closest to the door, standing and sitting, turn toward him.

"Everyone out!" Tom calls, shouting, projecting his voice toward the end of the car so everyone hears him. "Move, now – into the next car!"

The man nearest frowns at him. "What're you talking about, man? We're nearly at Grand Central."

Then, from the rear of the car, a woman's voice rises. "Is that *him*? Is he the man that jumped from the platform?"

Attention turns toward Tom. There's a commotion. Tom ignores the eyes. He moves aside from the door, trying to see the men who pulled on their masks. "Everyone needs to get through to the next car right now!"

There's abrupt gunfire, promptly followed by screaming, and the people in front of Tom dance as the bullets impact their bodies. Tom dives to the side, to his left, Beretta out. The car descends into chaos. People are running now. There's a stampede. They crush each other, trying to get through the narrow doorway and through into the next car. They trample the dead bodies. Feet stomp on Tom's back and legs as they try to flee.

Tom manages to crawl clear, away from the worst of the throng before they can do him serious damage. He tries to see down the car, toward the men in the gas masks. He catches glimpses through the rushing, pushing bodies. He sees one of them at the fore, a Sig Sauer MCX Rattler held out in front of him, searching for Tom, or else trying to catch sight of his fallen body to know the job is finished. Behind the man, there is movement. Something is happening. Tom can't see what.

Then, a sudden plume of grey begins to arise. It has the look and consistency of smoke, but Tom doesn't think it's smoke. He thinks it's gas.

The GB2.

## 64

The gas rises. It begins to spread.

The other passengers have seen it. They don't know what it is, but it alarms them as much as the gunshots. They push each other harder. Through the crush of the crammed, open door, Tom can hear their panic rippling through the next car, and likely down the rest of the train.

The gas is thick. When it lowers from the ceiling, when it settles, it'll be impossible to see through. It's like a fog, spreading. Tom remembers what Professor McCulloch said – upon ingesting, it's nearly entirely fatal. That once it dissipates it leaves no trace. No one will know what caused the choking death.

Still concealed behind the bodies of the people fleeing the car, Tom gets closer, crawling along the ground, keeping low, dragging himself along under the seating, making himself harder to see. The other men come into view. There are five of them in total. Tom sees Kit. He's masked, too. One of the men holds onto him – Tom assumes this must be

Lincoln. The other men are all armed, and aside from the Rattler it's with a mix of handguns – Glocks and Sig Sauers so far as Tom can see. One of them is carrying something that catches Tom's eye, surprising him. An M203 grenade launcher. It's hooked onto his combat utility belt. Tom isn't sure he's ever seen one in an active situation not attached to an M16.

That's a concern for later. Right now, the main concern, other than the gas, is the Rattler. Concealed under the chair, Tom raises the Beretta before the man can see him. He fires twice into his chest. The man goes down. The gas is lowering. The other men turn on the sound, but it's hard for them to see.

Tom huffs out air, clearing his lungs, preparing himself. He breathes in deep, filling his chest. Holding it, he rolls out from under the seats. He runs into the gas. He only has a couple of bullets left in the Beretta. The men are spreading out, searching. Tom reaches the first. They're not far from the dead man with the Rattler. Tom fires into his left thigh and the man drops to a knee. Tom shoots him through the mask.

The Beretta is empty. Tom pulls out the KA-BAR. The air is burning in his lungs. He crouches low, moving through the blinding smoke, grateful that it's at least non-corrosive. If it was sarin or soman gas, his skin would be burning. He'd be blinded.

He reaches the next man. He spins him. The man raises his Glock. Tom grabs his wrist and pushes it high. The gun goes off twice, the bullets hitting the roof. Tom couldn't risk one going wild and hitting Kit. He brings his knee up into the man's midsection. The man doubles. Tom can hear him coughing. Tom pulls the mask from his face, then hits him in the stomach again, causing him to suck in a deep lungful.

Tom pulls on the mask, continuing to hold his breath until the gas captured within can clear. He watches as the unmasked man falls back, choking, clawing at his neck until it's bloodied. His head turns bright red, like it's about to explode. His eyes bulge. His tongue protrudes. His neck looks thicker than it was. He's struggling to draw breath. The whites of his eyes turn red as the blood vessels burst. The man thrashes on the ground, rolling side to side, his feet beating out a tattoo on the car floor.

Then he's still. He's dead. Tom feels a cold horror at witnessing GB2's capability. Hearing about it is one thing, but seeing it firsthand is another. It didn't take long. Less than a minute. A painful minute, that probably felt to the man like an eternity.

Tom breathes through the mask. It's clear. Squeezing the handle of the KA-BAR tight, he moves on. He needs to be fast. He needs to clear this gas before it can do more damage, before it can move through the rest of the train.

He reaches the man with the M203. He's armed with a Glock, too. He's swinging it through the gas, searching for Tom. He sees Tom's approach. He sees the mask. It takes him a moment to realise it's not an ally. The moment costs him. Tom drives the KA-BAR downward, penetrating the fleshy space behind his collar bone on the left side. The man drops to his knees. Tom can hear him screaming through the mask. Tom pulls the knife out and drives it through the mask, through his right eye and into his brain.

He pulls the knife free and reaches for the Glock, but as he does so he feels himself rocked from behind, a mass throwing itself into him. Tom rolls through the impact and turns, sees the biggest of the men coming at him. He's holding a Sig Sauer. As he raises it, Tom is able to kick it out of his hand. It flies away, but the man is unfazed. He kicks at Tom, catching him in the centre of his chest with his big boot. Tom feels winded. He tries to roll back with the impact, to roll through, but the big man is fast and is already upon him. He kicks Tom again, this time lashing him across the chest and throat with his shin.

Tom falls back. The big man hits hard. Tom feels something roll against him on the floor. He grabs at it. It's cold to the touch. At first, he thinks it's a water bottle. It's not. It's a stainless-steel canister missing its top. It would have carried the GB2.

He swings it upward as the big man advances. He clubs at the man's chest and ribs, beating him back. Tom manages to stand, then brings the canister down onto the top of the man's head. It crumples on impact.

The big man shakes it off. He punches Tom in the chest. Tom drops, feeling like he might have cracked a rib. The man grabs at his skull. Tom realises what he's doing. He takes a deep breath as the mask is torn from him.

A robotic voice makes an announcement over the sound system. The speaker is directly overhead. Tom hears it loud and clear. *"The next stop is Grand Central Station."*

*Grand Central Station.* The reality dawns on Tom – the train isn't the target. The train is transportation for GB2. Grand Central Station – the busiest station in New York City, if not one of the busiest stations in the world – *this* is the target.

The big man punches Tom in the nose. He falls back, tasting blood at the back of his throat. He swallows it. He can't allow himself to take a breath. It takes all of his concentration to make sure he doesn't breathe.

He's landed next to the body of the man with the M203. Tom grabs it. It's loaded. The big man sees what he has. He backs off. Tom doesn't fire it at him. He turns, and fires it at the back of the train.

There's an explosion. A hole is blown through the back of the train. The door has been knocked out. Tom sees it fly away down the tracks.

There's a roar from the wind. Tom's ears pop with the change in air pressure. But the car begins to clear. The gas flows out of the hole.

"Mother*fucker!*" the big man roars, grabbing Tom and throwing him down the length of the car, toward the opening.

Tom keeps himself from falling out. The big man is advancing. Tom reaches for his KA-BAR, but he keeps it concealed. Waits for the big man to get closer. Tom is close to the hole he's blown in the back of the car. The big man approaches, arms wide, like he's going to throw him out onto the tracks.

Tom jabs the point of the knife toward his thigh. Again, the big man is faster than Tom expects. His arm shoots down and catches Tom's wrist, stopping the KA-BAR an inch before it can make contact.

But Tom isn't stopped. Isn't deterred. He keeps moving. Uses the big man's strength and stance and grip against him. Tom falls flat on his back and presses his boot into the big man's midsection and flips him overhead, onto his back. His grip breaks on Tom's wrist. Tom is quick to his feet. The man is turning onto his front, pushing himself up. He's close to the hole. Tom can hear the scream of the train's brakes. It's slowing, but it's still going fast right now. Tom kicks the big man across the face. He falls back, toward the hole. He braces himself either side of it. Tom kicks him hard in the centre of the back, forcing him through.

The big man falls. Tom catches the bottom of his legs, holds him in place hanging out the back of the train, doesn't want him to have a landing he could potentially survive. Tom feels the impact and vibration of the big man's body as he bounces off the tracks.

The train slows, pulling into Grand Central Station. It stops. It's well-lit here. Tom peers out the back, at the big man's body. Most of his head is gone. All that remains is a bloodied stump where it's been worn down by the impact against the tracks.

Tom hears a woman screaming. Others take up the chorus. They're out on the platform. They've seen the body.

Tom turns, looking down through the car. The gas is cleared. The people in the station don't realise how lucky they are. Tom looks at the fallen bodies, at the men he's killed, and the unfortunate passengers that were killed by them.

There's no sign of Lincoln. There's no sign of Kit.

Tom stands. The door between the cars is still open. He sees the people in the next car forcing their way out, desperate to get away. Lincoln and Kit could be hidden among them.

Tom goes to the nearest fallen body. He takes a Glock from it. He leaves the train. It's not over yet.

## 65

On the platform, there are gunshots. Two, straight up into the air. Most people hit the ground. Tom drops to a knee, Glock raised and ready. He sees what has happened. Lincoln, halfway up the stairs and maskless now, is trying to open a path through the bodies. He drags Kit along with his left arm. Lincoln looks back at the train, casts his eyes over the platform. He spots Tom. He spins and fires toward him with his Sig Sauer.

Tom dives flat, but it wasn't a well-aimed shot. The bullet is too high. It hits the train behind. Tom keeps his eyes up, watching Lincoln. Lincoln is already running, attempting to escape.

Tom pushes himself up and gives chase. "Everyone stay down!" he shouts, jumping over bodies, heading for the stairs. The people see that he has a gun too, and they're more than willing to comply.

Tom gets up the stairs and they're in a long corridor. He sees Lincoln and Kit running ahead of him. They're the only three here. Lincoln stops and spins, probably having heard

Tom's ascent. He scoops Kit up with his left arm, holding him against his body. He points the Sig Sauer at Tom.

"That's as far as you go, sweetheart," Lincoln says. "You can drop that gun right now."

Tom doesn't. He keeps the Glock at his side. He holds it out but he doesn't drop it. If he puts it down, he and Kit are both dead. "Let Kit go," Tom says.

Lincoln raises his eyebrows. He looks like he's about to laugh. "And why would I want to go and do a thing like that?"

"Because he's weighing you down," Tom says. "Let him go, and you can leave. You'll be a lot faster without him. Put him down, turn around and run, and I won't come after you."

Lincoln watches him. "You expect me to believe that, sweetheart?"

"I'm a man of my word."

"And if I don't?"

"I'll kill you."

Lincoln *does* laugh. "Oh, sweetheart – do you know what an absolute pain in my neck you've been this last week? And I didn't even know who you are until this morning." He laughs again, though Tom doesn't see what's funny. It's likely stress and exhaustion catching up to him. Frustration at his plan's failure. "And now here you are, *still* alive – and if you're still alive, then that means Arthur is dead. Arthur was a good friend of mine. The only friend I had left. Anyway, we're finally face to face, eh? You've decimated my organisation, darling. Do you know how much money you've cost me? Bloody hell, if anyone here is going to die, it's *you*."

"The longer you talk to me, the less time you have to escape," Tom says. "The cops are gonna be swarming this place soon enough. The FBI. Interpol. There's a lot of people coming for you."

"Sounds like it's already too late for me," Lincoln says. "But I can take the two of you with me."

He starts to level the gun, but Tom talks fast. "Put Kit down and I'll get you out of here."

Lincoln hesitates.

"You know I can do it. You haven't been able to stop me yet, right? I always find a way. I got on that train, didn't I? For Kit, I'll get you out of here."

Lincoln starts to smile. "You really think I need you? What makes you think I'm not capable myself, sweetheart? You've got nothing for me, Rollins. Maybe I'll kill the boy first, and you can watch. How's that sound, eh? I've got everything I need from him. I'll kill him, and I'll kill you, and I'll get out of here and do this all over again! Nothing will stop me this time. I'll gas this whole godforsaken city!"

Tom stares at him. He squeezes the handle of the Glock tight. He lowers it so it's at his side, almost touching his thigh. "Do you think you're fast enough?"

Lincoln stares back, watching him. "Faster than you, sweetheart."

"You sure? I'm American, Lincoln. We invented the fast draw. That's how George was able to kill your brother. That's how I'll kill you. You're just not quick enough."

Lincoln frowns. He has the gun raised already. Tom watches his finger on the trigger.

"We'll see about that," Lincoln says. He turns the gun toward Kit, toward his head.

Tom raises the Glock. He fires. He hasn't used this gun before. He has to hope it's in perfect working order, that there's nothing wrong in the barrel that could throw off the bullet's trajectory. Lincoln's men were professionals, though. He's confident they kept their equipment in fine working order.

The bullet goes through Lincoln's mouth, straight out the back of his neck, severing his spinal cord. Lincoln collapses, Kit on top of him.

Tom approaches, gun still raised though he's certain Lincoln is dead. Kit stands. There's blood matting his hair. He looks down at Lincoln. At his dead body.

"Don't look at that, Kit," Tom says, lowering the gun.

Kit turns away. Looks up at Tom.

"It's over," Tom says. He tucks the Glock into his waistband, next to the Beretta. "Let's go. Let's get out of here."

Kit steps closer to Tom. Kit slips his hand into Tom's. Tom holds onto him. They walk away.

## 66

Tom and Kit are outside of the station when Ella arrives, driving the badly damaged Ford.

The area is a mass of activity. Police, firefighters, and paramedics all swarm the scene, hurrying in and out of the building. Tom has disposed of the Glock. He still has his Beretta and KA-BAR but they're concealed, and no one is paying much attention to them anyway. No one is pointing him out to the cops. A lot of people who were in the train may not have got a good look at his face in all of the commotion, and the people who were waiting on the platform were face-down most of the time.

News vans are starting to pull up. Tom can hear a helicopter overhead. Ella gets out of the Ford and hurries to them. The blood on her face and in her hair has dried. She sees how Kit is holding Tom's hand. She smiles, briefly, and then her smile turns into tears. She's crying with relief. She stoops down and scoops Kit up in her arms, turning with him, then she turns into Tom and wraps an arm around him, too, holding both of them tight. Her arm is around Tom's neck, squeezing him. Her hand holds onto the hair at the back of his head.

She whispers into Tom's ear. "*Thank you,*" she says. Tom feels her tears running hot, pressing wet into his cheek. She kisses him there, then says again, "*Thank you.*"

Tom doesn't want to hang around for long. Doesn't want to get caught up in everything, to get tied down answering the same questions over and over, explaining what happened, how, when, and where.

"I need to slip away," Tom says as they part. "You can come with me, but I reckon they're gonna want to talk to you. You can either do that here or back in Vermont."

Ella looks around at the emergency vehicles and the people in uniforms. "It's safe now, isn't it?" she says. "It's really over?"

"They're all dead," Tom says. One of the scabs on Ella's face has cracked and a fresh drop of blood is running down her cheek. He wipes it away with his thumb. "But I haven't seen Ian. He might still be out there. I'm going to have to look for him."

Ella nods. She chews her bottom lip, still looking around. She holds tight to Kit, stroking his hair. "I'll stay," she says. "I'll talk to the cops."

Tom squeezes her shoulder, then turns to leave.

"Wait," Ella says.

He turns back to her.

"Will we see you again?"

"You'll see me sooner than you think," Tom says. "We'll say goodbye properly then." He pats Kit's back and then he slips through the crowds outside Grand Central Station, disappearing deeper into New York City.

## 67

It takes a week for Ella and Kit to get home. Tom is waiting at their apartment building for them. He gets out of the car and meets them at the entrance when he sees them. They're being dropped off by a taxi. Ella sees Tom coming toward them as the taxi drives away. Her face lights up. She hurries to him and they embrace.

"Have you been here long?" she says.

"Not long," Tom says. He smiles at Kit. Kit reaches out for his hand. Tom gives it to him. Kit stands beside him. "I thought I'd hang around a while, see when you got back. I told you we'd say goodbye properly. And I wanted to make sure you're both all right."

"We're fine," Ella says. "Come on up and we can talk."

Tom helps her with their bags as they head up, while still holding onto Kit's hand. The bags are new, recently bought. He assumes they've had to buy new clothing while they were still in New York City. Everything else they had was either lost or destroyed in various vehicles and Detective George Ross's apartment.

Finally back in their own apartment, their home, Ella dumps the bags in the centre of the living room floor and takes a seat, motioning for Tom to do the same. She takes Kit from him and sits him beside her on the sofa. Tom perches himself on the chair opposite.

"I assume you got out of New York City okay," Ella says.

"I didn't leave straight away," Tom says. "I hung around for a couple of days, trying to find Ian."

"I know you didn't find him," Ella says. "Because I have the answer to that question."

"Oh?" Tom says.

Ella nods. "He's dead. The cops and the FBI, they found the warehouse where Lincoln and his men were hiding out, making the GB2. In one of the rooms there, they said there'd been a fire. Their forensics got in there – they've been speeding everything along, trying to find answers because of everything that's happened – and they found trace DNA for Ian Farrow. They say he died in the fire, along with two others, but I didn't recognise their names. They said they worked for Lincoln, though, known members of his group."

"That's good to know," Tom says. "So that could be the end of GB2?"

"They haven't found any more of it."

"Who spoke to you?"

"FBI and NYPD."

"What else did they ask?"

"They asked a *lot* of questions about you."

Tom isn't surprised. "What did you tell them?"

"Well, they already knew your name," Ella says.

Tom grunts. Interpol were aware of him, and there were plenty of cameras in Grand Central Station. If the FBI and the NYPD didn't know who he was before, they certainly did after the events of a week ago.

"I answered their questions," Ella says. "I told them the truth. They asked where you were, and I said I didn't know. You'd disappeared outside of Grand Central. I think it frustrated them, but it's not like I was lying. I *didn't* know where you were."

"I'm sure I'll run into them again down the road. If they still have questions, they can talk to me then. But I'm not going out of my way to talk to them. There's nothing left to talk about. Lincoln and his men are dead." Kit is watching him while he speaks. "How's Kit been?"

"Better," Ella says. "They put us in a nice hotel, and Kit doesn't really like being away from home too long but I think he enjoyed the novelty of room service. All paid for by the FBI, too. We had a great time. I think we earned it."

Tom smiles. "Has he been drawing still? Writing?"

"He has," Ella says. "But no more *Fordham 1605*. No more formula."

"Oh really?"

"I think he knows it's over. I think he knows that the formula is dangerous, that he can't let it fall into the wrong hands. And I think *Fordham 1605* was a warning, for us. He was trying to let us know. I think Kit maybe knew what they were planning all along, and that was the only way he could tell us."

The intercom buzzes. Tom and Ella look at each other.

"Are you expecting anyone?" Tom says.

Ella frowns. She shakes her head. She gets up and goes to the intercom. Tom stands close so he can hear, making sure it's not a threat.

"Hello?" Ella says.

"Ella, you're home." It's a familiar voice. "This is Deputy – uh, I mean, this is Teddy Fuller."

Tom sees how Ella's knees almost buckle. He knows why. It's relief. Right now, she's talking to someone she didn't ever expect to hear from again. She thought Teddy Fuller was dead. They both did.

"*Teddy*," Ella says, breathless. "You're all right? It's so good to hear your voice."

"Well, I don't know if I'd say I'm *all right*." He chuckles. "But I'm still alive, and I heard you were on your way back home. I figured you'd get back about now."

"I'll buzz you in."

Ella hovers by the door, waiting for him. Tom returns to the living room. Kit watches him. Tom sits beside him on the sofa. "I'm gonna get out of here soon, Kit," he says. "It's been good knowing you. I know you're gonna look after your mom, but you all have my number. Don't forget that. You ever need me again, just call."

Kit shuffles forward. He turns toward Tom. He opens his arms. Tom leans down toward him, into the hug, wrapping an arm of his own around Kit's small body.

Teddy reaches the apartment. Ella lets him in. He's on crutches. His right leg is in a thick cast. "I'm really glad the elevator was working," Teddy says, laughing. There are some scars on his face, too. A split from his lower lip down his chin, and a deep gouge in his left cheek. He was never a big guy, but he's thinner now, too.

Ella embraces him. "I thought you were dead," she says. "I thought they'd killed you."

"Not quite," Teddy says. "But they did put me in hospital for a while."

From the sofa, Tom can see the way Ella and Teddy look at each other. The way they smile. How pleased they are to find that the other is still alive, and that they're reacquainted. Tom is happy to see it. Tom has high hopes for them both.

Ella assists Teddy into the living room. He sees Tom. "Rollins," he says. "I see you made it out the other side, too."

"Despite their best efforts."

Teddy hops closer to him, holding out a hand.

Tom stands and takes the hand. They shake. "I'm on my way out," he says. "I'll leave you all to get caught up."

"No, Tom, you don't have to go," Ella says.

He smiles at her. "This was never going to be a long visit. I just wanted to check in, to make sure you were both all right. To say goodbye properly. And now I know Teddy's alive, too. It's time for me to get going. I was heading out of Vermont when we first met. I've been here long enough."

"Do you have any idea where you're going to go?" Ella says. "Or are you keeping that to yourself?"

"When we were in New York, it got me thinking about New Jersey," Tom says. "I was thinking about visiting."

Ella frowns. Teddy looks surprised, too. "New Jersey?" Ella says.

"Freehold, specifically."

"Why Freehold?"

"It's the Boss's hometown."

"The Boss?" Ella repeats. Then her face lights up. "Oh, Springsteen? I didn't know you were a Springsteen fan, Tom." She shakes her head, smiling. "You really are a man of mystery, aren't you?"

"I figure while I'm so close, I should really swing by. I don't know when I'll be out this way again."

"Well, enjoy yourself out there." Ella takes his hand. She strokes it. She looks into his eyes. "Thank you," she says.

Tom turns back to Kit. He strokes his cheek with one finger. He nods goodbye to Ella and Teddy, and then he leaves.

# ABOUT THE AUTHOR

Did you enjoy *Trigger Point*? Please consider leaving a review on Amazon to help other readers discover the book.

Paul Heatley left school at sixteen, and since then has held a variety of jobs including mechanic, carpet fitter, and bookshop assistant, but his passion has always been for writing. He writes mostly in the genres of crime fiction and thriller, and links to his other titles can be found on his website. He lives in the north east of England.

Want to connect with Paul? Visit him at his website.

www.PaulHeatley.com

# ALSO BY PAUL HEATLEY

*The Tom Rollins Thriller Series*
Blood Line (Book 1)
Wrong Turn (Book 2)
Hard to Kill (Book 3)
Snow Burn (Book 4)
Road Kill (Book 5)
No Quarter (Book 6)
Hard Target (Book 7)
Last Stand (Book 8)
Blood Feud (Book 9)
Search and Destroy (Book 10)
Ghost Team (Book 11)
Full Throttle (Book 12)
Sudden Impact (Book 13)
Kill Switch (Book 14)
Choke Hold (Book 15)
Trigger Point (Book 16)

The Tom Rollins Box Set (Books 1 - 4)

Made in the USA
Middletown, DE
09 May 2025